Silver Springs
Mystery Series
Book 1

Murder
at the Summer
Cheese Festival

The Maplewood Crafters Club
Investigates In This Cozy Mystery

Jodie Morgan

DEDICATION

To Jim. Here's to many more adventures!

Thanks for your purchase! Get your surprise reader bonuses here: **cozycozies.com/pages/ss1thanks**

- **Audiobook ISBN**: 978-1-923587-01-4

- **E-Book ISBN**: 978-1-923587-00-7

- **Hardcover ISBNs**

  - **Dyslexic Print**: 978-1-923587-03-8

  - **Large Print**: 978-1-923587-04-5

  - **Regular Print**: 978-1-923587-02-1

- **Paperback ISBNs**

  - **Dyslexic Print**: 978-1-923587-07-6

  - **Large Print**: 978-1-923587-06-9

  - **Regular Print**: 978-1-923587-05-2

Published by Cozy Cozies

https://cozycozies.com

The moral rights of the author have been asserted.

All inquiries can be directed to: permissions@cozycozies.com

About The Book

When Laura Evans leaves her high-pressure Boston restaurant job for managing Silver Springs General Store's café, she's hoping for a change of pace.

Except the Summer Cheese Festival is fast approaching and an esteemed food critic is in town, ready to review the establishment for a second time. The first nearly closed the business. And the day after it hosts a pre-festival tasting...Laura discovers a dead body.

Suddenly Laura's boss Maggie is the prime suspect, her new job is in jeopardy, and her dreams of a peaceful Vermont life are crumbling faster than a block of cheddar. Determined to save her boss and her fresh start, Laura teams up with her observant landlady Evelyn Chan to uncover the truth.

But as Laura digs deeper, she discovers this charming small town harbors dangerous secrets...

This cozy mystery serves up the perfect blend of charm, community warmth, and intrigue. Ideal for readers who savor small-town settings, quirky characters, and clever puzzles.

Thanks for your purchase! Get your surprise reader bonuses here: <u>cozycozies.com/pages/ss1thanks</u>

ABOUT THE SERIES

In Silver Springs, everyone knows your name. And your secrets.

In this Green Mountain State town, Laura Evans isn't just the General Store's café manager...she's the town's unofficial detective. Alongside her observant landlady Evelyn Chan, Laura discovers dangerous secrets hiding beneath the picturesque veneer.

But Laura and Evelyn don't have to do it alone. They're members of the Maplewood Crafters Club.

This seemingly innocent club are also the town's secret helpers. Over craft projects and potluck dinners, they arrange random acts of kindness...and help solve mysteries.

What makes this series irresistible:

- A stunning setting

- Delectable culinary details

- Richly developed characters

- Ingeniously crafted mysteries with satisfying endings

If you love culinary cozies, craft and hobby cozies, Ellie Alexander, Agatha Frost, Laura Childs, Maddie Day,

Diane Mott Davidson, or Jenn McKinlay...or you enjoy books with new starts, close-knit communities, amateur sleuths, found family, personal growth, secret helpers, and food as comfort and connection...

You'll love Silver Springs. Because in Vermont's most charming town, the only thing more complex than the local craft projects are the secrets hiding just out of sight...

Thanks for your purchase! Get your surprise reader bonuses here: cozycozies.com/pages/ss1thanks

And there are more books coming soon, so if you'd like to read the next before anyone else...sign up at cozycozies.com/pages/newsletter!

TABLE OF CONTENTS

CHAPTER ONE

Two hundred and twelve miles from Boston, Laura Evans had hoped crushing disappointment wouldn't follow her. It had, but the morning whirlwind at the Silver Springs General Store café was an excellent distraction.

Cutlery clinked, the espresso machine hissed, and customers chatted while the August humidity hung in the air, even as ceiling fans whirled overhead. Starting as the café manager in summer perhaps hadn't been the best idea, but she had fall to look forward to.

"Macchiato for Shelly!" Eli Carter, her colleague and the café's resident barista, said.

"Are you out of those delicious scones?" a middle-aged woman asked.

"Not at all! You're in luck," Laura said. "Layla delivered a fresh batch just this morning."

Layla Ahmed, owner of Red Trillium Bakery next door, supplied the café's pastries and baked goods. On Laura's first day, a week ago, she'd tasted Layla's baking and understood what the fuss was about.

"Do you know if Layla's making those special herb and cheese scones for the Summer Cheese Festival?" the woman from before asked, leaning over the counter.

"Since this is my first festival, I'm not sure, but I'd be happy to find out for you!" Laura said.

"You're going to love it!" the woman said. "You must attend the Cheese Trivia. It's so much fun!"

Laura nodded with a smile and handed over the woman's to-go order.

The annual Summer Cheese Festival looming in less than two weeks had stirred the town into a frenzy. Everyone had spilled into the café with questions and the latest gossip. Everywhere she looked, someone needed something. A question answered, an order clarified, a hand lent.

"It seems I've wiped out the clean mug supply," Eli said, sidling up to the sink with an armful of dirty dishes. Today's shirt—always a shade of green—contrasted well with his dark-brown skin.

"Leave it with me," Laura said, pivoting and pushing up her sleeves. "I'm on it."

It was good, being part of a team again.

Maggie Brook, the store's co-owner and Laura's boss, descended the stairs from her office on the upper level. She was a tall woman with pale, freckled skin who favored simplicity, which reflected in her all-black wardrobe and no-nonsense attitude.

"Is everything ticking along with your team?" Maggie asked Laura, managing a quick smile.

"Keeping pace so far!" Laura replied.

"Just!" Jesse O'Connor added with a grin, selecting pastries for a customer.

"Good, good." Maggie's eyes dimmed. "Now brace yourself. The festival week's no picnic."

She nodded at them all and spun on her heel, heading to the retail section which occupied the rest of the building's first floor.

"Cinnamon roll and a latte? Caroline, yours is ready!" Jesse said.

"That's it!" a woman who must have been Caroline said, grabbing her order.

Jasmine Williams, another General Store employee, emerged from the back rooms. Her red-tipped box braids were pulled back, and she had a Woodland Watch badge—a local land steward organization she belonged to—pinned to her apron. She carried a stack of glossy pamphlets.

"The festival brochures have arrived! I'll put them on the table under the community notice board." Jasmine held one up for Laura to see, her smile bright against her dark-brown skin and sharp cheekbones.

"That's great, thank you!" Laura glanced at the proffered colorful foldout. It detailed event schedules, vendor profiles, and competition categories.

Jasmine smiled. "These are like reading the menu and thinking you've tasted the meal. Just wait till you see it in person."

The kitchen bell behind Laura chimed, and she turned to see a plate of buttermilk pancakes waiting. Anton Reynolds, the General Store's chef, nodded at her through the kitchen line. "Table three's order is ready."

Three golden-brown pancakes were topped with a pat of Whitman Family Creamery butter, a ceramic pitcher of local maple syrup beside them. Anton had added a fresh blueberry and raspberry compote and a light dusting of powdered sugar.

Laura thanked him and took the dish, transferring it to a tray before dropping it off to a delighted customer.

As the morning rush subsided, the café fell into an easy rhythm. Eli restocked cups by the espresso machine, Jesse arranged pastries in the display case, and Laura refilled sugar and salt shakers. The café hummed with conversation and the occasional hiss of the coffee machine.

"It's hard to believe you left Boston for our patch of Vermont," Eli said, reaching for another stack of ceramic mugs. "Are you still holding up okay? Two weeks in?"

Laura set down a just-filled shaker. "What can I say? There's something special about this town. It's all the thoughtful touches. The café has them too, like the little plant centerpieces. They always make me smile."

"See?" Eli said proudly, glancing at Jesse. "She likes my succulents."

Jesse grinned, the expression lighting up their pale face. "Alright, botanical prodigy. I'll let you win this time...but only because I'm feeling generous."

Eli rolled his eyes as he prepared a coffee, raising his voice over the hissing steamer. "Anyway, my grandpa always said it was the best little town this side of New England."

Jesse snorted, adjusting a cinnamon roll in the display. "Of course. The noble lie of the lifelong local."

"Says the arts school graduate who chose the country over city lights," Eli said, grinning.

"That's different," Jesse said, straightening. "I spent four years in Providence among people who treated exhaustion like a badge of honor. I was unsure what came next." They shrugged. "I visited here one October two years ago, and the entire valley looked like a painting. Two weeks later, I signed a lease."

"I've heard the fall colors here are breathtaking," Laura said, polishing water glasses. "My Gran always brought me in summer, so this'll be my first fall in town. I can't wait to see it for myself."

"Let's just survive the summer rush first," Eli said. "The festival's...a little chaotic."

Laura paused, cloth in hand, glancing at the chalkboard where Jesse had added a festival-themed illustration—a wheel of cheese wearing a tiny crown. "I've managed my share of busy shifts, but this'll be new."

"New is an understatement," Jesse said. "The whole town transforms. Every restaurant and café gets swamped with food writers, bloggers, and critics, all thinking they're the next cheese taster extraordinaire."

"Speaking of critics," Eli said, "last year's festival was something else. Remember that whole incident with Jeremy Blackwood? The poor guy looked as wilted as an over-watered plant when he lost his notebook!"

Jesse rolled their eyes as they passed. "It's just as well you found his notes for him. He treats them like state secrets." They must've seen Laura's surprised look, because they continued with, "Once upon a time, his reviews could shutter a place. Now? He's background noise. The last exposé worth mentioning was years back. Something about mislabeled halibut in Boston's fine dining scene."

A little girl, shy of four, stared at the chalkboard menu, shifting from foot to foot and chewing her lip.

Laura walked over and leaned down. "It's tough to choose! Would you like some help to decide?"

The girl nodded, studying her feet.

A woman who must've been the child's mother approached with a bashful smile. "Sorry, Dakota's taking so long."

"It's no trouble at all," Laura said, turning to the girl. "Hi, Dakota. I'm Laura! Want to tell me what you'd like to drink?"

"Dunno," Dakota replied with a tiny shrug.

Laura tilted her head. "What do you think about something warm? I could make you a hot chocolate."

Dakota's eyes brightened, and she nodded.

"Should we make it extra special?" Laura asked. "A little peppermint syrup? Some marshmallows?"

"Yes!" Dakota's voice grew more confident.

"How about whipped cream to top it off?"

The girl giggled. "Yeah!"

"Okay, great! Let's make it just the way you like," Laura said, leaning in like it was a secret.

Dakota's face lit up, and she gave a huge smile.

A minute or so later, Laura crowned her creation with an enormous swirl of whipped cream. She placed the finishing touch—a few marshmallows—on the saucer before placing it on the counter with a flourish.

"Here you go!" Laura said, smiling. "Where would you like to sit? I'll bring it over for you."

The girl beamed, admiring the cup like it was treasure. "Thank you! I wanna sit...over there!"

"Anytime!" Laura replied, and she meant it. Picking up the drink and placing it on a tray, she followed the mother and her daughter to Dakota's chosen table.

Dakota's mother mouthed a grateful 'thank you' as Laura set the hot chocolate in front of Dakota. As she walked away, Dakota pointed at the drink for her mother to admire, then looked back and waved at Laura, smiling.

Laura returned the gesture and turned to the sink, warmth blooming in her chest as she rinsed another mug. Moments like that lifted the job above the usual rhythm of tasks. Hard to name, but something about it was right.

Jasmine sidled up beside her at the sink, grabbing a stack of washed-and-dried plates ready to put away. "You've got some kind of magic. Dakota comes in every Tuesday with her mom. I've never seen her warm up to someone so quickly!"

"If I can make someone's day even a little better...I will," Laura said.

As she went about her work, Laura reflected on her last few days. At first glance, the General Store was just a shop...though she was beginning to see it as a community hub.

The main retail space sprawled across the first floor of the town's oldest mercantile shop, operating for a hundred and forty years, according to the weathered plaque. Exposed brick walls and timber beams spoke of craftsmanship from another era, while tall windows flooded the space with natural light.

The café occupied the front quarter, with mismatched wooden tables and chairs overlooking the Village Green. An antique counter served as the café's ordering station, its glass display cases filled with Layla's baked goods.

The retail portion had a curated collection of local products, artisanal foods, handcrafted items, and essentials. Reclaimed barn wood tables held things like corn, heirloom tomatoes, summer squash, honey, and handmade soaps. Floor-to-ceiling shelves lined the walls.

A carved wooden staircase led to the upper level, where Maggie's office was located alongside the staff break room and storage.

Behind the main building lay the courtyard, the carriage house where the co-owners, Maggie and her wife lived, and the old stables—used for storage and events. The third outbuilding was the old root cellar that'd been converted into the General Store's produce storage space.

Mosaic-tiled planter boxes lined the stone path connecting the buildings. The containers overflowed with blooms—black-eyed Susans, purple coneflowers, and daylilies, while the herb garden burst with fragrant basil, thyme, and lemon balm.

This place had stories to tell. Maybe Laura's would be one of them.

The café bustled with locals and visitors. It was the height of Vermont's summer tourist season, cars with license plates from Massachusetts, New York, and beyond, filling the Main Street parking spaces.

The work wouldn't be easy, but she was here for the long haul. For now, that was enough.

———◆———

Thomas Whitman, the Summer Cheese Festival head judge, entered the café, his proper posture a quiet display of his trademark attention to detail. His tanned skin spoke of his earliest years spent outdoors at Whitman Family Creamery. The last time he visited, he'd mentioned his toast was 'a touch overdone' but had complimented the excellent coffee. His eyes scanned the room with careful deliberation.

Someone was sitting at his usual table.

He might've been disappointed, but Thomas smiled as he surveyed the busy café.

Laura nudged Jesse. "Would you mind finishing this one for me, please?" she asked, pointing at the latte in progress.

Jesse nodded.

Laura slipped around the counter and approached Thomas. "Good morning, Thomas! So glad you stopped by. We've had quite the morning rush."

"Laura, great to see you," he said. "Busy morning indeed. Always good to see the local businesses thriving."

Laura nodded. "It's lovely seeing so much excitement around the festival. I'm glad I'm not the only one looking forward to it. Your usual table's taken. Would you like me to find you another that's just as nice?"

Thomas' eyes crinkled at the corners. "Change keeps the mind fresh, doesn't it? Though I admit to being a creature of habit." He glanced around the café. "Perhaps that corner table? The lighting is excellent for reading the morning paper."

"Perfect choice," Laura said, leading him to the spot he'd shown.

As he settled in, Thomas arranged his napkin on his lap. "The usual breakfast would be wonderful, if it's not too much trouble."

"Let me take care of that for you," Laura said before returning to the counter. "Jesse, would you mind putting in Thomas' regular order?"

Jesse flashed a quick thumbs up and glanced over at Thomas' table. "Thirty years in the artisanal food world and he still says please and thank you. Incredible."

"He's such a gentleman," Jasmine said as she collected a waiting meal from the kitchen window. "And a sharp mind, too, but you'd expect that from someone with so much experience. The town revolves around his opinion for those three days of the festival."

Laura checked the cold drinks stock. "I just hope my hospitality skills pass muster. I'd hate to be the reason for a festival scandal in my first month here."

Jasmine huffed a laugh. "Trust me, if Thomas has a problem with something, you'll know about it. But he'll tell you in the most courteous way possible."

Laura ferried orders and attended to customers. The café buzzed with energy around Thomas, and he nodded to familiar faces and exchanged a few pleasant words with an older couple at the next table.

When he finished, he approached the counter.

"Everything was delicious, as always," he told Laura. "Please give my compliments to Anton."

"Of course! I'll make sure he hears that. Have a wonderful day, Thomas."

<hr />

The older woman was tiny but determined, her warm golden-brown features alight with her usual cheer, weaving through the crowded café toward the counter.

"Good morning, Evelyn!" Laura said. "What brings you in today?"

"Seeing how my new tenant is managing!" Evelyn Chan replied with a twinkle. "And sampling a scone."

"Perfect timing," Laura said, stepping out from behind the bench and guiding Evelyn toward a table, pulling out a chair. "There's one with your name on it."

After Laura took Evelyn's order, the older woman asked, "How are you? And don't fib."

"I expected slower days, but honestly? It's been a good kind of busy," Laura said.

"Sounds like you brought the chaos with you," Evelyn joked.

"I hope not," Laura said. "My mom's already bracing for the 'I'm done' phone call."

"You're not going to, are you?" Evelyn said. It wasn't a question. "You're stronger than you think." Her eyes brightened. "Say! If you're free next Monday, which you will be because it's your day off, come to the Maplewood Crafters Club meeting. Silvia never missed it during her summer visits."

Laura smiled. "Gran always said the potluck nights were her favorites."

"You've got great timing, because it's the next one!" Evelyn said. "The other weeks are more casual. You're not obligated to bring food on those nights, though nobody complains if you do. Shall you come?"

Laura knew her landlady wouldn't take no for an answer.

"I'm looking forward to it," Laura said.

Evelyn beamed.

———◆◇◆———

Later, as Laura worked, foreboding settled over her. Again. After her third day on the job, Maggie had sat her down in the break room during a lull, fidgeting with a pencil.

"A bit of unpleasant news," she'd said, avoiding Laura's eyes. "Jeremy Blackwood's on the roster for the next festival committee meeting."

When Laura showed no recognition, Maggie explained—Jeremy was a food critic from Boston and a long-time festival committee member and assistant judge. Maggie's voice tightened when she mentioned his name.

"He said he's reviewing the store while he's in town," Maggie had added. "For the second time around. The last one eight years ago nearly finished us."

The knot in Laura's stomach tightened at the thought of tomorrow's meeting. At Hargroves—her previous hospitality job—one harsh review had cleared their reservation book for weeks—proof of how swiftly a critic could sink a reputation. She'd seen it happen firsthand during her fifteen years of building her career at one of Boston's most prestigious restaurants. All those fourteen-hour days, covering shifts, working overtime—all leading to that promised promotion to General Manager that'd vanished with the sudden sale of the business.

Her phone buzzed. A text from Danny.

"Hey sis! How's the new job going? Bet you're killing it!"

Despite her anxiety, Laura smiled. Trust Danny to check in right when she needed it.

She typed back:

> "It's going surprisingly well. You'd love it here."

Another message from Danny.

> "Great! We'll have to visit sometime! But seriously, you okay?"

Laura stared at the message, and rubbed her temples, remembering the phone call with her mother right before she'd moved. The conversation still stung with the precision only Bridget Evans could achieve.

"What if they don't appreciate you there?" she'd asked. "What if you don't fit in? And...a midlife crisis at almost thirty-eight? Really, Laura?"

The inevitable comparisons to her brothers had followed—Danny, the program director in New York, raising his son effortlessly despite his divorce, and Connor with his perfect California tech family.

And Laura. Falling short by being herself.

Still...underneath it all...Laura heard a loneliness her mother tried to hide.

She breathed in and out. The afternoon lull had settled in, bringing its own peaceful rhythm: chairs scooting back, low conversations, the espresso machine hissing. Customers lingered with a tranquility unlike anything she'd known in Boston, like there was no rush to get anywhere else. This was the breathing space she'd hoped to find in Silver Springs.

At least her Gran had supported the move—it had been her idea, after all.

Laura smiled as she remembered the wonderful surprise she'd found when she first arrived, all of two weeks ago. She had to hold onto that feeling.

The Summer Cheese Festival preparations loomed, and Jeremy Blackwood's name still sounded intimidating. But Laura wasn't without experience in handling difficult critics. They appreciated attention to detail and consistency. The General Store café could provide both.

Whatever happened, she wouldn't let Maggie down—not when she'd given Laura this chance. She'd come to Silver Springs seeking a new start, and facing challenges head-on was part of that beginning.

She would prove her mother wrong.

CHAPTER TWO

T he oversized crate wobbled. Laura, navigating between produce display bins, caught it just in time before the zucchinis met their demise. It was the day of the festival committee meeting, and it was already chaos.

"Look at you," Maggie said as she passed with a box of greens. Today, she wore a tucked-in linen shirt, midi-skirt, and work boots. All in black, of course. "I didn't know acrobatics were in your wheelhouse!"

From behind the counter, Eli gave Laura a thumbs up as he worked the coffee machine. "Smooth recovery."

Laura's face flushed as she laughed awkwardly.

The farmer, Toby Evers, who'd brought the delivery, walked in with another crate of salad leaves and set it down on a shelf. "That's the last one."

He nodded to Maggie and headed through the back entrance, the revving of his truck a few minutes later signaling his departure.

Laura arranged the kale, mustard greens, and sweet corn on the shelves. Satisfied, she passed Jasmine, stifling a smile. Jasmine had the unfortunate task of helping the affable but hapless Norman Buckley to choose an item from the menu. The man's indecisiveness was legendary.

Laura reached the counter, where Jesse stood plating up a fresh batch of scones for the display case.

Maggie followed. "Laura, if you've got a second, I need help with—"

The front doorbell jingled.

A short, well-dressed man in his fifties entered the bustling store. His porcelain face wore a sour expression, like he'd just bitten into an unripe plum. He raised a skeptical eyebrow at the colorful preserves and relishes in an antique cabinet. His tailored linen shirt, burgundy bow tie, and expensive shoes seemed offended by the General Store's rustic vibe. He adjusted his wire-rimmed spectacles on his aquiline nose.

Maggie's eyes darkened, and she ducked down underneath the counter, muttering something under her breath.

"What's wrong?" Laura asked.

"Don't get him looking this way," Maggie hissed. "I haven't got the capacity."

"Who is—" Laura began to ask.

The man advanced toward the counter, clasping his hands behind his back, chest raised. "Good morning."

Laura steadied herself before putting on her best professional smile. "Good morning! Welcome to—"

"Yes, yes," he said, knitting his eyebrows together. "I'm Jeremy Blackwood."

Laura blinked a few times before recovering. Right...the food critic. "Oh! It's a pleasure to meet you, sir. Since you're here ahead of the other committee members, may I offer you something while you wait?"

Jeremy ignored her and leaned over the counter. "Maggie, I've always found the ostrich approach most unbecoming." He straightened, a smirk tugging at his lips as he deigned to glance at Laura. "A late breakfast, thank you. Let's see if your culinary offerings have improved. Though I daresay it's unlikely."

"Of course," Laura said.

Maggie's cheeks reddened, and she curled her lip as she rose from her hiding spot.

Jeremy sauntered toward a corner table and took out a notebook, jotting a few things down.

Maggie stifled a groan. "Can't believe it's almost time for the committee meeting already. Are we sorted?"

Laura nodded, gesturing to a large table at the far side of the café. "I've made sure it's all in place. Drinks, muffins, everything's set."

"Perfect," Maggie said, exhaling. "Those foodies call themselves adventurous, but they always ask for the plainest snacks."

Laura stifled a chuckle.

Benjamin 'Ben' Ashby, a tall youth with an earnest expression, and freckled skin, chose that moment to enter from the back. He helped with maintenance jobs around town when he wasn't at his father's hardware store. He zigzagged his way in, balancing boxes of lights and extension cords stacked high enough to block his view. Maggie dodged around him, doing her best not to become one with the tangle as she hurried away.

Ben opened his mouth as he approached Laura—probably to say something silly—but stopped dead in his tracks.

From behind his temporary cover, he leaned in and whispered, "Is that...Jeremy Blackwood?"

Laura gave a slight nod.

Ben let out a low whistle before continuing. "I'm installing these out the front, but if you need someone to keep him calm, I'm available. Just don't ask me to keep him happy. That's beyond my skill-set."

Laura had to hide a smile.

The festival committee meeting had come and gone. Among the attendees had been Jeremy, Maggie, Thomas, of course, and several others. Diana Martinez was one: festival committee member, judge, and the owner of Mountain Valley Dairy, a local creamery and a General Store supplier. Rosalind Prescott, the festival director and committee chair, often came in for herbal tea. And Alexander 'Alex' Caldwell, the marketing manager, did his weekly shopping on Fridays. The rest, Laura didn't know by name.

Everyone except Maggie had left the building...and Jeremy. He remained at the table for some time, oscillating between making thoughtful noises and writing.

Laura monitored him in-between other duties until she filled a crystal pitcher with ice water and selected the newest of their printed menus. She approached him, but Jeremy ignored her arrival, continuing to scribble.

"I brought you some water, Mr. Blackwood," she said, placing the pitcher on a plate to catch any drips. "And here's our lunch menu. Take your time. The ham and Whitman Family Creamery cheddar on brioche is especially good. Layla Ahmed bakes the brioche each morning, and the reserve cheddar is receiving wonderful feedback for its depth of flavor."

That got his attention. He looked up from his notebook, his eyes narrowing. Jeremy swiped the menu from Laura's hands and cast an eye around the store, before his gaze landed on her.

"And you are?"

"I'm Laura Evans, the new café manager," she said. "It's a pleasure, sir. We're grateful to welcome someone of your reputation."

His eyebrows shot up, and his lips curled into a smile. "So they've brought in fresh blood to salvage this establishment. Did Maggie mention I'm writing a review?"

"She did," Laura said. "We're looking forward to hearing your feedback. Everyone here takes pride in making sure each dish feels special."

Jeremy chuckled. "I look forward to sharing my...thoughts."

"Take all the time you need, and if anything on the menu raises a question, I'm happy to help."

As she walked away, he couldn't resist having the last word. "I would've thought Maggie herself could spare a moment in her busy day to greet me. What a shame..."

———◆◇◆———

The café grew busy as locals filtered in for lunches. Maggie emerged from her office and joined Laura at the counter, looking rattled but determined.

Laura handed a slice of carrot cake to a customer and leaned closer. "Jeremy's still here, just so you're aware."

"I know," Maggie said with a groan. "He's here to poke around and see what falls apart." She plated up a few sandwiches before putting them on the higher shelf for Jesse to take out. "His last review nearly did us in. I won't let that happen twice."

Laura tried to look reassuring. "We've got a great team and we'll give it our all."

Laura delivered Jeremy's lunch: a summer squash and herb frittata, sharp cheddar slices, and walnut flour flatbread. It was an elegant presentation, even if Jeremy was predisposed to find more fault than flavor. He picked up a forkful of frittata, tasting it like a detective gathering evidence.

"How are you finding everything so far?" she asked, breaking the silence.

"Served at a suitable temperature," he replied, pausing for effect. "That's an improvement."

Laura suppressed her laughter. "Is there anything else I can bring for you?"

"Not at present."

She nodded. A ribbon bookmark sat on the open page in Jeremy's notebook. The end had a tiny, silver, sparkling cheese wheel pendant affixed to it.

"What a lovely bookmark," she said. It seemed sentimental for a man so sharp.

He nodded but otherwise ignored Laura's compliment, snapping the book shut. "I see the store has made many changes since my last visit."

She nodded. "There's something special about what's happening here."

His smile was cruel. "Let's hope it continues. This festival might prove pivotal in its...future."

As the early afternoon wore on, the café buzzed, but Laura's focus stayed on Jeremy. He took his time with his meal, jotting the occasional note. She was about to head over to Jeremy's table to refill his water when Jeremy glanced at his phone, stood, and made for the exit. Laura maneuvered around a table of chatty retirees, overhearing part of his conversation as he passed.

"Yes, we'll need to discuss those consulting arrangements," he muttered, the words barely audible over the lunch rush's clatter.

———◆———

Laura climbed the last step to the stables' mezzanine floor they were using for the pre-festival tasting, carrying several boxes of crackers. The two ceiling fans spun high overhead. It was a more intimate space than the grand Town Hall chambers where the festival would unfold. The stables were one of many sites for pre-festival events held throughout Silver Springs. All part of the effort to drum up interest and ensure a high turnout when the big three-day event arrived.

"Looks like we're in the home stretch!" Jasmine looked up from where she was arranging cheese samples on slate boards. "What else can I help with?"

Laura smiled with relief and brought the boxes over to Jasmine. "Would you mind placing the crackers to the left of each setting? And could you please fill the water pitchers? I'll go over everything one more time."

Jasmine nodded and did both tasks while Laura distributed the handwritten information cards for each cheese variety, ensuring the aging times and milk sources were visible for the tasting participants.

After they'd completed those jobs, Laura consulted her checklist. "Looks like we're all ready. I'll just check the chairs are—"

"In perfect sight lines." Jasmine finished, her dimples appearing. "Though I'm sure our esteemed critic will have something to say about it. Last year, he made us change the entire room layout because 'the afternoon sun would 'compromise the integrity of the flavor profiles.'"

Laura chuckled, double-checking the festival badges for each tasting participant were laid out on the table near the landing. Everything was ready.

The stairs creaked, and Laura turned to find Jeremy standing there. The gleam of his silver pocket watch—was, much like the man himself, polished to perfection.

"Good afternoon, Mr. Blackwood! The tasting doesn't begin for another twenty minutes, but we've just finished setting up if you'd like a moment to look around," Laura said, proud of how steady she kept her voice.

Jeremy frowned as he swept his gaze across the room. "I hope this temperature won't mask the subtle notes in aged cheddars. And these cheese knives—" He produced his notebook from his messenger bag. "I hope they're sharp enough not to crush or tear."

Jasmine stepped forward, holding a pocket thermo-hygrometer. "We've been monitoring the temperature since nine this morning. It's holding steady."

Jeremy's eyebrows rose. "At least someone here understands proper procedure." He turned back to his notebook, missing Jasmine's quick grin at Laura.

He finished jotting down whatever he'd wanted to note before his voice took on a calculating edge. "I've been doing some fascinating research. Uncovering some...surprising details." He patted his messenger bag. "This year's festival might prove more enlightening than anyone expects."

As Jeremy's words lingered, goosebumps rose on Laura's arms. Outside, more tasting participants gathered.

Jasmine cleared her throat. "I'll do one final check on the temperature of the aged cheddars."

Jeremy stalked through the room, his critical eye surveying each cheese display. He paused at the Mountain Valley Dairy section, where several award-winning varieties sat.

"Interesting amber hue," he said. His expression remained neutral, though something flickered in his gaze.

The floorboards near the stairs creaked again, and Maggie arrived, her pixie cut disheveled, with Diana close behind.

Jeremy nodded at them both. "Good afternoon." He turned to the cheesemaker with a barely disguised sneer. "I was just pondering how resourceful it is to base your company's branding on the rather astonishing tale of your family's historic cheese recipe. So...creative."

Her bronze-skinned face flushed a deeper tone. "We've used that method for generations."

"I'm sure you have," he said, then turned his attention to Maggie. "And you! The ambiance of your charming establishment for the tasting—how clever. It must be comforting for Silver Springs to relive its past before the future catches up."

Maggie's jaw tightened. Laura exchanged a glance with Jasmine as she busied herself straightening the already-perfect serving utensils, trying to look absorbed in the task.

"We're doing what we can, with what we've got," Maggie said as her fingers dug into the side of the tasting table, where a small crack in the antique wood waited for repairs. "A little respect wouldn't go astray."

The room's temperature dropped several degrees.

"Thomas," Jeremy said. "Perfect timing. I was about to share some...explosive findings."

The festival head judge had arrived during the exchange. His curated artisanal-professional appearance—crisp oxford shirt with rolled sleeves and dark premium denim—matched his cordial but strained expression.

Thomas' hand went to his festival badge, adjusting it, as he said, "This isn't the best time to discuss this. We're here to focus on the tasting."

"Are we?" Diana stepped forward from where she'd been double-checking the arrangement of her cheese samples. "Because I've been fielding Jeremy's pointed questions about my family's recipes."

"If we're questioning things—" Jeremy reached for his messenger bag.

"That's enough." Rosalind's voice cut through the tension. The festival committee chair and director stood at the top of the stairwell, her perfect posture radiating authority. "This is a pre-festival tasting, not an inquest."

Alex emerged from behind Rosalind and scurried in, his pale, almost translucent skin appearing even more washed out under the stables' overhead lights.

"Still cooking up those whiz-bang strategies, Caldwell?" Jeremy ignored Rosalind's words, his tone far from friendly. "From what I've found, certain parts of your genius reputation might be...over-exaggerated."

Alex flushed and buried his face in his notebook.

Laura circulated with a tray of apple slices, trying to appear casual as she offered refreshments to the tense group. She could smell the interplay of aged cheeses—sharp cheddar, nutty alpine, buttery brie—beneath an undercurrent of anxiety.

"The evidence speaks for itself," Jeremy continued.

"That'll do." Maggie's voice had a no-nonsense edge. "This isn't the time or place. If you're here to—"

"I'm here to reveal the truth," Jeremy shot back. "Though I understand why some might prefer comfortable lies."

Thomas caught Rosalind's eye as the woman's alabaster skin went paler, if possible, a silent message passing between them. Alex shifted, his gaze darting to Diana, who gave him a shake of her head.

"I believe," Rosalind said, "the other attendees will arrive—" she checked her watch. "In less than five minutes. Professional decorum is non-negotiable." She gave Jeremy a pointed look. "For everyone."

"Of course," Jeremy said, grinning, and he winked at Rosalind. "But I do hope you'll all find my keynote speech at the Summer Cheese Festival awards ceremony...enlightening." He paused for dramatic effect before saying, "I have some interesting revelations planned that'll captivate everyone's attention."

Rosalind's mouth tightened into a thin line, Thomas grimaced, Alex's pen stopped mid-scribble, Diana's knuckles whitened around her cheese knife, and Maggie's eyes darted around the room, looking anywhere but Jeremy.

———◆———

The pre-festival tasting wound down in a flurry of goodbyes and lingering conversations. Laura maneuvered through the crowd, collecting empty trays as attendees drifted toward the exit in small clusters.

"Magnificent textures in that Alpine variety," a woman in a floral dress said to her companion. "I told Edna she must try it before they sell out."

Near the top of the stairs, Diana huddled with Alex, their voices low but animated as they discussed something about promotional materials. Rosalind swept through, thanking attendees and checking items off her clipboard. She stopped to speak with a cheesemaker, and their conversation quickly turned secretive.

"He's getting desperate," said the vendor. "Five years ago, his column was syndicated in twenty newspapers. Now it's down to what, three? He used to expose real scandals in the food industry."

Rosalind nodded, her voice low. "These days he's just stirring up drama to stay relevant."

"Do you need help with those?" Jasmine asked, gesturing to the stack of cheese boards Laura was balancing.

"I've got it, thank you," Laura replied. "Could I ask you to grab the water pitchers?"

"Already on it," Jasmine said, moving toward the refreshment table.

Near the entrance, Thomas, Maggie, and two committee members Laura didn't recognize stood in a loose circle. Their conversation drifted toward her.

"—submit the final vendor layouts by tomorrow morning," Maggie was saying.

"I'll ensure it's on Rosalind's desk first thing," one committee member replied.

Thomas checked his watch with a slight frown. "I should head home. The day starts early tomorrow."

"Any big plans for the evening?" the other committee member asked. "I'm thinking about reviewing those new entries from the Hammond Cooperative."

"Nothing so productive," Thomas said. "I'll probably spend it in my shed tinkering with that old motorcycle again." He let out a self-deprecating chuckle that drew sympathetic smiles from the group. "Been trying to fix the thing for months now. I'm hopeless with anything mechanical."

"Let someone else handle it, Thomas," Maggie suggested. "Life's too short to waste on lost causes."

"Speaking of which," the first committee member interjected, "did you hear about the disaster at last weekend's Burlington Wine Expo? Apparently, their keynote speaker—"

The conversation moved on, and Laura noted how Jeremy lingered by the display boards, jotting something in his notebook. Thomas broke from his group with a friendly wave to his colleagues, nodding to Jeremy before heading to his car. All around her, dozens of conversations continued as the last attendees trickled out, the successful tasting event concluding in a buzz of anticipation for the festival to come.

CHAPTER THREE

The following morning, Laura arrived at the General Store just as the first streaks of sunlight painted the sky. She lingered by the door, drawing a deep breath and letting the familiar scent of coffee and baked bread settle her nerves. This morning, she was determined to channel her energy into getting things organized. With the Summer Cheese Festival approaching—and its crowds and chaos—she was grateful for the distraction.

Laura checked her to-do list for the day. First item? Double-check the stables, ensuring everything was in its proper place after yesterday's event.

The old stable building looked dramatic in this light, its weathered wooden sides glowing against the lightening sky as she opened the stables' main sliding doors.

A draft carried the earthy smell of aged wood from the interior, the usual cool of the building replaced with an odd humidity that clung to her skin. She flicked on the light switch.

Her throat constricted. There was a form sprawled on the concrete floor.

Jeremy Blackwood. His position indicated he'd fallen from the mezzanine above.

For a moment, Laura stood frozen, her mind refusing to process what her eyes were seeing.

She hurried over, dropped to her knees, heart hammering, and checked his pulse. Nothing. Laura pulled back, an involuntary gasp escaping her lips. She fumbled for her phone with trembling fingers.

"Nine-one-one, what's your emergency?" The dispatcher's calm voice seemed surreal.

"I—need to report—" Laura steadied herself. "An emergency. A man—he's in the stables. The Silver Springs General Store. No pulse. He's not breathing. He's...he's gone."

"Are you safe? Is there anyone else there?" the dispatcher asked.

"I'm alone," Laura said. "I—I wasn't expecting anything like this."

"Can you identify the person?"

"His name—his name is Jeremy Blackwood." Laura said, bile rising in her throat. "He is—I mean was, visiting for the festival. He was a food writer."

The dispatcher took her through a series of questions—her name, the exact location, Jeremy's condition. Laura answered mechanically, her eyes never leaving Jeremy's form. Her hand shook so badly she had to press the phone tighter against her ear.

"Emergency services are on their way," the dispatcher assured her. "They should arrive within minutes. Should I stay on the line until they get there?"

"I—" Laura's voice caught. She closed her eyes and drew a long, steadying breath. "I'll call Maggie—she's my boss. She should come." Her tone was steadier now, though the calm was mostly surface. "Thank you."

"All right, I'll let you go. Help is on the way. Call us back if anything changes."

After hanging up, Laura dialed another number. "Maggie, I'm so sorry...something's happened. It's an emergency."

Maggie excused herself from whatever she was doing and asked, "What's wrong?"

"I'm in the stables...I found...Jeremy Blackwood." Laura forced the rest out. "He's...dead. I've already called emergency services."

Maggie gasped as sirens wailed in the distance, growing closer.

Laura took in the tragic scene before her, her breathing coming in shallow gasps. She ordered herself to focus even as her mind screamed at her to look away, to run, to be anywhere but here.

Jeremy's glasses had shattered against the concrete floor. Next to him, his gleaming pocket watch lay in pieces. The broken face pointed at ten-o-seven, as if time itself had stopped at that moment.

She straightened, her pulse racing so hard it throbbed in her temples.

His messenger bag sat discarded on the floor beside scattered papers, though his notebook with its cheese wheel pendant was nowhere in sight. The absence was significant somehow.

Laura leaned in for a closer look, swallowing hard. Strange. The bag had these...dark blue ink splotches.

Next to it sat a page scrawled with nonsensical amounts and dates, labeled as 'arrangement'. The handwriting was frantic. Was this part of the 'revelations' he'd mentioned at the pre-festival tasting?

Laura looked up at the mezzanine. He'd fallen—but why? And while that theory explained the papers everywhere, it didn't account for the missing notebook. Maybe he'd left it somewhere?

She stepped back, the concrete floor tilting beneath her feet. What was she doing? This was a crime scene.

She began pacing near the entrance, chewing her lip, waiting, doing everything she could to avoid looking at Jeremy. Her mind spun with fragments of yesterday afternoon's tasting event. Jeremy had talked about 'fascinating research' and 'surprising details.'

Was it an accident? Or had someone lured him back here, to stop the revelations from coming to light? She didn't want to believe it.

Someone burst through the open stable doors, and she jumped.

"Laura!" Maggie rushed toward her. "Oh! Oh, no." Her hand flew to her mouth, and she staggered back a step.

"The...police are on the way," Laura said. "I called them as soon as I saw."

Maggie nodded, still staring at the scene. "I just can't believe..." Her voice cracked, eyes darting to the mess of papers. "This is terrible, Laura."

Her boss looked stricken, but there was a flicker of something else in her expression.

———— ◆◇◆ ————

Morning light crept across the General Store's courtyard as two officers secured the stables' doors with evidence tape. The old building's weathered wood appeared more worn in the growing daylight, its familiar silhouette now holding dreadful secrets.

From behind the main General Store building, onlookers gathered in the alleyway, their hushed voices carrying. A few curious faces peered over the back gate, withdrawing when one police officer gestured for them to move away.

Laura fanned herself, the humidity making her cotton blouse cling to her skin. Even the heritage apple trees, their leafy branches heavy with ripening fruit etched against the brightening sky, seemed to creak, adding to the unsettling sensation that'd settled over the General Store grounds.

Beyond the gate backing onto the alleyway, Laura could see the rear of Ashby Hardware. Several times a week, Pete would cut through the alley to grab a coffee. Could that be how someone got in?

Through the General Store's back entrance, staff members cast worried glances toward the courtyard while Maggie maintained some semblance of a normal opening time routine. There was nothing normal about this day, not anymore.

"Excuse me." A voice drew Laura's attention.

An athletic-looking woman with olive skin approached, her curly dark hair tied back into a bun. She carried herself with the authority of someone used to taking charge, though her expression was kind. A red dress shirt with rolled sleeves, chunky lace-up boots, and dark jeans added to that impression.

"Are you Laura Evans?" the woman asked.

Laura nodded.

"I'm Detective Sergeant Ramirez. Thank you for waiting. I know this has been challenging." Her eyes searched Laura's face. "I have a few questions for you. Can you do that? I'll need to record it."

A few beats passed, then Laura summoned what was left of her strength, and nodded.

Ramirez pulled out a portable digital recorder. She spoke into the device, explaining the context, before turning back to Laura. "Before we begin, I need to ask. Who owns this establishment?"

"Maggie Brook and Kathleen Quinn," Laura replied. "I'm the café manager."

"And you report directly to them both?"

"Yes, I do."

Ramirez nodded. "Can you walk me through what happened?"

"I went to the stables because I just wanted to make sure everything was tidied up after yesterday's tasting," Laura paused, the memory of what she'd found making her voice waver. "That's when I...saw him."

"You did the right thing calling us," Ramirez said. "First, you mentioned a tasting?"

Laura explained the event the General Store had hosted the day before.

Ramirez frowned. "When you...entered the stables, did you notice anything else amiss?"

Laura hesitated. "There were...broken glasses, a smashed pocket watch stuck at ten-o-seven, and papers all over the floor. His bag had...ink spilled on it. But the notebook I saw him using—it was missing. One page left behind had dates and amounts and a title: 'arrangement.' I don't know...he was hinting at something big yesterday. That might be what he meant? It sounded like he was onto something."

Ramirez' eyes narrowed. "I see. Who would've been in the stables last?"

"It was just me and Jasmine Williams tidying up afterward," Laura replied. "We hold events up on the mezzanine floor."

"Wait," Ramirez interrupted, glancing toward the stables. "I noticed when I arrived—there are no locks on these doors. Why?"

Laura shifted. "I think Maggie never felt the need for locks. They've never had a break-in or any security issues as far as I know."

"I see," Ramirez's tone sharpened. "This is a serious oversight. The lack of basic security measures is problematic, especially now. This needs to be addressed immediately. I'll discuss this with your bosses."

Laura nodded, feeling a flush of embarrassment.

"Who was here yesterday afternoon?" Ramirez asked.

"There were lots of people—vendors, committee members, and attendees." Laura said.

"Did anyone stand out?"

Laura hesitated, her instincts telling her to be careful. "Jeremy kept saying his speech at the upcoming Summer Cheese Festival would shake things up. He seemed excited about it."

Ramirez paused. "Did he single out...anyone in particular?"

"Yes...Diana Martinez. He was critical of the story behind her cheese, like he didn't believe it."

Ramirez arched an eyebrow. "Anyone else?"

"He commented on Maggie Brook, my boss, too. He implied she was avoiding the future, whatever that meant. Jeremy hinted Alex Caldwell's reputation was built on shaky ground. He said he had interesting revelations planned for his keynote that would captivate everyone's attention." Laura swallowed hard. "And now...he's gone."

Ramirez nodded, considering. "And what time did everyone leave?"

Laura shook herself, trying to overcome her anxiety and focus on answering. "Around...four pm."

"Detective Sergeant? There's something you should see."

They turned at the sound of a man's voice. It was one of the patrol officers, and his badge said, 'Littlefield.' He flashed an evidence bag containing...a festival committee badge. The heritage cheese wheel logo, the elegant typeface showing who it belonged to, and the purple color.

Laura's stomach plummeted.

"Is something wrong?" Ramirez asked.

"That badge...it belongs to Diana." Laura's voice shook.

What did it mean? Was she the last person to see Jeremy alive?

Ramirez shut off the portable recorder. "Thank you for your time, Laura. Would you mind heading back inside? And can I use one of the rooms upstairs? I want to speak with the staff."

⸺⚬⸺

Laura sat in the General Store's upstairs breakroom, cradling a coffee mug's glazed clay, and she took a sip: an Americano with cream. It'd only taken Eli two times to memorize her coffee order. Her temples throbbed.

"You should eat something," Jasmine said, sliding a plate of toast closer. After finding Laura pale and trembling near the counter, she'd guided her upstairs and fixed her a light breakfast. "It might help you feel better."

Laura nodded. "Thank you. You're very kind." She forced herself to take a few bites, but her stomach churned.

"Anyone would be shaken after what you saw," Jasmine said. "Finding Jeremy like that..."

The events of the morning replayed in Laura's mind. What if the secrets Jeremy had threatened to reveal were something someone would...take a life for?

"Do you want to talk about it?" Jasmine asked, "I'm here for you. You're not alone in this."

Laura took another deep breath and nodded. She needed to talk to someone. Thank goodness for Jasmine.

CHAPTER FOUR

Laura emerged into the main retail space, where the cheerful morning bustle had been replaced by hushed, anxious whispers. Her heart still thundered against her ribs.

Maggie stood near the checkout, her brow furrowed, fingers drumming a relentless rhythm on the countertop. She'd insisted on keeping the store open, though the police had cordoned off the stables. An older regular arrived, and Maggie seized the chance to help him select his weekly shopping.

Upstairs, Ramirez had commandeered the break room. Maggie had already faced her line of inquiry. Now it was Jasmine's turn. At the café counter, Eli's hands shook as he made an espresso. Jesse stood near him, reorganizing the pastry display, wearing a worried expression. Laura busied herself refolding dish towels, her ears straining to catch snippets of conversation around her.

"Laura, can you come over here please?" Maggie called out, gesturing at the growing line of customers and the old-fashioned cash register, its drawer stuck halfway open like a shocked gasp. "This old thing's acting up. Can you take the counter?"

Laura nodded, and began taking people's orders while Maggie fiddled with the till, muttering to herself.

"Kathy thought it added character...today of all days...can't even—" She gave the register a shake. "Blast it, the sliding bit's gone. Just what we need. If only—" She clamped her mouth shut, shoving the drawer closed, and it thankfully stayed that way. Her phone beeped in her apron pocket and she fished it out, groaning at the screen. "It never ends. I'm knee deep already and now there's more?"

She hurried toward the back door. Laura grabbed a damp cloth and headed to help Eli clear the empty tables. Jesse had moved to assist retail customers.

Eli looked up from stacking cups and saucers. "Thanks, Laura."

"Of course. Are you doing okay?" Laura asked.

Eli shrugged, but avoided her gaze. "I feel like I should be the one asking you that. Wish people would stop asking me questions about what happened. What would I know? Except...I hope it has nothing to do with it, but I can't help but think...I overheard Jeremy on the phone the other day. He got real sharp with someone, and said, 'You'll regret it if you don't.'"

Laura straightened. "Can I ask—do you remember who he was talking to? And did you let Detective Sergeant Ramirez know?"

Eli shook his head for the first question, and nodded for the second, stacking the last piece of errant cutlery onto a tray. Jeremy must've been involved in something that led to his death, but what?

Jasmine emerged from upstairs, her interview with Ramirez finished. She steadied herself with a deep breath as she picked up a coffee order.

Jesse heaved a sigh before ascending the stairs for their turn.

———◆———

"Good morning, Laura," Katie Fowler called as she approached.

She was an assistant at the Village Skein, Silver Springs' local yarn store. Laura checked the time. Katie appeared every morning at nine forty-five, like, well, clockwork.

"Or not so good," Katie corrected herself.

"A busy one," Laura replied, forcing a smile as she scribbled four coffee orders: a vanilla latte for Rebecca, the yarn-dyer; a cappuccino for Nell, the no-nonsense owner; a double-shot espresso for Ruby, a part-time employee; and an Americano for Katie.

Laura tore off the slip and affixed it to the coffee machine.

Katie leaned in. "Such a tragedy. Maggie must be relieved."

Laura stiffened.

"His review when they opened nearly destroyed their business," Katie said with a knowing nod, lowering her voice. "Everyone knows how much they hated each other. And it's not just Maggie who had issues with him. Apparently, there's someone telling the police they overheard Diana threatening Jeremy at the farmers' market recently. Something about how she'd 'do whatever it takes' if he didn't stop poking his nose into things that didn't concern him. I shouldn't be spreading rumors, but that's what everyone's saying. Between that and her festival badge being found at the scene..."

She accepted her change and swept away to wait with the other to-go customers.

Laura's stomach clenched. This was useful—but it was still gossip, and that could be damaging. Yet it wasn't malicious—more a way of navigating a town where news was the currency of belonging.

Mrs. Merriweather, who always had black coffee and a blueberry muffin, paused after ordering. "I heard about the trouble. You let me know if you need something, alright? It was such an awful thing for you to discover."

Laura's throat threatened to close for the umpteenth time that morning. At least in this instance it wasn't for a terrible reason. "Thank you. That's very kind."

———◦———

Laura wove between tables, clearing away dishes and refilling waters. Locals and visitors sat clustered together, their low voices drifting to Laura's ears.

"...happened right here. A dead food critic. Such a scandal."

Laura's stomach clenched.

"Right in Silver Springs!" someone else exclaimed.

"Didn't Maggie have issues with Blackwood?"

Someone scoffed as they sipped their tea. "The worst review he ever wrote!"

It hadn't even been two hours since she'd discovered Jeremy! She pushed through her tasks as whispering voices closed in from all sides.

"And at the General Store, of all places!" someone said, shaking their head.

Another clucked their tongue. "Poor Maggie, this must be dreadful for her, on top of everything."

CHAPTER FIVE

P erched like vigilant birds at their window-side vantage point, Martha Henderson and Judith Yoon, friends of Evelyn, surveyed the café's comings and goings. Martha, vice president of the Historical Society, and president of the Good Neighbor Guild, fidgeted with her napkin. Judith, a former editor at a New York publishing house who now contributed puzzles to the Maplewood Memo, glanced toward the counter with concern. She tapped her pen against a half-completed crossword in front of her.

Laura steeled herself. Though she'd served Martha and Judith often, a strange mix of familiarity and awkwardness settled in as she approached.

"Remind me to pick up those door stoppers before Pete closes," Martha was telling Judith.

Judith nodded. "Good thinking. I need a lightbulb anyway. And you know how close his store is to the alleyway." She leaned in, a conspiratorial look crossing her warm-beige complexion. "We may learn something interesting!"

They registered Laura's arrival and looked up.

"Laura, dear," Martha said, her voice softer than usual, eyes searching Laura's face. "We heard you were the one who...found him."

Judith patted Laura's forearm. "Such a terrible thing to experience. Are you alright?"

Laura's voice wavered. "I'm...managing. It means a lot you asked. What can I get for you both today?"

After taking their order, Laura turned to leave, but Martha leaned forward. "The whole town's talking about what this means for the festival. Jeremy was supposed to be our keynote speaker at the awards ceremony, but now..."

"Without an assistant judge, the contest portion might need to be restructured," Judith finished for her, brow furrowed.

Martha's eyes darkened, her pale skin taking on a rosy hue, as it always did when she was concerned.

"And you know how Jeremy was," Judith started.

Martha stifled a groan. According to Martha, Judith tended to get her hands deep into other people's pies.

"He was always digging into everyone's business. I can't help wondering if—" Judith stopped herself. "Some people might breathe easier with him gone, is all I'm saying."

"We survived another rush," Eli said, tidying the pastry display, eyes downcast.

Laura heaved a sigh, rolling her shoulders.

Jesse's gaze swept to Laura as they wiped the espresso machine. "Even after a wretched morning, you pulled through with such poise. I don't know how you manage it."

Jasmine emerged from the stockroom, carrying a stack of boxes, her shoulders tense. "Neither do I."

Laura gave a wan smile as she cleaned the counter. "Thanks, all of you. Despite...everything that's happened...being here is still so much better than Boston. There, customers wanted their food yesterday. Here, everyone remembers your name and wants to check on you."

"Classic Silver Springs," Jesse said, cracking a brief smile. "You'll get cornered by Mrs. Lawson's stories of her grandchildren in Connecticut, ambushed by Mr. Fleming's composting tips, and if Dr. Patel's nearby—hope you like birds."

"You can't sneeze in this town without someone asking what's wrong and offering to bring you soup," Eli said, restocking sugar packets. "It's sweet...and a little much."

Laura raised an eyebrow. "I'm guessing you all already know my life story?"

Jesse shrugged. "We know you worked at some fancy place in Boston..."

"Hargroves," Eli said.

"Right. And you're Silvia's granddaughter. That alone earns you the town's collective trust," Jesse continued.

"And," Eli said, "You...left Boston. Something happened at work."

Jasmine shot him a look. "Not that it's anyone's business."

Laura rolled her eyes with a weary smile. "And here I thought I could keep one thing to myself."

"Don't worry," Jesse said. "The rumor mill means well...mostly. And for what it's worth, we're glad you're here."

Laura balanced on the wooden step stool, arranging jars of blackberry preserves on the top shelf.

"Shift it left," Kathy said, handing Laura another jar. "Late summer's our showpiece—strongest hue, best light."

Kathleen 'Kathy' Quinn, a former architect, co-owner of the General Store, Maggie's wife, and Laura's other boss, scrutinized the arrangement with a discerning gaze.

Laura repositioned the jams. "Such beautiful colors. Did Maggie make these?"

"Sure did," Kathy said, her voice softening. "It's been a morning. How are you coping? Finding Jeremy like that...that's not something you just brush off."

Laura fought to stop her hands from trembling as she took another jar. "I'm...trying to stay steady."

Kathy frowned, twisting her wedding ring, the only thing decorating her tanned, weathered hands. "Town's already buzzing. Vicious stuff. All because Maggie raised her voice at Jeremy. She's been a cornerstone here for decades and now they're painting her as a suspect."

"The police haven't confirmed anything," Laura said, stepping down from the stool.

"Not officially, sure, but Ramirez asked about her whereabouts three separate times." Kathy's voice cracked. "This festival carries a significant portion of our summer revenue. With Jeremy gone and Maggie under the microscope, there's already talk of scrapping the whole thing."

Laura shook her head. "We're not letting all this fall apart—not if we can help it."

———————•◦•———————

The police had wrapped up their initial investigation and departed, allowing Ben to install a combination lock on the stables' doors. The additional heavy-duty padlocks Maggie sent him to buy were out of stock at his dad's store, but he'd ordered them in.

Laura hoped the locks would be enough of a deterrent.

Maggie had sequestered herself in her office for three hours now. Laura couldn't just stand by and let her boss stew up there by herself. She should check on her and see how she's doing. Laura busied herself preparing a proper afternoon tea—Earl Grey with a splash of milk, plus a few shortbread cookies.

Laura knocked on Maggie's office door. A startled rustle of papers, then Maggie called out.

"Who's there?"

"It's Laura. I brought up some tea."

A moment of hesitation before: "The door's open—don't mind the mess."

Maggie sat at her desk looking exhausted—eyes dull and shoulders hunched. Laura placed the tray on the desk. Her boss' hands trembled as she reached for the teacup.

"Thank you, that's...thoughtful," Maggie said, letting out a joyless laugh. She took a sip of tea. "Ramirez has all but stamped 'guilty' on my forehead."

Laura froze. "Wait a second. What reason would they have?"

"They found notes in Jeremy's bag. Pages of 'consulting fees' charged to me," Maggie said. "Which isn't true, I've never paid him a dime."

"That's strange. Something's off," Laura said.

"It's nonsense," Maggie said, rubbing her forehead. "They've told me I can't leave town—like I'm going to bolt with the festival breathing down our necks. I'm holding on. Kathy sees through it, of course. She always does."

"There's no way they actually believe you'd—" Laura trailed off.

As Maggie shifted in her chair, a large sheet of paper partially covered by other documents caught Laura's attention. A hand-drawn blueprint of the General Store, with detailed annotations in Maggie's handwriting, had the stable area circled in red marker.

Maggie scrambled the papers, covering the diagram. "Just some repair plans I've been working on. I started them ages ago—nothing to do with any of this mess."

Laura nodded, tearing her eyes away from the blueprint as she fought to keep a neutral expression. "I should get going, but I'm here for you."

Maggie had a strained smile on her lips. "The tea was perfect, thank you."

Laura didn't reply for several seconds. "Of course," she stammered. "Any time."

As she descended the stairs, Laura's heart thudded. She liked Maggie. Still...the red circle around the stables,

Maggie's strange behavior, and the mysterious consulting fees were strange.

One question kept nagging at her.

Why was Jeremy at the stables that night, anyway? Had someone met him there? Or had someone lured him there, knowing the building would be empty, hours after the pre-festival tasting ended? Unless Jeremy had a reason to be there, it made no sense. Whatever had brought him to the stables was the key.

Laura kicked off her shoes. Every muscle ached. The apartment felt too quiet after the chaotic day. Her phone buzzed against the kitchen counter.

Laura sighed, shoulders slumping. "Hi, Mom."

"Laura." A sharp intake of breath. "It's all over the news here. A murder at your workplace?"

"It's in the right hands, Mom. The police are on it."

"A food critic? Wasn't he the one who gave your boss that terrible review years ago?"

Laura's stomach tightened. "Yes, that's true."

"So she had a motive." Bridget's voice wavered. "You need to come home. Before you get dragged into this."

The floorboards creaked as Laura paced the small kitchen. "This place...it feels right. I'm not giving that up."

"Your home is in Boston. Where you have connections." Bridget sighed. "I didn't want you to move away. Now this has happened, I can't help but feel...this is another reason it wasn't the right choice."

A tense silence stretched between them.

"I'm sorry, Mom. I have to go." Laura's fingers tightened around the phone.

After a long pause, Bridget said, "Please, Laura. Think about what I've said. I only—want you to be safe."

"I will."

After hanging up, her phone buzzed soon after. Again? It wasn't her mother, though. It was Connor.

"Heard about what happened. You okay? Need anything?"

"I'm managing as well as I can. Thanks for checking in."

"Let me know if that changes."

He responded.

Laura contemplated her reflection in the darkened window, her skin pale and drawn, eyes shadowed with unwanted knowledge. She wouldn't be going back to Boston.

CHAPTER SIX

The fresh smell of lime enveloped Laura as she entered Evelyn's apartment. Her breathing steadied, her muscles relaxing as her landlady welcomed her.

"Come sit in the living room. I'll only be a moment," Evelyn said.

Laura sank into a plush armchair, and Oscar, Evelyn's dark-brown Burmese cat, padded over. He circled her ankles, then settled on her lap, purring as she ran a hand over his soft back. Monty, Oscar's brother, with a light bluish-gray coat, remained on the windowsill.

A cream-colored sofa with knitted throws and patterned cushions sat facing the windows. Colorful landscapes hung on the walls, and a wooden coffee table featured Evelyn's crocheted sunflower coasters. The loveseat matched Laura's chair, its floral upholstery draped with a crocheted Afghan with deep pink, green, and ivory squares.

Bookshelves lined one wall, holding mysteries, biographies, and craft books alongside family photos and pottery. In the corner, a lush fern, a jade plant, and African violets sat near the window. Beyond the living room, the spacious dining area held an antique sideboard and a large wooden table.

Evelyn bustled in, setting a tray with key lime pie and two glasses of iced cider on the coffee table. "Something to cool us down on this hot day."

Laura took one glass, letting the cider seep through her. "Thank you. They...really seem to think Maggie's involved."

Evelyn shook her head, cutting a slice of pie for Laura. "Honestly. As if Maggie's the only one Jeremy ever crossed. What exactly are they basing it on?"

"The notes in Jeremy's bag started it," Laura said. "He was keeping detailed records of consulting fees billed to Maggie."

Evelyn's eyebrows rose.

"She promised she had nothing to do with it, but people haven't forgotten the review. It hurt her business badly."

Evelyn stared at her. "And they believe Maggie's grief turned so bitter it boiled into something violent? Absurd!"

Laura nodded. "Detective Sergeant Ramirez seemed convinced it shows Maggie was trying to buy a second chance through Jeremy."

"That's not like her in the slightest," Evelyn said, frowning. "Unfortunately, the police only need motive and opportunity to make assumptions."

"She's not someone I'd ever expect to be involved with this," Laura said. She accepted the plate Evelyn handed her as Oscar continued to purr on her lap. "They let Diana go within an hour, but they're still hounding Maggie. Diana's badge was at the crime scene! And she and Jeremy had such a tense exchange." Laura paused, considering. "Although...now I think about it..."

Evelyn leaned forward. "What did you just put together?"

Laura swallowed. "Earlier today...I noticed Maggie had been tucked away in her office, so I made some afternoon tea and went to check on her."

"That's thoughtful of you," Evelyn said.

Laura sighed. "I noticed...printouts of the General Store's building plans on her desk. It was covered in her notes and the...stables were circled. When she saw me looking, she covered it with other papers and brushed it off, saying it was for renovations—but something about her tone felt..."

"Suspicious?" Evelyn frowned. "Something tells me the full story hasn't come to light. Have you read Jeremy's review?"

She hadn't, so she found the article on her phone, reading a few lines aloud.

"A culinary catastrophe. The General Store Café takes perfectly good locally grown ingredients and transforms them into inedible..." she scrolled down. "Their food was awful. The server was untrained and provided the sloppiest of service, as if they had no hospitality experience whatsoever." Her eyes widened. "He called it 'a testament to incompetence' and 'the worst farm-to-table dining experience in New England.' I can understand why Maggie would be upset. Furious, even. But to do something like that...I just don't see it."

Evelyn nodded. "Maggie doesn't strike me as having done something like that! However, someone else might've, especially when you consider his reputation for uncovering scandals. Perhaps..."

"Do you think...someone killed him to keep their secrets safe?"

Evelyn let out a sigh. "The only thing I know is this is a terrible situation. Still, it'd benefit you to be aware of the man Jeremy was."

"Okay...let's see what comes up," Laura said, typing his name into her phone's search engine.

Most of Jeremy's press mentions appeared in gossipy food magazines and lifestyle blogs. The decline was striking—abundant coverage dwindled to sparse mentions in the past two years.

Ten years ago, Jeremy's name appeared in respected outlets and alongside major restaurant reviews. Five years ago, he'd been writing for second-tier publications. And recently? Mostly blog appearances and local festival coverage. His star had been fading long before he died. Jeremy's declining career might explain his abrasive personality at the tasting, but it didn't explain why someone would kill him.

Evelyn gave her a gentle smile. "Perhaps there's a way you could lend a hand."

Laura looked at her. "You mean...get involved? I don't know, this is serious. I might just make a mess of things."

"You're part of this now, Laura. You care too much not to be," Evelyn said. "And what if you make things better?"

"Evelyn, someone died! I'm just the new café manager. I could make things worse! What if I end up pointing fingers at innocent people? Or what if the killer realizes I'm asking questions? Finding him...it was awful."

Evelyn set down her mug and leaned forward. "Laura, I've lived here for forty years, and if there's one thing I know, it's that stories travel faster than the truth. The police don't know who's been nursing what old hurt or hiding which family skeleton. But I do. And so do you, if you pay close enough attention."

"Why me? What could I do?" Laura asked.

"When I was younger, something similar happened. A man was wrongly accused of stealing from the community fund. People turned on him overnight. His business collapsed, his family was left to fend for themselves. They cleared his name six months later, but the damage was already done. And I stood by, watching it unfold. It was a terrible time for our town, a reminder of how quickly things can unravel. My late husband Charles always said in such times, you see people's true natures. That's why I won't sit by. You heard the café whispers. If we leave this to unfold on its own, Maggie's reputation, and the store, may not survive."

Laura smoothed Oscar's fur. "This isn't something I've ever done before...I'm out of my depth."

"You have a good eye for people, Laura," Evelyn said. "You spot the unspoken nuances—a tired smile, a hesitant question. And you respond with kindness. That's rarer than you realize."

Laura was silent for a long moment. "It's not that I don't care. I just...wouldn't know where to begin. My Mom phoned me today...and it didn't go well."

Evelyn's expression softened. "And how is Bridget?"

"She caught the news and called me immediately," Laura said, stabbing her fork into the pie. "She told me coming here was a mistake."

"And what did you tell her?" Evelyn asked, sipping her cider.

"That I'm staying," Laura said. "She wasn't happy about it."

"Parents. They see us as we were, not as we are."

Laura picked up her fork again. The pie's cool, creamy filling melted on her tongue. "This is incredible. And...thank you. It helps to talk about it."

"Anytime." Evelyn smiled. "Rather than focus on what you lack, concentrate on what you have. I've known most people in this town for decades. They'll talk to me in ways they never would to the Detective Sergeant. And you're new, which means people will either underestimate you or try to impress you with what they know."

Laura bit her lip. "I don't want to regret doing nothing. Maggie saw something in me. She trusted me with her café and gave me the job. I can't ignore what's happening."

Evelyn nodded. "In that case, let's get to work. Who else had something to gain from Jeremy's silence?"

Laura considered. "Diana didn't take it well when Jeremy brought up her family's methods."

"I imagine she didn't," Evelyn said. "Though I daresay Jeremy gave more than one person cause for resentment."

"How would I make up an excuse to talk to her? Or anyone else?" Laura asked.

"That's why you've got me!" Evelyn said, her eyes twinkling. "I've known Diana since she wore pigtails. And you see what others overlook. Together, we'd make quite the team."

Oscar stirred on Laura's lap. Monty gave a flick of his tail.

"If we're going to speak to Diana, consider it arranged." Evelyn opened her phone and began typing. "She's a busy woman, but she might have time to squeeze us in, especially if I mention you're interested in learning about her cheese."

Oscar nuzzled closer against Laura as Monty stretched and jumped down from the windowsill.

Evelyn's phone buzzed. "She said we're welcome to drop by tomorrow evening."

"I'm not sure I could do this without you," Laura said.

Evelyn smiled. "You don't even have to ask. I'm always here for you." She glanced at the mantel clock. "Would you look at the time! I insist you stay for dinner. No arguments. Tonight's risotto."

Laura's stomach growled, and they both laughed.

"I'd really appreciate that, thank you. I guess my stomach agrees."

The rich aroma of garlic and herbs filled Evelyn's kitchen as Laura added another ladleful of stock to the absorbent rice.

"Perfect technique," Evelyn said, chopping fresh parsley. "You're no stranger to the kitchen, I see."

Evelyn's kitchen was a cook's dream, with pots hanging above a worn block island and an impressive collection of cookbooks. As Laura stirred, her eyes wandered to a colorful spine: 'Spice. Steam. Stir.' by Rachel Wu.

"I love her recipes," Laura said. "Your daughter has such an incredible talent for combining flavors."

Evelyn beamed. "The way Rachel marries old and new techniques is extraordinary, though I suppose a mother's praise carries a hint of bias."

"No, really," Laura said. "Her chapter on umami in comfort foods changed how I approach cooking! She's incredible."

Evelyn grinned. "She'd be delighted to hear that. And she comes by every so often. Are you interested in meeting her?"

Laura's spoon froze mid-stir, her cheeks flushing pink. "You'd...introduce me?"

"Of course I would," Evelyn said. "Rachel loves meeting fellow food enthusiasts." She checked the roasting vegetables. "Excellent. Five more minutes."

———◇———

Laura and Evelyn settled at the dining table. Steaming bowls of root vegetable risotto sat in front of them, alongside a crystal bowl of colorful salad.

"This is delicious," Laura said after her first bite. "Thank you for asking me to join you."

"My pleasure," Evelyn replied. "Sharing a meal with a new friend is always a delight." After a comfortable silence, Evelyn continued. "So, tell me. How are you really settling in?"

"I'd just started to...but now..." Laura began, pushing a piece of carrot around her bowl. "I'm not sure. I'd finally found my footing...then this happened. It feels like I'm missing something important about the townspeople. I can't believe someone here committed a murder!"

"You're sharper than you give yourself credit for," Evelyn said. "The trick is learning when to trust your gut." She frowned. "Another food critic scandal...remind me to tell you sometime about the run-in Rachel and I had with one last year."

As they finished, despite everything, a quiet sense of belonging settled over Laura—stronger than anything she'd known in months.

CHAPTER SEVEN

The sky stretched forever above the dairy as Laura parked her car. A gust of warm evening air brushed her face as she and Evelyn trudged up Mountain Valley Dairy's drive, muddy from the recent rains.

Three dogs sprinted across the field. Laura bent to pet them, struggling to find a head to scratch amidst the furry blur. She counted an Old English Sheepdog, an Australian Shepherd, and a Golden Retriever as they wiggled and jostled.

Evelyn laughed. "We should've brought some treats!"

Tearing down the hill came another figure, human-shaped this time.

"Scoundrel! Rascal! Get back!" It was Diana, breathless. "Perry! Come on, you lot!" With a colorful bandana around her neck, she looked part farmer, part artist.

The dogs bounded away, plonking themselves down a few meters away from them, tails wagging.

Diana opened the farm gate. "Sorry about that. You'd think I never fed them."

Laura grinned. "I was tempted to sneak them home with us. Surely they're no more trouble than Evelyn's cats."

"I'll pretend I didn't hear that," Evelyn said, embracing the farmer. "How are you, Diana? It's been too long.

I've missed seeing you at the Friends Of The Library meetings."

Diana sighed. "I know...the dairy keeps me so busy, especially this time of year with festival preparations. Hello again, Laura."

"Thanks again for having us! I haven't tasted the cheeses on their own yet, but I've loved every dish Anton's made with them," Laura said.

Diana's eyes brightened. "That's wonderful to hear. I can't give you a tour today, but I'd love for you to try a few of our signature cheeses."

"I know you're busy, so we won't stay too long," Laura said.

"Nonsense," Diana said. "I'm happy to have you both. And you should come to the pre-festival tour we're hosting soon. That's when you'll see the entire operation. The aging rooms, the production facilities, everything."

"We wouldn't miss it," Evelyn said.

At this hour, the usually busy farm lay still. Diana led them away from the dairy buildings and toward the farmhouse, which housed the visitors welcome area, a series of offices, and staff areas. Scoundrel, Rascal, and Perry scrambled to follow. Diana paused outside their kennel and put them to bed.

"August," Diana said. "It's the best of times, it's the worst of times." Her smile wasn't all wry, and her eyes were bloodshot. "The festival's great for business, terrible for sleep. But with everything else..."

They went down a hallway and entered a small, cluttered office. A half-finished knitting project and a chalkboard with the day's task list sat upon a rough-hewn desk.

"Make yourselves comfortable," Diana said. "I'll get everything we need for the tasting." From the bench, she grabbed a wooden board featuring three distinct cheeses, water glasses, and plain crackers. "I've selected three of our most popular varieties for you to try. A fresh chèvre with herbs, our six-month aged cheddar, and our eighteen-month alpine-style."

"Everything looks wonderful. The aroma alone is mouthwatering," Laura said.

"The chèvre is best sampled first," Diana said. "Notice the brightness, the herbal notes. The cheddar has a sharpness. And the alpine—you'll taste notes of caramel, toasted nuts, and a slight fruitiness."

"Exquisite," Evelyn said. "You've outdone yourself this year, Diana."

Laura nodded. "It's easy to see why these have taken home awards."

Diana beamed. "Thank you. That means a lot." She sipped her water. "I'm hoping the judges at the festival will agree."

Laura glanced at Evelyn before asking, "With everything going on...I just wanted to check in. How are you?"

Diana's smile faded. "You mean with Jeremy's death? It's been...terrible. I know how it might look, my festival badge being found there. I must have dropped it at the tasting. That's all."

"Was he...talking about your cheese, then?"

"He was making claims," Diana said. "About the methods we use. Saying they're not as 'traditional' as I say they are. Thought he could get a rise out of me." Her phone rang with a sharp trill and she jumped. "I'm so sorry. Could you wait here?"

Laura moved closer to the entrance, pretending to examine a cheese award hanging on the wall. Diana's voice reached her through the doorway.

"Yes, I saw your message. No, I couldn't call you back right away. I've had visitors. And you know I've been busy. The pain in my backside, yes. But now he's gone, we can proceed as planned."

Laura recoiled, but she forced herself to keep listening.

"I understand your concerns, but too much is at stake for all of us." Diana's voice became firmer. "We've worked too hard to let him destroy everything."

Moments later, the door burst open.

"Things," Diana said, running a hand through her hair, "are hectic. I'm so sorry. I can't do this right now."

"We understand. Thank you again for your time, Diana," Evelyn said as she stood. "And do come by if you need anything. My home is always open to you."

Diana nodded, her eyes wild.

<hr />

"That was an experience," Evelyn said, as they headed back to the car.

Laura fumbled with the keys before getting them in the ignition. The sedan sputtered to life.

"Did her whole mood shift when we said his name, or was it just me?" she asked.

Evelyn nodded. "That call seemed to change everything. She could hardly usher us out quickly enough."

Laura backed the car down the driveway too quickly, wincing, and she told Evelyn what she'd heard Diana say. "Could she have meant Jeremy?"

"It could be innocent," Evelyn said. "Perhaps just business plans, tangled up with someone else's ambitions. Not everything revolves around Jeremy, though I wouldn't rule him out yet."

"I want to believe it's nothing, but it's hard to ignore the timing."

Laura turned onto the main road. They drove in silence as roadside trees and farmland gave way to scattered houses, approaching the town.

"This is turning into a mess," Laura said.

"I have just the thing. Remind me to show you my murder board method once we're back," Evelyn said.

Laura nearly swerved. "I must've misheard you. Your what?"

"From all the mystery novels I've read," Evelyn said. "It may sound fanciful, but once you arrange the clues and connect them, the truth often obliges."

"You've dealt with situations like this before?" Laura asked.

Evelyn laughed. "Strictly theoretical, of course. But I have a corkboard, index cards, and a generous bundle of Martha's leftover yarn. We'll stop by Northern Necessities. Supplies first, then sustenance."

The grocery run had yielded more than just snacks—Evelyn's dining table had disappeared under sticky notes, markers, and a mountain of index cards.

"What comes after the murder board?" Laura asked.

Evelyn pursed her lips. "We should have a word with Thomas and Rosalind. If Jeremy had anything up his sleeve, they're likely to know."

"What about Alex?" Laura asked. "He looked panicked when Jeremy brought up his 'genius' thing."

"Well spotted," Evelyn said, uncapping a blue marker. "He's on the list. Shall we put our heads together?"

Laura reached for a stack of index cards.

"Our little web is looking like progress," Evelyn said, stepping back to survey their growing array of connections. "We make quite the detective duo."

Laura smiled, surprising herself. "You know...you might be onto something."

CHAPTER EIGHT

Laura parked in front of Alex's bungalow on the town's outskirts. Its earth-toned exterior, adorned with brackets and square columns, contrasted with the forested surroundings.

Evelyn got out. "Alex and his wife moved out here a few years ago. He said he needed the quiet for his creative process."

"I didn't realize he lived out this way. Seems isolated."

"Some prefer it," Evelyn replied. "He's always been a man who...keeps to himself. Speaking of which, his neighbor finds him rather odd. Alex's wife has been spending more and more time with her family in Tennessee."

Evelyn nodded toward the front porch, where a line of garden gnomes stood at attention. "In summer formation, as expected." She chuckled. "Alex enjoys keeping them on seasonal rotation."

Laura lifted an eyebrow.

Evelyn shrugged. "Some questions are best left unanswered."

They approached the porch, and Laura rang the doorbell.

"Just a minute!" Alex called, his voice sounding winded.

Thuds and rustles sounded from inside, then a door slammed. Alex stood in the doorway, flushed and breathing hard, with damp hair. He wore a blue long-sleeve cotton buttondown open over another t-shirt, both oversized and thrown on. Strange, considering the warm weather.

He blinked at them. "Evelyn? And...you're that...new café manager from the store. Lily? Lisa? No, Laura? I wasn't expecting—"

"Good evening, Alex!" Evelyn cut him off. "Please forgive the intrusion. Are we interrupting?"

He hesitated, glancing over his shoulder. "Not at all. I'm sorry, but...is there something I can help you with?"

"Your festival brochures are wonderful," Laura said. "Evelyn told me you were the one behind the design?"

Evelyn nodded. "The Crafters Club was discussing them earlier this week. Martha was taken with the color scheme. A compliment's best delivered in person, don't you agree?"

Alex's expression shifted. "That's...kind. Though it's rather late for a design consultation...if that's what you want."

"Please don't worry if now isn't ideal. We can come back another time," Laura said.

"No, no, it's fine," Alex said. "I could use a short break." After a moment's hesitation, he stepped aside. "Come in."

Inside, the entryway bookshelf overflowed with agricultural books and design magazines, partially concealing a towel and a compact set of hand weights. As Alex steadied a stack of journals, his sleeve slipped back, revealing a surprisingly muscular forearm. He tugged it down. Alex ushered them through to the living room.

"Please, make yourselves comfortable," he said, gesturing toward a modern-looking sofa with stiff cushions.

Laura perched on the edge, while Evelyn settled beside her with a bemused glance.

"Can I get you something? Coffee? Tea?"

"Some water would be lovely, thank you," Evelyn replied.

Alex bobbed his head and disappeared into the kitchen. When he returned, he carried three glasses of water.

"Thank you," Laura said. "Everything you've done for the festival looks incredible."

Alex sank into an armchair opposite them. "You think so?"

"They've caught everyone's eye," Evelyn said. "They're so pleasing and well-designed."

"Jeremy didn't think so. It doesn't matter, now he's..." The corners of Alex's mouth twitched downward. He gripped his glass, hands trembling.

Evelyn leaned forward. "It's a shame he couldn't see the thought and care you put into them."

"He accused me—of being unoriginal! Of having—" Alex shook his head. "It's absurd!"

He fiddled with a fountain pen, blue ink stains on his fingers. Alex's elbow brushed a teetering stack of papers, sending them cascading to the floor. Laura crouched to gather the scattered sheets, picking up a brochure with bold print and elaborate designs. Several were in European languages.

"Just research materials..." he mumbled, shoving the brochures into a nearby set of drawers. His phone rang in his pocket and he flinched.

"Don't let us keep you. Do you need to take that?" Laura asked.

"No, it's nothing," he said, though his fingers twitched toward his pocket.

"It seems the committee was rather...tempestuous this year?" Evelyn asked.

"You could say that," Alex said. "Jeremy and Rosalind had quite the blow-up right after the tasting event."

"Did something happen?" Laura asked.

He shifted, glancing at his watch. "Rosalind accused Jeremy of tampering with 'reputations' and 'lying about everything.' She pointed right at him, like this, and stormed off before he could defend himself."

His phone buzzed again. Alex pulled it out and glanced at the screen, his face paling before he shoved it back in his pocket. In the room's corner, a small wooden table held a framed photo. It showed Alex in a suit, beaming beside a cheerful woman in a wedding dress with curly brown hair.

"How is your wife? I don't believe I've met her," Laura said.

He gave a tight-lipped smile. "She's well. She's visiting family in Tennessee this week." He rubbed his temples. "I wish I could've gone with her—get away from all this mess for a while—but the police asked the committee members not to leave town."

Laura's eyebrows rose. "The whole committee?"

Alex's face flushed. "I—well, yes. Standard procedure, I'm sure."

Laura nodded. Did that mean Ramirez suspected someone among them? She forced herself to refocus on the conversation. "I hope she had a safe trip down there and she enjoys her visit. Changing the topic, but if you don't mind me asking...did Jeremy ever mention what his keynote was about?"

Alex's eyes flickered. He twisted the cap of his fountain pen until it clicked off and on again. "He—told me he would shake things up."

"I've been wondering what he was trying to say," Laura said.

"I—don't know either. He...mentioned something about committees and reckless decisions? Jeremy liked his drama. That much was clear."

"It's such a dreadful thing," Evelyn said. "I hope they find out what happened."

"I—should have seen it coming," Alex muttered. "It's just—" He stopped, pressing his lips together before shaking his head. "Nothing."

"Thank you, Alex. We should let you get back to your evening," Laura said.

"Yes, we shall," Evelyn agreed. "So nice to see you."

The two women moved toward the front door, stepping outside. Laura glanced back to see Alex's head pop out, scanning the road. He pulled the door shut, locking the deadbolt with a sharp click behind them.

———◆———

Laura observed the bungalow across the road from inside her car. "Do you think his nervousness is just his personality, or was something bothering him?"

Evelyn sighed. "Likely both. He's not the only one with secrets."

Alex stood at his window, half in shadow, half in light. His shoulders were hunched, and he paced, appearing to be talking to himself. A conflicted man...but, about what?

Laura parked in the alleyway behind the Morrison Building, a three-story Victorian. Warm light spilled from Evelyn's second-floor windows above the darkened Mountainside Stories bookshop. The building had once housed her late husband's medical practice on the first floor, but after Charles passed ten years ago, Evelyn had closed the practice. Now Mountainside Stories occupied the space, while she kept the second floor and rented the top to Laura.

She sighed, switching off the engine. "So many pieces, and none of them fit."

Evelyn unbuckled her seatbelt. "Why don't you join me upstairs? A meal might help us make sense of this."

Laura smiled. "That would be wonderful, thank you."

CHAPTER NINE

Laura slipped in through the General Store's side entrance. Her mind still reeled with the recent events, but that morning, a text from Danny had temporarily buoyed her.

"Saw the news about your boss. That's terrible! Want me to come visit? I give great hugs!"

Despite everything, she'd smiled.

"Thanks, but I'm managing okay. Tell Callum his aunt says hi!"

"Will do! He misses his favorite aunt. Stay strong!"

As she entered the quiet building, condensation had fogged the windows in the humid morning air, tiny trails of water painting streaks on the glass. She wasn't alone. Kathy jumped. She'd been hunched over an architectural triangular ruler, protractor, and drafting compass. A partially constructed breakfast sandwich sat on graph paper with precise lines drawn around it.

She gave a sheepish grin. "Woke up at three am with an architectural blueprint for the optimal breakfast sandwich. Couldn't resist prototyping it."

Laura stared at her.

Kathy shrugged. "Sometimes simplicity's the superior design. Coffee?"

Laura burst out laughing, and even Kathy had to join in.

The older woman set aside her drafting tools and grabbed the French Press next to her, selecting a mug. "Coffee's already underway."

Laura's eyes flicked to the espresso machine. Why wasn't she using that?

Kathy followed her gaze and snorted. "That contraption? Absurd!" She grinned, pouring Laura a coffee. "Lost half a day decoding the manual. It was in three languages—English allegedly among them, though you'd hardly know it."

Laura smiled and thanked Kathy before taking the mug. "Is Maggie feeling any better today?"

Kathy nodded. "I insisted she sleep in. Obstinate to a fault, that woman. She was determined to be here at dawn."

"She deserves a breather. We'll make that happen," Laura said.

Kathy rolled her eyes. "Good luck with that!"

Wrapping her hands around the mug, Laura breathed in the invigorating smell of the brewed coffee and savored the quiet, knowing it wouldn't last. The blend had hints of roasted nuts and dark chocolate. Delicious, as ever.

Kathy set her sandwich-in-progress on a plate and grabbed her cup, filling it with the last of the liquid from the French Press. "Better finish logging yesterday's shipment. I'll be in the cellars."

Laura nodded as the back door clicked. Her gaze drifted to the stairway leading to the second floor. She was alone. Now was her chance.

A twinge pinched her stomach. Kathy had been nothing but kind to her these last few weeks. What would she think if she caught Laura snooping through her wife's office? She stepped away from her mug, drawn to the stairs. Every instinct said stop. But if Maggie and the store's reputation was being threatened...

The café stood empty, silent but for the creak of wooden floors beneath her steps as she crossed to the kitchen. She grabbed a pair of food-grade gloves from a drawer. Ridiculous, maybe—but if the police ever searched Maggie's office, explaining her fingerprints on everything would be worse.

Slipping the thin gloves on, she crept toward the stairs, each creak of the floorboards making her wince as she grew closer to Maggie's office door. Was this...a good idea?

Maggie's desperate expression these past days...the whispers around town...she needed to know.

Laura steeled herself. She'd only be a minute. She turned the knob, surprised to find it unlocked. Strange, but then again, Laura had never seen Maggie lock it—probably because she trusted her staff. The store building itself was always secured, and Maggie didn't keep cash up here.

She slipped inside. Maggie's office was as cluttered as ever, with paper stacks teetering on every surface. Laura sifted through the nearest pile, careful not to disturb any other items on the desk.

The first few pages were innocuous—a vendor's catalogue and inventory lists. A flash of red caught her eye as she sorted through the papers—an envelope with a red stamp. She picked it up, revealing a stack of them underneath the first. Final notices. That's strange. Why would Maggie leave them so late? Unless...she tugged the desk drawer open. Even more final notice bills. She snapped it shut.

Is that why Maggie had been so flustered? Even before...Laura bit her lip. This only confirmed one thing. Maggie needed help. If Laura didn't do something, who would? Laura double-checked nothing seemed out of place, and peeled off her gloves, heading back to the café with blood pounding in her ears.

She grabbed her coffee cup off the counter and took another sip. That was a mistake. The rich flavors? Muted. The temperature? Lukewarm. She poured it down the sink, and strained away the grounds left in Kathy's French Press, now empty, and put them in the compost bin. She was ready. For whatever came.

Laura headed to the linen cupboard near the back entrance to replenish the dish towels, her hand reaching for the handle. The phone rang. She hurried back to answer it.

"Good morning, this is Silver Springs General Store. Laura speaking. How may I be of help?"

"Laura! Your bosses asked, and I have delivered! As usual! I'm out by the back gate if you wouldn't mind doing the old open sesame."

"Of course! I'm on my way," Laura said, hanging up the phone, unable to stop the smile stretching across her features. She grabbed the gate key and headed outside.

Isaac 'Izzy' Lennox bounced on his heels. Behind him sat his old pickup truck, loaded with wooden crates.

He was an employee at Goldenleaf Apple Farm, one of the General Store's many suppliers, and a Silver Springs Players member, the community theater group. He was the fastest friend she'd ever made. In his mid-twenties and twelve years her junior, Izzy reminded her of a younger version of her middle brother. They'd crossed paths on her second day in town when he'd visited her as part of his one-man welcoming committee. He'd brought food, helped her unpack, and given her a tour of the town, because that was just the sort of young man he was.

"Morning, morning, morning!" Izzy sang out before she'd even reached the gate. "Great day for deliveries!"

He leaped onto his pickup's tray, his golden-brown skin visible at the cuffs of his patched shirt. As always, he'd braided his long, curly hair back into a bun. He grabbed the first crate and hefted it toward the front, before jumping down again to grab it.

"Hi, Izzy! Here, let me help you," Laura said, swinging the gate open.

"Always so kind." He grinned and handed her a box, grabbing two for himself and balancing them as they headed to the store.

As they walked, his demeanor softened as he said, "Hey, I heard about what happened. Are you holding up okay? Anything you need? Always happy to arrive with some food if the fridge is looking a little empty."

It was so like Izzy to check in on her. "I'm managing," she replied with a wan smile. "Thanks for asking."

Izzy gave her a nod and a knowing look. Like her brother Danny, he had an uncanny ability to sense when something was amiss without pressing the issue. Both shared that rare gift: boundless enthusiasm tempered by a graceful sense of when to step back and hold space.

Laura set her box down by the counter, and Izzy followed in her wake, depositing his two in a neat stack before racing back outside for more. Laura chuckled as he whizzed past, unpacking the first box and placing the new batch of apples on the display tables.

"Thanks again for your help with my mess of a closet back at my apartment," Laura said when Izzy returned with two more boxes. "I couldn't have managed without your truck. You've saved me a dozen trips."

"Not at all!" Izzy set down his load, smiling. "The least I could do. That's what friends are for."

The unloading complete, Izzy pulled an invoice from his pocket. "I can't forget the paperwork or Vernon will have my head." He brightened. "And the obligatory reminder. Come to the next show we're putting on! Wind in the Willows!"

Laura signed the delivery slip and handed it back. "Sounds wonderful. I look forward to it."

With a cheerful salute, Izzy headed for the door. "Great, gotta run! Apple deliveries, fruit and cider, wait for no man!"

Laura called after him as he bounded out the door. "Thank you, see you later!"

⸻ ◆ ⸻

"Laura! The sun shines today, and no one's yelled at me yet. A record, I'd say."

She turned, her arms full of linens, to see Ben standing in the doorway.

"Morning! You're early. May I offer you something to drink? Coffee?"

"If you can be bothered with a decaf caramel latte with lactose-free milk, that'd be great, thanks," he replied and took the pile from her. "How are you this morning?"

Laura nodded with a tired smile. "I'm doing okay. Thank you."

Ben set the heap down, organizing each dish towel into its place while Laura started up the espresso machine. It gurgled into life.

"And before you say anything about my coffee order," Ben said, his back to her, bustling around the tool cupboard in one of the back rooms. "I don't make the choices. My taste buds do."

Laura laughed. "I won't judge you for that! I'll have it ready in a moment."

Once she'd made Ben his requested beverage, Laura began the familiar pre-opening routine. She placed freshly baked scones on a tiered stand. What little was leftover would go to the Good Neighbor Guild's Meals That Matter program.

As she worked, she asked, "Busy morning ahead? How are things going at the stables?"

He heaved a sigh. "Let's just say last week it was a welcome mat for trouble. The combo lock's on, but we're waiting on the delivery for the heavy-duty reinforcements. I've got loads of other fixes lined up in the meantime. Still waiting on those anti-climb spikes for the swing gate, though. Kathy locks it up tight each night when she gets home, sure, but—"

"Where does she go?" Laura asked.

"Her other job." He said it as if she was supposed to know. "Renovating old interiors?"

Another job? And at night? Strange. Didn't she have enough to do at the store?

"Anyway," Ben continued from the back room, "If someone really wanted in? Hop, skip, and they're on the grounds."

Laura nodded. "There wasn't much stopping someone, was there?"

Ben re-entered, carrying an assortment of equipment, and glanced over. "No. Funny, you're the second person in a week to ask about security back there."

Laura placed a mug on the shelf, trying to sound casual. "Really? Who was the first?"

"Ramirez," he said. "She even requested the security footage from the back of Dad's shop."

Laura's hands faltered as she reached for another mug. "I guess I've been thinking about it, that's all."

Ben walked over to face her, arms folded, a hint of a self-satisfied smile tugging at his lips. "Really, Laura? Most folks just mutter over coffee and hope someone else deals with it."

"I see you've been keeping an eye on things," Laura said.

Ben shrugged. "Yeah, I don't blame you. It's all been...a bit much. Especially for Maggie." He perked up. "But hey, I've been around a while. I might pick up a few things that could help."

A small smile tugged at Laura's lips. "I'd...appreciate that. Thank you. But...we need to be careful."

"Consider it done," Ben said. "Careful is my middle name. Right after Wilbur. Which, in my defense, I didn't choose."

Kathy burst in, arms full of boxes. "Ben! Morning."

"Kathy!" he said, a grin in his voice. "Is it chaos yet, or are we still pretending we have it under control?"

Kathy rolled her eyes, but in a good-natured way. "Too soon to say." She addressed the next part to Laura. "Give me a hand with Tracy Mitchell's delivery?" She set the boxes down on an empty table.

Organic basil and parsley took an entire box, each bunch fragrant and vibrant. Dill, cilantro, and chives filled another. A third box had an astonishing microgreen array: tender pea shoots, amaranth with deep red leaves, radish sprouts, sunflower shoots, and delicate mustard greens.

Kathy checked the boxes. "Tracy threw in a few extras. Knows the value of goodwill. The woman's a gem."

"What if we featured them?" Laura asked, already thinking of creative ways to display them.

"Good idea. Let's clear some space," Kathy said.

They did just that, then gathered metal buckets and filled them with the aromatic herbs and some water from a jug.

As they worked, Laura glanced at Kathy. "If it's alright to ask, was it Burlington where Maggie went the night...it happened? I heard something about visiting a friend."

Kathy's face was serious now. "She said the words, sure...but it felt off. Like there was more under the surface. I trust her, but something didn't ring true."

On his way outside, Ben asked, "Please tell me you don't believe the rumors."

"Don't put words in my mouth, kid," Kathy said, but her tone wasn't unkind. "I don't. This town! Rumors swirling like a summer storm."

———◦———

Later that morning, Maggie bustled in.

Jasmine, standing behind the counter polishing glasses, raised an eyebrow. "So much for sleeping in."

Maggie smiled despite her haggard expression. "Give me a chance. I woke up at eight!" Her gaze swept across the space, landing on the herb display. "Great! Tracy's delivery came. It looks wonderful."

Laura started on another espresso as Maggie approached.

"How are you feeling today?" Laura asked.

"Better," Maggie said. "Nothing coffee can't fix."

Laura handed Maggie her drink. The timing of Maggie's absence had been nagging at her. If Maggie had been in Burlington the same night as the...she stirred her own coffee, choosing her words carefully.

"Kathy and I were chatting," Laura said. "She mentioned you were in Burlington that night, visiting a friend?"

Something flickered across Maggie's face. Her fingers tightened around the cup.

"Yes," Maggie said, interested in wiping the already clean counter. "Just catching up with an old college friend. Alice. We don't see each other often."

"That sounds lovely. I'm so sorry you came back to such a terrible morning," Laura said. "Can I ask, did you stay overnight?"

Maggie's eyes darted up, then away. "Yes, I did. Too late to drive back home." She gave a too-bright smile. "Better check on those pastry orders for tomorrow. Never enough hours."

As Maggie retreated to her office, Laura's mind swirled with unanswered questions. Maggie's evasiveness left Laura feeling unsettled. It was clear she was concealing something.

Eli, Jesse, and Jasmine had the café under control, giving Laura a chance to slip away for a well-earned lunch break. As she passed the retail section, voices drifted from a cluster of customers gathered around a display table.

"...heard the bills were piling up. Could be motive enough if you ask me," a woman said.

"Terrible shame," another voice chimed in. "The General Store's been here forever."

Laura's chest tightened as she left the café and headed toward Ashby Hardware. The rumors were spreading fast. The jingle of the bell above the shop door welcomed her arrival.

Pete looked up from sorting screws into small labeled drawers. "Laura! What can I do for you?"

"Good morning, Pete," Laura said with what she hoped was a calm smile. "Do you have any hooks? I've got some art I'd love to put up."

He motioned for her to follow him down the aisle. "Got just what you need back here." As they walked, he lowered his voice. "How's Maggie holding up? I imagine she's taking it hard, poor woman."

"Kathy made sure she slept in this morning," Laura said.

Pete grinned. "That's our Maggie. Has to be strong-armed into taking time off." His expression sobered. "Just wish folks weren't gossiping. I don't believe a word of it."

"Really? You don't?" Laura asked before she could stop herself.

"Of course not! It's just..." He sighed. "I heard Ramirez has been all over town asking about her. And, I don't know if this is true, and you didn't hear this from me, but...there are rumors going around that the police found something in Jeremy's apartment. Detailed notes about the General Store's debts."

Laura's eyes widened. "What was he going to do?"

Pete shrugged. "Not sure. Apparently, he'd written something in the margins about 'how he could use this against Maggie.' Just...wish I could help clear up this mess." He stopped in front of a shelf lined with containers of small hardware—screws, bolts, hooks, and more.

"Here we are," Pete said, selecting a box of hooks. "How many would you like?"

"A dozen, please," Laura told him, and they headed to the counter, where Pete began ringing up her order.

He'd just said he'd be willing to help...she had to take the chance.

"Your place has a view of the alley, right? Did the police come by?" she asked.

Pete nodded. "Sure did! And...they found something, too." He grinned. "Are you...looking into things yourself?"

Laura hesitated, then nodded, admitting defeat. Pete was a sharper fellow than she'd expected. Just like his son.

Pete handed her the hooks and said, "Since it's for Maggie, I'll show you. Might be something there."

He opened a file on his laptop next to him and flipped it around so she could see the screen—time-stamped from the night it happened. Laura leaned closer, scrutinizing the grainy footage.

"There!" Pete pointed at a shadowy figure moving away from the carriage house entrance toward the stables, disappearing from view. A black jacket and loose pants obscured any details, hiding their identity—and intentions. They were of medium height and had a lanky build. The timestamp showed nine-forty-five pm.

He fast-forwarded the video playback until it showed ten-ten pm. The figure exited the stables and moved with more urgency back toward the carriage house before disappearing from the camera's range entirely.

"It's hard to tell who or what they were up to," Laura said, pulling out her purse.

"Exactly," Pete agreed. "Keep me posted on what you find?"

"I will. And that's just what I needed, thank you." Laura smiled as she tucked the hooks into a pocket in her bag.

She headed toward the door, but he called after her. "How's the apartment working out?"

Laura turned, her eyes brightening. "It's slow going, but it's getting there."

Pete nodded. "Glad to hear it. Listen, we've got a proper drill and level. If you need any help, just say the word. Ben or I will be there."

Laura smiled. "That's so generous, thank you. I may just do that."

She left the hardware store, the temporary warm feeling dissipating as the figure in the footage gnawed at her. Was it an outsider who knew the grounds well enough to strike when everyone was gone? Or someone closer to home, making it look that way?

She needed more pieces before the picture made sense. She tried to focus on what she knew: Maggie's insistence she was in Burlington, Ben's theory about the gate, and Kathy's doubts.

Next to Pete Ashby's storefront, vibrant dahlias spilling from green buckets framed the entrance to Rosie's Garden, the local florist. A few steps away, behind the smudged glass of a red metal newspaper dispenser, the Maplewood Memo's headline screamed in bold type: 'Mysterious Death At General Store: Foul Play Suspected.'

She fumbled in her pocket for change and inserted it into the slot.

Before reading the front-page article, her eyes caught the familiar header of 'The Local Lowdown' by Hazel Thorton—usually her favorite part of the paper for its witty take on county happenings.

The front-page article was brief but loaded with insinuation: 'Sources close to the investigation report local business owner Maggie Brook is under scrutiny following the suspicious death of renowned food critic Jeremy Blackwood. Brook's establishment, which received a scathing review from Blackwood years prior, was the scene of the tragedy.'

Laura's stomach clenched. The article contained just enough facts to seem credible. No direct accusations, but the message was clear to any reader.

Several townspeople huddled around their own copies. One woman nudged her companion, whispering something that prompted both to stare at Laura. Folding the paper and tucking it under her arm, Laura hastened back to the General Store, the weight of their gazes following her.

———◦———

After returning from her errands, Laura slipped away to the break room, grateful for the quiet moment to herself. Before she fixed herself some lunch, there was something she needed to do first. After pulling out her phone and tapping open the notes app, she began typing.

The door swung open. Laura locked her phone screen.

It was Jasmine, balancing a tray with two plates and glasses of water.

"I thought I'd join you for lunch," Jasmine said, setting the tray down. She slid one plate toward Laura. "You haven't tried the dill and goats' cheese tartine yet. It's life-changing."

"I really appreciate that. Thank you."

The tartine looked amazing with its golden brown pastry crust filled with eggs, goats' cheese, and fragrant dill.

Jasmine sat across from her. "So, what were you working on when I walked in?"

Laura hesitated, then sighed. "Can I trust you to keep it quiet?"

"Of course," Jasmine said, leaning forward.

"I've been...investigating what happened to Jeremy," Laura said, her voice lowering. "Something about the case against Maggie doesn't sit right with me."

To Laura's surprise, Jasmine didn't look shocked.

Instead, she nodded. "I wondered. All the questions, all that casual people-watching you pretend isn't obvious..."

Laura gave an abashed smile. "Be honest. Does this sound ridiculous?"

Jasmine took a bite of her tartine. "Not at all! Maggie gave me a chance when everyone else overlooked me. These rumors are nonsense. I'm game if you are."

"That would be incredible, but, are you sure?" Laura asked.

"Absolutely. Just tell me what you need."

Laura chewed a piece of tartine, savoring the sharp tang of the cheese against the pastry's buttery sweetness. "I saw Pete this morning. He showed me some security footage from that night."

Jasmine's eyes widened. "And?"

Laura reached for her water. "Someone wearing black was lurking, but it's hard to say who."

"No way! You think it could help clear Maggie?"

"Maybe it's enough to make the police rethink things," Laura said.

"On that note...Jeremy's grudge collection didn't begin or end with Maggie, you know," Jasmine said.

Laura paused mid-bite. "How so?"

"He and Rosalind weren't exactly friends, but something had changed recently," Jasmine said between mouthfuls. "And he'd been getting under Alex and Diana's skin too. He kept acting like he was sitting on some grand revelation. It was the same story with Thomas at every cheese competition. So many tense interactions."

"I hadn't heard that before," Laura murmured, putting down her plate to type all that up. "And yet they all continued to come back, year after year, to work together during the festival?"

Jasmine shrugged. "You can't avoid people you don't like in small towns." Her eyes widened. "Speaking of tensions, have you heard about the guy who used to be a judge?"

Laura hadn't.

"He became a judge two years ago but he suddenly quit just before last year's festival. The official story was 'personal reasons,' but...he and Rosalind had this massive blow-up during a committee meeting. Half the town heard them shouting at each other."

"Do you know what the fight was about?" Laura asked.

Jasmine shrugged. "Something about 'integrity of the process.' Whatever it was, he stormed out, and announced his resignation the next day. Some say Rosalind threatened to expose something about him if he didn't follow her 'guidance' on the winners."

Laura glanced toward the window of the break room, watching the movement of distant townsfolk below and the clouds passing by above. She'd need every clue she could find to solve this.

And now, with Jasmine's help, she might have a better chance of discovering them.

CHAPTER TEN

Laura had expected the café to be a little quieter, but the chatter was deafening. The whole town had decided Saturday afternoon was the perfect time for coffee and a side of rumors.

What could've caught their attention now? Hopefully, it wasn't something to do with Maggie.

Jesse darted between tables, their arms laden with plates. "If one more person asks me about Jeremy Blackwood," they said quietly as they passed Laura, "I might make up some wild stories just to see their reactions."

Laura hid her smile as she set down a plate of food for a customer. Jasmine stood behind the counter, pouring beans into the grinder with her brow furrowed.

As Laura approached, Jasmine looked up, beckoning her with a tilt of her head.

"You won't believe what the café regulars are convinced of this time."

"What's going on?" Laura asked, stacking several dirty cups into the dishwasher.

"Word is," Jasmine said, "the autopsy results got leaked. They're saying—"

Table five's diners, having finished deciding, now waited for service.

Laura turned to Jasmine and gave her an apologetic look. "I'm so sorry. Hold that thought." She headed over to the waiting customers to take their order. "Good afternoon! What would you like to—"

"Did you hear the news about Jeremy Blackwood?" a woman with a floral scarf interrupted, eyes wide and eager.

Laura blinked, afraid to ask.

"You know," another woman said. "A love bite! Right on his neck!"

"So much for that impervious bachelor act," an older man chimed in, shaking his head with mock pity.

Laura tried to keep her expression neutral, though her mind raced with possibilities. She opened her mouth to speak, but the man leaned forward, eyes glinting, brandishing a gossip magazine.

"That's not all," he continued, loud enough for the entire café to hear. "This Boston mag says they found a lady's undergarment inside his apartment!"

Gasps and murmurs erupted around the café. A few heads turned, trying to glimpse the article.

"Imagine the scandal!" the other woman said.

The woman wearing the floral scarf nodded. "I wonder what poor soul mistook him as attractive."

How rude! Laura attempted to maintain a neutral expression. "What can I bring you today?"

The woman in the floral scarf smiled. "I'll have the roasted tomato soup. And some of that delicious sourdough."

"Make that two," added the older man with a grin.

"And I'll have the goat's cheese on rye, please," the other woman said.

Laura jotted down their orders and hurried back to the counter to hand them off to the kitchen, her mind spinning. If Jeremy had a secret romantic entanglement, it added a new dimension to everything. Was there a connection to what had occurred? If that were the case...it couldn't have been Maggie, surely! Still...why was he at the stables? It made little sense.

She turned back to Jasmine, helping her prepare another round of pastries for afternoon tea customers. "Thanks for waiting," she said. "So...what were you just saying?"

Jasmine gave a wry smile as she plated up raspberry danishes. "Table Five beat me to it, huh? A love bite. That raises more questions."

Eli made a noise of agreement from where he stood behind the espresso machine.

As Laura took another order, Maggie descended the stairs. Her pixie cut stuck out at odd angles, as if she'd been raking her hands through it all day. Dark circles shadowed her once-bright eyes. Maggie paused by the display table, an unfocused expression on her face, as if she were lost in another world.

A voice came from the back corner. A stage whisper if there ever was one. "It's only a matter of time before they arrest her."

Laura's pulse quickened. She cast a glance at Maggie, who now stood staring at the local honey. She needed to change her approach—fast—if she wanted to get to the truth.

———————⊲◦⊳———————

Laura pushed through the storeroom door and stopped short. Maggie was hunched in the corner beside the shelves of dry goods, clutching the day's edition of the Maplewood Memo. Her hands trembled, the paper crinkling between her fingers.

"Maggie? Are you alright?" Laura asked, stepping closer.

Maggie's eyes remained fixed on the newspaper, her face ashen. "Mrs. Hartwell handed this to me. She said I'd want to see what they'd printed about me. I can't believe Cecil from Riverbank Produce told the Memo I once said I'd 'never forgive' Jeremy for that review. We were having a laugh at the farmers' market just last week!"

"This is just meant to provoke, not inform," Laura said, taking the paper from Maggie's hands. "You don't deserve this kind of treatment."

Maggie shrugged. "The Detective Sergeant called this morning. Full of questions. She said she's swamped with so-called 'tips'—everyone suddenly remembers something odd. And she's chasing them all down. The Memo's itching for a headline. Murder sells. Especially with a tidy villain to pin it on."

Laura folded her arms. "They're jumping to conclusions with no facts."

Maggie ignored this, her expression forlorn. "Enough moping for me. We have customers."

———◆○◆———

The afternoon crowd thinned, leaving behind only a few lingering customers. Laura exhaled as the noise level dropped, giving her a chance to think. Kathy had commandeered a table in the corner, her computer screen casting a dim glow across her determined face. The trackpad and keys clacked as she pounded them. She banged a fist on the table. Several heads turned before returning to their conversations.

Laura made her way over. "Is everything alright?"

Kathy gave a wry smile. "Spreadsheets! I'd rather strip layers of paint with a butter knife." She shoved the computer a couple of inches forward and rubbed her temples. "Maggie handles inventory management, but with everything...thought I'd assume control."

"Do you think some afternoon tea would help?" Laura asked.

Kathy nodded. "Good idea."

Laura was about to ask what she'd like when Kathy got up, grabbed an apple from a display table, and crunched into it before sitting back down.

She leaned in toward her boss. "Can I...please have your help with something after work? It's...important."

Kathy's eyes narrowed, then softened. "Something to do with you-know-who?"

Laura gave a nod.

Kathy let out a long breath, her eyes flicking back to the spreadsheet. "Sure."

———◄◊►———

Anton had already started on a batch of pasta salad when Laura joined him in the kitchen. A small tower of summer vegetables sat next to a bowl of fresh herbs, and the bright, fresh scent of basil and lemon wafted through the air.

"How's everything going?" Laura asked.

Anton flashed a thumbs up, gesturing to the large mixing bowl filled with cooked pasta. "Mind helping for a few minutes?"

Laura smiled. "This is a treat. At Hargroves, I barely got to step into the kitchen."

Anton smiled and nodded as he tossed the pasta with diced tomatoes and fresh mozzarella.

Jasmine poked her head in. "Are you all good back here?"

"Could use a hand," Anton said, nodding her over.

Jasmine gave a quick smile. "Jesse and Eli have the café handled."

"Great, thanks," Anton said, handing her a knife and pointing to some bell peppers. "Laura's getting into the cooking spirit."

"We'll make a chef out of you yet," Jasmine said with a wink. She took her spot at the stainless steel bench, dicing vegetables to add to the bowl.

"How's Maggie?" Anton asked.

"Tired, by the looks of it," Laura replied. "Kathy said she had a sleep in, but it looks like she was up half the night working."

"You mean worrying," Jasmine said, adding herbs to the mixture. "Poor thing. Can't believe they're still after her."

"It's awful, how many people are assuming the worst," Laura said, frowning as she sliced red onions.

Jasmine sighed. "When you've been around here long enough, you see how quickly people jump to conclusions." She reached for the olive oil and vinegar, drizzling it into the bowl. "And how easily they don't consider other angles."

Laura nodded, her mind considering everything she'd learned so far. But as she diced vegetables, her thoughts settled, and she caught herself humming an old tune—something she'd picked up from her dad. Anton smiled, and to her surprise, joined in as they worked.

———————◦———————

Only the refrigerator's white noise and the aroma of baked goods remained once the last patrons trickled out. Laura wiped down tables while Maggie stacked chairs. She always claimed she had far too much to do, but she still liked helping with the menial tasks. Especially when she needed a distraction. Eli cleaned the espresso machine, Jesse packed away clean dishes, and Jasmine reorganized the display stands.

Laura paused beside Maggie. "How are you holding up?"

"It depends who you ask," Maggie said.

Before Laura could respond, Kathy strode in. "That's it, honey. Off you go."

Maggie frowned. "I'm fine. Just need to—"

"Nope," Kathy said, shaking her head, though her smile was kind. "You need rest. Go home and relax. Or at least pretend to."

Maggie attempted to protest, but sighed. "Fine..." She gave Kathy a tired smile. "Thanks, my love." She leaned in to give her wife a quick kiss before heading out, her shoulders slumped.

How much longer could Maggie hold up under the pressure? Laura shook off her concern and turned to Kathy, who was already stacking some of the leftover pears into a basket.

"Do you still have a spare moment once we've finished up?"

Kathy's eyes met hers. She paused, then nodded.

The café became a liminal space after closing time, now empty except for Laura and Kathy.

Kathy sat astride one of the bar stools and faced her. "So. What are we talking about?"

Laura hesitated. "I'm so sorry if this is out of line, but I need to ask. Do you know anything about those 'consulting fees' they found in Jeremy's bag?"

Kathy stiffened.

Had Laura overstepped? She tried to push forward. "Please know I'm only asking because it might make a difference."

Kathy's eyes darkened. "Why do you need to know?"

Laura froze. "Because I'm worried about her. She's struggling, and I want to help." She forced herself to take a deep breath. "Evelyn and I...we're trying to make sense of all of this."

Kathy gave her a sharp look. "You're investigating?"

Laura tensed. "Trying, yes. I just...I can't shake the feeling something's off. But we need—"

"Evidence." Kathy nodded and heaved a sigh. "Can't believe I'm entertaining this, but fine. I don't like seeing her like this. Maggie's always managed the finances. I deal with the tangible. I've got the login credentials around here somewhere..." She spent several minutes hunting on her phone. "Here we go." She retrieved her laptop, opening it and clicking around, muttering to herself. "No...that's not the interface I remember. Wait. This might be it." She frowned at the screen. "Odd layout. Hold on." She stopped scrolling. "This doesn't bode well. I suppose, but it's hard to say. I haven't reviewed this data before."

"What is it?" Laura asked.

Her boss heaved a sigh. "These statements are displaying cash withdrawals from Maggie's savings account. The amounts don't correspond with what the police mentioned, however...the chronology all conforms." Kathy rubbed her forehead, staring at the screen. "Why would she withhold this information? Eight years together, and she's always managed our finances. Never felt the need to scrutinize her methods."

The timing was uncanny, but...why cash? Maggie concealing the transactions from Kathy implied a larger scheme. So much for hoping this'd clear things up. Now the situation was muddier than ever.

Laura swallowed. "Is it possible she didn't realize it could be relevant?"

Kathy sighed, squinting at the screen as if it might give her some explanation. Uncertainty gnawed at Laura. She needed to think. Needed to piece together what information they had. She slid her stool back from the bench, but Kathy's voice stopped her in her tracks.

"Wait," Kathy said. "I'm checking our joint credit card statement and..." Her face paled. "This can't be right."

"What are you seeing?" Laura asked, leaning forward.

"A charge from a gas station outside Burlington. On the night Jeremy died." Kathy's voice trembled. "Maggie told me she was visiting her friend Alice in Burlington and drove back the next morning. And the time...nine-thirty-seven pm. Why would she be refueling?"

Laura's heartbeat quickened as Kathy stood and closed her laptop, her expression hardening.

"Enough of this. Time for some answers."

Kathy strode toward the stairs, and Laura hurried after her, catching up as they reached Maggie's office. Kathy threw open the door.

Maggie's surprise gave way to concern. "Kathy? Laura? What's wrong?"

Kathy powered up the laptop, placing it on Maggie's desk, jabbing at the screen. "Care to explain this? And while you're at it, tell me about these cash withdrawals you've been making from your savings account? For months?"

Maggie's face fell as she glanced between the screen and her wife. "Kathy, I can explain—"

"Heck! You'd better," Kathy cut in, her jaw clenched.

Maggie's shoulders slumped. "I wasn't in Burlington just to have dinner with Alice. I was picking up your anniversary gift."

"My...what?"

"Remember that antique architectural drafting set you saw in that specialty shop last year? The one with the brass instruments?" Maggie's voice softened. "Alice helped me track it down. The owner lives outside Burlington. Alice and I drove there to pick it up after dinner—she was in on it the whole time."

"And...the withdrawals?" Kathy asked.

Maggie nodded. "I've been saving for it bit by bit, withdrawing small amounts at Maplewood Credit Union when depositing funds. I didn't want you to notice a large sum missing all at once." She looked at Kathy. "It was supposed to be a surprise."

Kathy deflated. "An anniversary gift? Maggie! We're in the middle of a murder investigation where you're the prime suspect, and you didn't think to mention this?"

Maggie looked down. "I...didn't realize...but I suppose with the notes found in Jeremy's messenger bag..."

"I understand wanting to keep it a surprise," Kathy said before pressing a kiss to Maggie's forehead. "But in a situation like this..."

"I know," Maggie said. "I just wanted it to be perfect."

Laura hesitated, not wanting to intrude on the moment but needing to ask: "Maggie, I don't mean to push, but is it possible someone might have noticed these withdrawals? Maybe...they saw a pattern?"

Maggie considered this. "I suppose it's possible, though unlikely. The tellers know me, but they're discreet. I can't imagine who would've paid enough attention."

Laura nodded, though a chill ran through her. Had...someone noticed those withdrawals and seized an opportunity to frame Maggie?

"Thank you for sharing that, Maggie," Laura said. "I should head off."

"And I've got a few tasks to tidy up," Kathy said. Turning to her wife, she continued, "Time for you to finish."

Maggie gave a defeated nod. Once they were both downstairs, Kathy gave Laura a look.

"Don't worry about Ramirez. We'll tell her everything. Last thing I need is her discovering it on her own and accusing us of withholding evidence."

Laura nodded and tried to put on a smile. "You and Maggie, the General Store, the customers...we'll get through this. I promise."

She would make sure of it.

Kathy smiled. "Thanks, Laura. Now, on home."

———◆———

That evening, Laura knocked on Evelyn's door.

"Good evening," Evelyn said. "What a lovely surprise! I'm just about to put the kettle on. Join me for some tea?"

"Yes, please," Laura said. "There are a few things I wanted to tell you."

Evelyn directed her to the living room. "Excellent! Make yourself comfortable."

Oscar padded over, circling Laura's ankles with a soft meow before jumping into her lap after she'd settled in her usual armchair.

Evelyn appeared with a tray holding a teapot and two cups. "You look like someone with a discovery to share."

"It's something Jasmine told me today," Laura said, accepting the cup Evelyn offered. "And what Kathy and I discovered."

Evelyn's eyebrows rose as Laura recounted the story of what had happened after work. "That's a relief. Though I wish Maggie had said something earlier!"

"Me too. Still, there are a few things that don't add up."

"That's why we're investigating," Evelyn said after a sip of her tea. "And now, what did Jasmine mention?"

"She told me about a former festival judge. Jasmine said he quit last year after an argument with Rosalind about integrity. Apparently, half the town heard them shouting at each other, and Rosalind threatened to expose something about him if he didn't follow her advice on the winners."

"I heard about that," Evelyn said. "For him to resign so publicly...it was quite the scandal."

Laura leaned forward, careful not to disturb Oscar. "Do you think this connects to what Jeremy was investigating?"

"It might," Evelyn agreed.

Laura considered. "Do you think...we should talk to him?"

Evelyn pursed her lips. "If I remember correctly, Judith might have a mutual connection with him."

"Do you think she could help arrange a conversation?"

"I'll speak with her," Evelyn said. "Hopefully, if he's willing...we may learn something."

CHAPTER ELEVEN

M ondays held a special place in Silver Springs'
weekly rhythm. While most people marked it
as the start of their workweek, for Laura, it was
her day of rest. And in the evenings at six-thirty
pm...The Maplewood Crafters Club gathered in Evelyn's
second-floor apartment in the Morrison Building. Just as
they'd done so for almost thirty-five years.

Silvia, Laura's Gran, was the first in the Evans family to
attend, and tonight, Laura would be the second. Her Gran
had always cherished it, explaining it as a cross between
a craft group and a social gathering. Still, whenever she
mentioned it, there was always a twinkle in her eye.
Like...Laura was missing something.

Laura spent the entire day organizing the last of her
belongings. Three weeks post-move, the apartment finally
was home. A lightness lingered in her chest—maybe from
the orderly space, or maybe from parting with half her
old things, now sitting on the shelves of the Silver Springs
thrift store. They hadn't fit in her car, so Izzy had dropped
by with his old pickup and a tarpaulin, cheerfully hauling
it all away.

Pete had dropped by that morning, as promised, and
hung the paintings up for her. Her favorite, an abstract

piece by an artist she'd met at a SoWa open market in Boston, had pride of place on the wall behind her couch.

Pacing in the hallway, the old kitchen wall clock showed there was still half-an-hour to go. She went to check her bag to make sure she had everything. The spiced aroma of the box of cranberry-orange muffins she'd bought from Layla's bakery drifted out. Also inside was her crochet project and hook that'd spent the last three years languishing in a cupboard in her old Boston apartment. Waiting was all that remained. She'd be patient.

———◆———

Fifteen minutes early, Laura knocked on Evelyn's door. The patience she'd tried hard to muster hadn't lasted. Besides, she was being helpful. She could assist Evelyn. She shouldn't have to prepare everything by herself! Laura had hardly let her knuckles graze the door when it swung open, revealing Evelyn in a cherry-red blouse. Her reading glasses perched low on her nose, and a wide smile lit up her face.

"Laura! How lovely." She took Laura by the arm. "Come along inside now. Are you ready to see what we get up to?"

Laura laughed. "Yes, I am! I arrived a little early, I'm afraid—but I brought muffins. I hope that's alright."

Evelyn beamed. "Now that's a grand entrance. Cranberry-orange muffins from Layla and a smile to match. You're clearly Silvia's granddaughter."

She placed the box on an antique sideboard in the dining room, next to stacks of plates, cutlery, and drinking glasses laid out ready. Oscar raced into the room, rubbing against

Laura's leg while Monty examined her with a discerning gaze. Soft lighting cast a gentle glow across the space, and handmade quilts draped over furniture. The scent of citrus wafted through the air, and she took a big sniff, making Evelyn smile.

"I've got a lemon drizzle cake in the oven," Evelyn said. "And a potato salad ready in the fridge. I hope you came with an appetite."

"That sounds and smells delicious!" Laura said. "Can I help you with anything while we're waiting on the others?"

"The only task on your list tonight is choosing a good seat," Evelyn said. "Today's your day off!"

Laura was about to object, but Evelyn waved her off, so she did as instructed. The setup differed that evening. Two armchairs had been pushed closer together, leaving space for a floor cushion in front of the coffee table. For the cats?

Oscar followed her, jumping into her lap before she'd even settled in. Smiling, she gently pushed the indignant cat aside to make room for her crochet project. The scarf, half-finished and wrinkled from its long dormancy, spilled out. The tangled skein was hand-dyed Targhee wool she'd bought from a dyer in Boston—a deep forest green. She'd purchased it during a rare afternoon off, wandering through the yarn shops in Cambridge, dreaming of cozy evenings that never materialized amidst the demands of her previous career.

Laura sent thanks to her past self for including notes of the pattern and where she was up to. And it was a miracle she still had the pattern downloaded to her phone! Her fingers fell into a familiar rhythm, the yarn sliding through her hands as Oscar purred.

Voices drifted in from the hallway. Her pulse quickened. If the others were friends of Evelyn, they'd welcome her with open arms. Hopefully.

———————◆————————

Martha and Judith came into the room, Judith's large tote overflowing with colorful yarn. Laura rose and Oscar slid off her lap, landing on his feet with a disgruntled meow.

Martha smiled. "Laura! It's such a pleasure to see you here. I know you're going to enjoy yourself." Her tone was warm, but laced with an undertone Laura couldn't place.

"Yes, wonderful to see you. Welcome!" added Judith.

She patted Laura on the arm, then shared a knowing glance with Martha as the three of them settled back into chairs. Judith's yarns spilled across the table, while Martha's remained in her project bag, feeding through a guide hole on the side.

"May I ask what you're both making? The colors are lovely, Judith," Laura said.

Judith's eyes twinkled. "I'm crocheting a new Afghan. Evelyn recommended the pattern." She held up a strip of connected squares, each a vibrant hue. "It's a join-as-you-go design, so I don't have to spend hours at the end putting it all together."

Martha chuckled. "I'm working on something a bit more predictable." She pulled a half-finished circle of overlay crochet from her project bag. "A set of coasters for the Good Neighbor Guild potluck auction."

"You've got me curious now—what makes it predictable?" Laura asked.

Martha smiled. Both Martha and Judith's phones chimed, and they reached to check them almost simultaneously, smiling at their screens.

"Just the others giving us an update on their arrival," Judith said, noticing Laura's inquisitive glance.

The doorbell rang, followed by a cheerful greeting in a southern accent. A lanky woman strode in, clutching a backpack in her long fingers. She wore cargo pants and a t-shirt printed with an Eastern Bluebird.

"Evening, y'all." Her gaze landed on Laura. "Well now. You're new!"

Laura got up from her chair again to shake the woman's hand. "Hi, I'm Laura. It's lovely to meet you."

"It's a pleasure!" the woman said. "I'm Francesca Palermo, which makes me sound like some Old Hollywood movie star, so just call me Fran."

Laura smiled.

Martha nodded at the bluebird print. "Fran's our resident birder. She works at the Twilight Pines State Park."

"Birds are my thing. What can I say?" Fran said. "You'll catch on soon enough." She rummaged in her backpack and pulled out a small embroidery hoop with fabric stretched across it, showing Laura the intricate outline of a bird taking shape in black thread. "Been working on this spotted towhee for a while now."

"Such lovely work," Laura said.

"Thanks!" Fran replied, settling onto the floor cushion.

So that's what it was for.

Fran noticed Laura looking and grinned. "Evelyn insisted on making me this after I kept refusing a chair.

I've always preferred solid ground, but I appreciate the comfort."

Evelyn entered with four others trailing behind her: an olive-skinned man with a mess of curls, a short older woman wearing a denim sleeveless vest, a man wearing a peaked cap, and Jasmine. They crowded into the room.

"Now then, allow me to make introductions," Evelyn said. "This is Laura, just arrived from Boston, and already settling in at the General Store as the café manager."

A chorus of welcomes followed.

"I'm Yanni Petros," the curly-haired man said with a playful salute. He had an accent she couldn't place. "I run Wanderer Pantry. Pleased to meet you."

"Marcela Torres," said the woman in the sleeveless vest. She walked over to where Laura was sitting and shook her hand. "I'm the Town Clerk."

The man in the peaked cap tipped his hat. "Christopher O'Reilly." He spoke with a lilt that hinted at his Irish roots. "Call me whatever amalgamation of those names strikes your fancy. I used to get paid for carpentry, now I do it for fun."

"Lovely to meet you all," Laura said.

"So, Laura," Christopher began.

Fran groaned. "Here we go."

Christopher ignored her, focusing his attention on Laura. "I've got a riddle for you: what has keys but can't open locks, and space but no room?"

"A keyboard," Judith said.

Christopher glared at Judith. "You were supposed to give her a chance to answer!" He saw Laura's puzzled expression and grinned. "I'm testing material for The Whittled Word, the quarterly amateur newspaper I run.

Riddles and wordplay keep the mind sharp." With a glance at Fran, he continued, "Some say my jokes are terrible, but I consider myself a humor connoisseur."

Laura laughed, and gave Jasmine a hello. Oscar jumped into her lap.

Jasmine smiled at Laura. "Looks like you've been made right at home."

"First time at the Crafters Club?" Yanni asked. "You're not sure what you've got yourself into, I imagine." He winked and dropped onto the couch, digging into his bag.

Laura smiled.

Fran stared at her embroidery hoop, needle, and thread. "I'm trying to finish this, but at the rate I'm going, I'll still be here next year!"

"It'll be done before you know it." Marcela took a chair, her cross-stitch thread ready to go. She also pulled out a coloring book, lying it open beside her to a half-filled-in page with a complex radial design.

Yanni set out supplies for a miniature amigurumi moose in progress. He had a fancy hook.

"Is that an ergonomic handle? It looks so comfortable," Laura said.

Yanni brightened, holding it up. "You've spotted my pride and joy! It's an ergonomic bamboo handle with a steel hook. Saves my wrist after hours of work on my project."

Christopher settled into a corner chair, propping a sketchpad on his knee, and began drawing with a graphite pencil.

"What are you sketching?" Laura asked.

"It's my favorite covered bridge. I love the structure and heritage of it. A reminder of days past."

"I know just what you mean. I've always loved them too," Laura said.

"We're so glad you could join us, Laura," Martha said.

Laura smiled, her slight anxiety from before fading away. "This is lovely. Thank you all for having me."

Conversations sparked up, mingling with the aroma of lemon drizzle cake still in the oven. Laura relaxed back into her seat and picked up her work again.

———◇———

The discussion turned to recent events.

"I'm not saying the competition isn't fierce," Judith said, busy with her crochet Afghan squares, "but I hear the Summer Cheese Festival judges are a little set in their ways with who wins in certain categories."

Martha nodded, her hands never pausing. "Certain winners have become predictable."

"Those rumors! Always circling," Marcela said as she threaded her needle. "They've never proven it."

"Of course there's favoritism!" Judith said. "Though now Jeremy Blackwood is out of the picture...maybe it will go away."

Martha snorted. "Really, Judith! It's more likely to increase. That man made his living exposing things, not profiting off them."

Judith raised a skeptical eyebrow. "I always thought there was something fishy about that man. And now look what's happened."

Laura glanced up from her scarf. "That's true. He didn't exactly avoid confrontation." Her words tripped out before she could catch them back.

Judith latched on. "Secrets and scandals! Two of my favorite things. It's no surprise someone'd had enough of him."

Martha tsked.

"Not only that," Judith said. "I heard Jeremy found something big. Something so scandalous, several people wanted it buried along with him. You know what I think? They're all in on it. Rosalind, Diana, the other judges, Alex, the entire festival committee! They're all in cahoots. They had to shut him up before he exposed them."

"Don't be ridiculous, Judith!" Martha said.

"Groups," Fran muttered. "Doesn't matter where, what, or why, you can't escape the politics. Best avoid them."

"My dear woman, you attend one every week," Judith said, and Fran let out a huff of laughter.

———◆———

Evelyn announced dinner, and they proceeded to the dining table. Everyone's containers for the main course stood waiting on the sideboard, with serving utensils, plates, glasses, bowls, and cutlery. Evelyn beamed as she set down the potato salad.

Judith had gone all out with a platter of Swedish meatballs smothered in a creamy sauce.

"Old family recipe," she declared.

Jasmine had brought a quinoa salad with colorful roasted vegetables and a drizzle of pomegranate molasses. Martha's was a casserole dish filled with scalloped potatoes and ham. Fran had brought a rustic pizza, topped with wild mushrooms and herbs. A trio of tamales belonged to Marcela, each wrapped in corn husks.

"There's shredded chicken, pork, and spinach," she said, pointing out the different bundles.

Yanni's offering was a freshly baked loaf of sourdough and an enormous container of rainbow pasta salad. Fusilli spirals tossed with olives, feta cheese, cherry tomatoes, and an array of bright peppers. He cut a slice of bread for everyone. Christopher had contributed a large corn and cheddar quiche.

"Everything looks absolutely splendid," Evelyn said. "I'm so grateful you could all come."

Everyone helped themselves, the room buzzing with chatter as they filled their plates with food and settled around the dining table.

"Here's to the finest company a Monday evening could ask for!" Evelyn said, as glasses clinked together.

———◆———

Empty dishes and the scents of warm comfort food lingered as Evelyn crossed to the kitchen and returned with a tray. "I hope you've left space, because dessert waits for no one," she said, setting down a freshly baked lemon drizzle cake. Before everyone reached for a slice, Evelyn hurried back and came out with a second platter.

"And here are some cranberry-orange muffins, courtesy of Laura."

Laura laughed. "I wish I could bake like that, but they're all Layla from Red Trillium Bakery's doing."

"Excellent choice! Her food is always delicious. Thank you, Evelyn," Martha said as she helped herself to a slice of the cake. "And you too, Laura."

"That Layla knows how to bake," Yanni added, biting into a muffin. "You tell her I said so."

Fran sighed in contentment. "I need to come to the General Store more often. Don't get much time off, though."

Christopher raised an eyebrow at Laura, helping himself to a piece. "Will we see you next week? Or have we scared you off?"

"You've all been so kind. I'd love to keep coming," Laura said, taking a muffin and a slice of cake.

Evelyn looked delighted. "We'd be terribly put out if you didn't return. Of course we'll have you."

Judith nodded. "With a spread like this, we'd be offended if you didn't."

"You're going to like it. Especially with everything we get up to." Jasmine gave her a mysterious smile.

The group exchanged knowing looks.

CHAPTER TWELVE

E velyn swore Silver Springs' best kept secret was
the library. Next to the Town Hall, facing the
Village Green, sat an unassuming but lovely Victorian
building. It housed the library and the Silver Springs
Historical Society. According to Evelyn, no newcomer
to the town should be without a library card.

Laura understood Evelyn's excitement on entering
the building that evening after work. It was the second
time she'd been, but the first she'd given the place a
proper look. Oak paneling and stained-glass windows
greeted them, casting the foyer in warm, colorful light.
A spiral staircase wound through the center. Laura's
gaze traveled up past rows of bookshelves and display
cases to where the ceiling opened into a grand skylight.

"What an incredible space," Laura said.

"I promised you a treat," Evelyn replied with a broad
smile, leading the way to the front desk. "And we've
only just begun."

A familiar face hunched over a table in the reference
section—Judith, surrounded by puzzle books and draft
grids for what looked like crosswords and sudoku.
Laura nudged Evelyn, who grinned.

"You never interrupt the genius while she's at work," Evelyn said.

While waiting in line, a man ahead of them clutched a book and tapped his foot against the floor. He wore overalls and a flannel shirt, and a satchel bursting with papers hung against his slight frame. Blue ink stained his fingers. It was Alex.

The first person in the line, having checked out their library books, walked away, and the librarian turned her attention to the man next in the queue. "Hello, Alex!"

"I'm…I'm…" Alex said, stumbling over his words in his eagerness to respond.

"Alex! What a delightful surprise," Evelyn said, and he jumped before whipping around.

Laura couldn't help but smile. "Good evening."

His expression didn't match hers in its enthusiasm, voice pitched higher than normal. "Good…evening. Fancy—seeing you here."

Evelyn nodded. "Laura's one of us now, so of course, a library card is in order."

Alex nodded, only half-listening.

"What about you?" Evelyn asked.

Alex clutched his satchel tighter. "Me? Just returning some books."

The librarian smiled at the group. "Evelyn, always lovely to see you. And this is Laura, did you say?"

Evelyn introduced Laura to the Adult Circulation Librarian, whose name turned out to be Joyce Adler.

Turning back to Alex, Joyce said, "I've confirmed your prior reservation for the shredder this evening." She must've seen Laura's expression as she let out a laugh. "We have a Lending Exchange program here at the library. We loan out everything from painting easels to screwdrivers. Some things you can take home, others you have to use here in the Lending Exchange room." She nodded at Alex as she gestured to a side door. "The shredder's there ready."

"There's nothing quite like the satisfaction of cleaning things out, is there?" Evelyn said.

"Yes, just—clearing out old files. Committee papers we don't need anymore. Spring cleaning, you might say." Alex let out a forced laugh. "Though it's August."

Joyce gave him a horrified look. "Shouldn't those be archived?"

"Some things don't need to be kept," Alex murmured. "Especially early drafts with...errors." He gripped his satchel even tighter as he edged away. "Good night, now."

A book cart thwarted his attempt to leave. He tripped, his satchel flying open and sending papers fluttering through the air. Laura knelt to help gather them, reaching for a sheet that had skittered under the book cart just as Alex lunged for it. They nearly bumped heads, but her eyes caught on a line of text just before Alex snatched it away. It was a printout of email exchanges between him and—Jeremy Blackwood? Discussing something about marketing campaigns and...payments? Her heart raced.

Alex clutched the paper to his chest, cheeks flushed as he stuffed it back in the satchel. His hands trembled as he fumbled to secure the remaining sheets. For a moment, his eyes met hers.

"I can't—" he started, then stopped, shaking his head. "I need to..." But he couldn't finish the sentence.

Laura picked up a paper near her foot and handed it over, maintaining a neutral expression. "Here, I'll help."

"No, no, thank you!" Alex insisted, jamming the last papers back into his satchel. He dashed toward what must've been the Lending Exchange room.

Joyce had watched the entire exchange with a bemused smile. She turned her attention back to Laura and Evelyn. "Now, what can I assist you with?"

Evelyn clasped her hands together, smiling. "A library card for Silver Springs' newest resident, please."

Joyce grinned. "Excellent!"

Evelyn and Joyce guided her through the process, but all Laura could think about was how strange Alex was behaving. It seemed she had another piece of information to add to the growing list.

———◆◯◆———

Joyce handed Laura her new card with a smile. "A very warm welcome to our newest member of the Silver Springs Public Library!"

Laura thanked her.

Joyce turned to Evelyn. "Sometimes I wonder if you're responsible for most of the new signups."

Evelyn chuckled. "Now you're an official member," she said to Laura. "I insist on giving you the grand tour."

Joyce beamed. "What a wonderful idea! I'd offer to show you around myself, but Evelyn knows this building so well."

"Forty years of patronage will do that," Evelyn said, winking. "First stop is fiction." She gestured to the rows of shelves. "Mystery, romance, science fiction, literary...what do you prefer?"

"Historical fiction is my favorite...though I love a good mystery now and then," Laura replied.

"Mysteries! You have excellent taste," Evelyn said, winking. "Joyce, you'll want to add Laura to the list."

Joyce looked up from helping another patron. "I should! Laura, I'd recommend joining the Mystery Book Club! They meet every other month in the Robinson Room. I'll add you to the email list if you'd like."

"That sounds lovely," Laura said. "Thank you!"

They continued past reference materials and periodicals until they reached a cozy corner filled with comfortable armchairs.

"This is the reading corner," Evelyn explained. "Many good stories have been devoured right here."

Laura sighed. "It's been a while since I just curled up and read."

Evelyn winked at her. "That's what the library's digital lending system is for! There are many audiobooks. Joyce will have you listening in no time."

"You always think of everything. Thank you, Evelyn," Laura said.

They rounded a corner near the non-fiction section, bumping into Martha, who balanced a stack of books.

"Evelyn! And Laura, what a pleasant surprise," Martha said, setting down her burden on a nearby table. "Getting acquainted with our little library?"

"Yes! Just got my card," Laura replied, holding it up.

"You really are your grandmother's granddaughter," Martha said. "One of her favorite things in Silver Springs is the seasonal book sale." She smiled and nodded at Evelyn. "You're in the company of the woman behind the idea. She helped the Friends Of The Library start it all those years ago, and it continues to be one of our biggest fundraisers. You missed a spectacular winter sale last year." Martha's eyes twinkled with mischief. "Wasn't it good, Evelyn?"

Evelyn's relaxed demeanor faltered. "It was...eventful."

"Have you told her about what happened to the book you found and—"

"I'll explain another time," Evelyn cut in, her cheeks pink. "When we have more time for...elaborate stories."

Laura looked between them. "Now I'm curious."

"All in good time," Evelyn said, steering Laura toward the next stop on the tour.

***

Laura arranged panini filled with roasted vegetables and brie on a tray in the display cabinet in the café the next day, sunlight streaming through the windows in golden shafts. She stepped back to inspect her work. Satisfied, she let her gaze roam over the mid-morning bustle around her. Kathy chatted with a customer about reclaimed wood, while Jasmine carried in boxes from a delivery truck. Laura's mind, however, was preoccupied with how many regular customers whispered as they sat at tables, stopping whenever Maggie rushed past.

The bell above the door chimed, and Rosalind entered. Every hair was in place, and her elegant dress was high end, but there was no mistaking the dark circles under her eyes.

Laura was behind the counter in an instant. "Good morning, Rosalind! What can I prepare for you today? Your usual herbal tea?"

"Triple-shot espresso," Rosalind replied. "Festival stress. I'm running on fumes today."

Laura recorded Rosalind's order and placed it next to the others for Eli. "You're juggling so much. I admire that."

"I'm barely hanging on," Rosalind said with a tight smile.

Laura gave her a sympathetic look. "I heard you visited Boston, a city I used to call home until recently. Did it treat you well?"

Rosalind's eyes widened. "It was productive. Lots of meetings."

"Back-to-back, I bet," Laura said.

Rosalind fumbled in her purse. "Yes, thank you for taking my order. I'll wait over here."

She declined a receipt and stepped away from the counter to wait, tapping her foot against the tiled floor. Laura watched her go for a moment. What had happened in Boston? Or was it really just meetings?

<hr>

The morning crowd had come and gone, leaving the café in relative quiet. The lunch rush would begin in an hour. Kathy had left on a supply run, and Maggie was nowhere to be seen, leaving Laura with little to do other than tidy tables.

Perhaps the stables warranted another inspection. The police had cleared the scene, and Ben had mentioned he would fix a few things there. Maybe, as long as she was quick about it...Jasmine, Jesse, and Eli could manage just fine on their own for a few minutes.

Laura called to her coworkers. "I'm going to check in with Ben. I'll be back soon!"

She exited the building and crossed the grounds to the stables, recalling Kathy's worried expression. Laura shook the memory off and pushed ahead, hoping for more clues to clear up the mystery before things got worse.

Ben was already there, as expected. He braced one shoulder against the weathered wood of the stable door, steadying it while his other hand worked a cordless drill. Two shiny new heavy-duty padlocks—just in from his dad's hardware store—lay on an overturned bucket beside him. Tools spread across a worn canvas drop cloth. Every few seconds, he'd step back, squint at his handiwork, then resume working.

"Need anything while I'm here?" Laura called, raising her voice over the drill's persistent buzz.

Ben turned off the drill and said over his shoulder, "Oh, Laura! All good here, thanks!"

Laura nodded. "I'm going to take a quick look inside. See if there's anything I missed."

"You got it!" he said, giving her a wink as he stepped aside to let her pass.

She scanned the interior and her eyes fixed on the spot where Jeremy Blackwood had fallen. She climbed the stairs to inspect the mezzanine floor. Once there, a section of the balustrade askew caught her attention. Touching the wood, it shifted under her hand. Was this...where it had happened? She shivered.

"Did you find anything?" Ben called from below. He'd finished setting the second padlock into its place.

Laura took a breath. "Nothing new..."

The unsteady wood was only further proof he'd hit the balustrade and fallen. Nothing that'd help with the investigation.

A minute later, Ben called through the entrance. "And...done! Locks installed. Do you think you could help me give them a quick once-over?"

"Happy to help, but something caught my eye. Do you mind coming up for a moment?"

Ben joined her on the mezzanine and crouched to look at the spot she'd pointed out. He sucked in a breath. "Yikes. This is the spot, huh?"

Laura didn't have to answer the question.

He nodded. "Not looking forward to fixing that...but I'll make sure it's solid."

They both hurried back to the stairs, about to head to the first floor to test the locks, when Laura triple-checked the floor to see if she'd missed anything. It seemed...she had. Something...so tiny, so faint, it was easy to miss. She dropped onto her knees to look closer. It was a small paper scrap wedged between two floorboards.

Ben crouched down beside her. "What's that?"

Laura frowned. "I'm not sure. Would you mind staying right there? Best not to touch anything just yet."

Ben scoffed and assumed a guard position, squinting around as if someone might jump out from a hiding spot and steal the piece of paper. "As if I would."

Laura climbed down the stairs, exited the stables, and crossed the grounds toward the main building. She returned carrying food-grade gloves and a plastic zip-bag. With them on, she retrieved the paper, unfolding a note with writing scrawled in an unfamiliar hand: 'General Store Stables. Nine forty-five.' Nothing else.

A chill ran down Laura's spine. Jeremy's watch had stopped at...ten-o-seven.

"What is it?" Ben asked, peering at the scrap from a safe distance.

"I have a feeling...Jeremy and...the murderer prearranged to meet at this spot. Still...who invited who?"

Ben shivered. "Jeepers. To think it happened here!"

Laura nodded. "Once we double-check the locks, I'll take this to Detective Sergeant Ramirez on my lunch break."

They hurried toward the door at the first floor entrance. Ben stood on the outside with Laura on the inside. He locked the padlocks.

Laura slid, pushed, and pulled against the doors to be sure. "All good!"

Ben nodded as he let her out, locking up and pocketing the keys. "I declare these doors hooligan-proof."

What a relief to be out of that building.

"Alright! Next up, trimming that hawthorn bush back by the gate and setting up the security light," Ben said, waving his arm in its general direction. "Shouldn't take too long."

"Careful you don't end up looking like a pincushion," Laura said.

He grimaced. "No promises."

Ben's prediction of how long his next task would take proved correct, at least on initial inspection. Less than fifteen minutes later, he burst into the café, breathless. Laura turned, halfway through stacking the dishwasher with yet another load.

"Laura, got a second?" Ben asked, making a gesture that could only represent putting on gloves, and motioning her over. Had he...found something else?

She dried her hands, picked up a fresh pair of gloves and a plastic zippered bag, and caught up with him just outside the door. "What's going on?"

He ignored the question, picking up speed. They reached the back gate. He'd trimmed some sections of the hawthorn bush, but if you looked closely...right where the hedge touched the gate, near the hinge...was a small piece of material caught in the thorns. It was black and seemed water-resistant.

"Whoever left this must've been in a hurry!" Ben said. "Do you think—"

Laura nodded, mouth set in a grim line. She slipped on the gloves and put the other potential piece of evidence in the bag she'd brought.

Walking to the Silver Springs Police Department an hour later, Laura held her tote with the evidence tucked inside close to her body. Before she'd slipped out of the General

Store, claiming she'd needed to run an errand, she'd placed a few dollar bills in the tip jar to pay for the equipment she'd used in collecting the fabric and paper scrap. The red brick building was just up ahead. Reaching the worn concrete steps, she hurried inside.

The sound of chatter and phones ringing filled the air, intermingling with a steady rhythm of keyboards clacking and papers shuffling. Laura approached the front desk, and the administrative assistant looked up and gave her a smile.

"Good afternoon," the woman said.

"Good afternoon. I'd like to speak with Detective Sergeant Ramirez, please," Laura said. "It's about...the Jeremy Blackwood case."

The administrative assistant nodded. "Of course. I'll let her know you're here. Please take a seat."

Several minutes later, Ramirez strode out from the back. "Laura?"

Laura stood, her heart racing as she reached into her tote bag.

"I have something important you should see," she said, pulling out the two sealed plastic bags and holding up the one containing the fabric scrap. "Ben found this caught on the hawthorn hedge by the General Store's back gate when he was doing maintenance work. It looks like it was torn from someone's clothing."

Ramirez examined the bag, then looked up. "And the second item?"

Laura hesitated before handing over the other bag. "We found this tucked between the floorboards in the mezzanine level of the stables." She indicated the visible writing through the plastic. "It says 'General Store Stables. Nine forty-five.' No signature, no date."

Ramirez' eyebrows rose as she examined the note. "And you collected these items yourself?"

"Yes," Laura said. "With gloves, of course. I didn't want to contaminate anything."

Ramirez' expression shifted as she frowned. She took both bags. "Laura. I appreciate your initiative, but this is evidence in an active murder investigation. You should've called us immediately upon discovery rather than handling it yourself."

Laura's cheeks flushed. "I was only trying to help..."

"Even with gloves, you've compromised the chain of custody," Ramirez continued. "Evidence needs to be collected by trained personnel following proper protocols. Your intentions were good, but this complicates things for us."

"I'm sorry," Laura said. "I didn't think—"

"No, you didn't," Ramirez said, though her tone softened as she continued. "That said, thank you for bringing these in rather than keeping them to yourself. We'll get them logged and sent for analysis."

Laura nodded, not meeting Ramirez' eyes. "Is it possible these are relevant?"

"We'll see," Ramirez said. She motioned Laura toward an interview room. "This way, please. I'll need a formal statement about when and where these items were found, who discovered them, and who handled them. And Laura? In the future, if you find anything that might be connected to this case or any other, please call us first. Don't touch it, don't collect it. Just report it. Understood?"

"Yes, of course," Laura replied, head down. "I won't make the same mistake again."

CHAPTER THIRTEEN

The break room occupied a modest corner of the second floor, tucked away from the bustle of the café and retail space below. A square wooden table dominated the center and mismatched chairs surrounded it—all also made of wood, with colorful cushions tied to the seats. Along one wall, a kitchenette featured the essentials: a kettle, microwave, toaster, and refrigerator plastered with local touristic magnets. Cups, bowls, and plates sat on a shelf above, most handmade by local potters.

The opposite wall housed a row of lockers in blue, each labeled with a staff member's name on a little placard in Maggie's handwriting. A small pinboard hung beside the door. Someone—perhaps Jasmine—had pinned up several instant photos of the staff and their smiling faces at various events.

A bookshelf in the corner held an eclectic collection—novels and old cookbooks with dog-eared pages. A thriving potted spider plant sat on the highest shelf.

Back from her trip to the police station, Laura's head swirled with more questions than answers as she used the rest of her lunch time to update her notes on the investigation. Her cheeks still burned as she relived

Ramirez' reprimand. The evidence was in proper hands now—that was what mattered. She'd made a mistake, yes, but her intentions were good, and it was an error she wouldn't make again.

She checked her phone's notifications and grimaced. Three missed calls from her mother already today. She couldn't leave it any longer.

"I was about to imagine the worst," Bridget answered.

Laura pinched the bridge of her nose. "I promise I wasn't ignoring you. I was just caught up at work."

"I read the news this morning," Bridget said, a faint sigh escaping. "About those financial records. They made it sound so...certain. That she was paying him off. My heart just sank."

Outside the window, sunlight dappled the courtyard, peaceful and ordinary.

Inside, Laura's pulse sped up. "I don't think that's how it really happened. I think someone's setting Maggie up."

Her mother was quiet for a moment, then a short, nervous laugh. "And you know this...how, darling?"

"I've spent some time looking into it, and I think I understand more now," Laura said. Wait. What? She'd—

"You've been what?" Bridget's voice jumped up an octave. "Laura Jaqueline Evans, please tell me you're not...involving yourself in a murder investigation."

The middle name.

"I'm just trying to get a clearer picture by asking a few questions, that's all. To understand."

"Questions?" Bridget's voice trembled. "Laura...what if you ask the wrong person? The thought of you...of something happening...I just want you to be safe. I raised you to be smart, to be careful."

"I'm not rushing in. I know what I'm doing," Laura said, trying to keep her voice level.

"Really, sweetheart?" Bridget asked, her voice soft. "Because from where I'm sitting...it feels like you walked away from such a safe career. And now this. Working in that place, and getting caught up with your boss, who the police suspect of killing someone. It's...a lot for me to process. I worry."

"I know, Mom. I'll be careful."

Bridget sighed. "Laura, I really think—okay. Be safe."

She ended the call. She couldn't go back to Boston. No matter what Bridget Evans had to say about it. The door opened, and Laura looked up to see Jasmine's head poking around the frame.

"Can I...talk to you for a second?"

"Yes, of course," Laura said, putting her phone away and motioning her friend over.

"So, that rumor about the love bite? Not so much a rumor. A friend of mine who works security at the Medical Center overheard the examiner confirm it."

Laura's pulse quickened. "So Jeremy was seeing someone? Do we know who it was?"

"That's what's got everyone talking. Usually, Jeremy's romantic life was an open book. He was notorious for dating food critics and celebrity chefs to boost his profile." Jasmine leaned in closer. "But this? Complete mystery. No sightings, no social media hints, nothing. He kept whoever it was under wraps, which is out of character for him."

"If he kept them a secret," Laura said, "that says a lot."

Jasmine nodded. "I wanted to say...have you seen this?" She handed over her phone.

It was an article from a Boston gossip magazine dated just yesterday. The headline read: 'Fall Of A Culinary Critic: Jeremy Blackwood's Fading Influence.'

Laura leaned closer, scanning the piece. The article described Jeremy's financial troubles, citing 'sources close to the critic' who claimed he was in significant debt. Most surprising were the documents found in his home suggesting he'd been preparing to file for bankruptcy. And according to former colleagues, he became obsessed with finding his 'comeback story'—a scandal big enough to restore his fading reputation. He began compiling dossiers on industry figures, documenting patterns, and inconsistencies that might reveal impropriety.

"But this is unusual," Laura read aloud, "because industry insiders report Blackwood always seemed flush with cash, sporting expensive new clothes and booking reservations at high-end establishments. It appears he came into a windfall in the months before his death. One can only speculate about the source." Laura sat back in her chair. "If Jeremy was desperate for money, that could explain the 'consulting fees' allegedly paid by Maggie. But she denied any such arrangement..."

"Where did his sudden wealth come from?" Jasmine finished her thought. "And that reminds me. You won't believe what I heard from my friend. Apparently, they found a handwritten note in Jeremy's pocket that read: 'I need to clear a few things up, but I don't want Lou to find out. Meet me at Moss Ridge Preserve at ten-thirty pm.'"

"Lou...he's Diana's husband, isn't he?" Laura said, her eyes widening. "But if Diana wrote that note, why would Jeremy end up at the stables instead of Moss Ridge?"

"Maybe there was a second note? Or a change of plans?" Jasmine shrugged. "Either way, it's strange."

"Thank you, Jasmine," Laura said, smiling. "I really appreciate your help with this."

Jasmine nodded. "Always happy to."

———◦———

Leaving work through the front door, Laura's phone vibrated in her pocket.

A message from Evelyn.

> "Haven't heard from you. Are you all set?"

> "Nearly there!"

Her phone buzzed again.

This time, a call from Evelyn. "Laura! I'm in the parking lot. Are you nearly here? We mustn't dawdle. This case won't solve itself." Evelyn chuckled before hanging up.

Laura rounded the corner and slipped into the narrow path next to the Morrison Building leading to the alleyway behind. Her small blue sedan sat ready, and next to it with an expectant expression...stood Evelyn, a light lace shawl draped over her arm and her handbag by her side.

"There you are! A fashionable thirty seconds late." Evelyn looked up from her watch with a twinkle.

Laura opened the car door for Evelyn, then sat in the driver's seat. She turned the ignition, and the engine protested with a series of reluctant coughs before shuddering awake.

Evelyn smiled and patted the dashboard. "A reliable old soul, just like me. And now, to visit Thomas."

Laura arched an eyebrow. "We're really just dropping in? No warning?"

"Festival or not, I've never known Thomas to turn down a chat," Evelyn said.

"I can't argue with that," Laura said with a laugh, putting the car into reverse.

Evelyn retrieved a small tin from her bag. Once Laura had backed out, Evelyn selected a homemade honey snap from the container and handed it to her.

"Investigators require proper sustenance," Evelyn grinned. "Worry not. I shall chart our course."

Once again, she'd thought of everything.

Laura put the car into drive and let the comforting flavor of the snap dissolve her remaining doubts. Evelyn gave her the first set of directions to Thomas' property. Laura turned onto the road.

———◆———

Few pedestrians remained on the otherwise clear sidewalks as stores shut for the night. Downtown unfolded before them as they drove. Evelyn instructed Laura to make a right turn—one Laura nearly missed. Evelyn began to question the distraction, but her gaze tracked where Laura had been looking before. There, charging down the street with hiking sticks in hand, strode Martha.

"Is there a reason Martha's in such a hurry?" Laura asked as they drove on.

"Just doing her daily exercise. Speed-walking, no doubt," Evelyn said. "Even after her knee surgery, Martha hasn't slowed down. Lawrence thought giving her some Nordic Poles might cheer her up. They've worked too well. She hears 'take it easy' and thinks it's a challenge. Just like how she treats her weekly bingo club at the Senior Center—always striving for that win."

They left the shops behind and entered a residential area, driving along a tree-lined street. The roads became narrower and more winding as they went, the outlines of mountains visible beyond. They passed a bungalow hidden behind a few trees. Alex's place. Parked out the front of his driveway—

"Did I just see a police car behind us?" Laura asked, glancing up briefly at the rearview mirror.

"It was indeed," Evelyn said, shifting around in her seat to peer through the back window. "I wonder what they're doing there?"

Laura paused. "Do you think this could be tied to Jeremy?"

Evelyn frowned. "Perhaps. Keep going straight. We'll cross the Deer Brook bridge soon."

———◦———

A farmhouse appeared up ahead as they wound up the driveway, a small formal garden surrounded the house with manicured trees and bushes. They parked next to a shiny black four-wheel drive and climbed out. When Evelyn pressed the doorbell, a sweet, complicated chime rang through the house.

One minute. Two. Nothing. No signs or sounds of movement from inside, except a dog barking from somewhere. Laura rang the bell again, adding a vigorous knock for good measure.

"No one's answering. Looks like he's out," Laura said.

"Give him another minute," Evelyn replied, not appearing in the least surprised.

Footsteps approached from within, and the front door swung open.

Thomas blinked at them, finding himself in a situation he hadn't written into his schedule. "Laura? Evelyn? What a surprise!"

After a brief pause, he ushered them in. He wore his usual attire—premium denim, and a tailored shirt—but this evening he'd rolled up his sleeves and wore an apron that read, 'Life Is Better With Cheese.'

"We thought we'd pay you a visit," Laura said, smiling after having read what was written on Thomas' apron.

"I hope we didn't come at a bad time," Evelyn added.

His brief shock turned into a smile. "No, no. I was just barbecuing in the shed. Why don't you come out the back with me?"

"That's most generous of you, Thomas. Thank you," Evelyn said.

———◦○◦———

Thomas led them along a path toward a well-built shed behind the house—more workshop than storage space. Solar-powered garden lights illuminated their way as delicious cooking smells wafted from the open shed door.

The front area seemed more like a custom gourmet kitchen than a tool storage space. It was as neat as everything else, like he wanted everything in the universe arranged just so.

A stainless steel counter lined one wall, and shelves above contained jars and kitchenware. A tabletop ceramic grill with sizzling steaks sat next to a stovetop and oven. Above it, a large pipe connected the exhaust fan to a hole in the ceiling, ventilating the space while still letting the delicious smells of the steak linger. Laura's stomach growled despite the honey snap.

A black and white border collie bounded toward the visitors, tail wagging.

"This is Bailey," Thomas said, as the dog leapt around them. He crouched, his face softening as he gave Bailey a thorough scratch behind the ears. "Adopted him from Stonefield Animal Refuge two years ago. We've been inseparable ever since, haven't we, buddy?"

Bailey responded with a bark, pressing his nose against Thomas' hand for more attention, which Thomas provided with a chuckle. The dog seemed to sense something and began circling Evelyn, sniffing her pants.

"He smells your cats," Laura said to Evelyn, laughing.

Evelyn bent to pet Bailey. "What a friendly fellow you are."

The back of the shed was as organized as the front, with tools hanging on peg boards and labeled storage bins lined up on the floor. Several outlets along the wall powered a charger and grill. In the corner, an electric motorcycle lay disassembled, its parts laid out neatly on a tarp.

"Looks like someone's been hard at work," Laura said, gesturing to the bike.

Thomas followed her gaze. "I've been attempting to repair it for months. It's handy for checking fencing." He chuckled. "I like the odd tinker, but I'm no mechanic." He walked over to the sink and washed his hands, then picked up a set of tongs, turning the steaks. "These are done. Fancy staying for dinner?"

Laura hesitated. "We don't want to interrupt."

"Not at all!" Thomas said. "Please, I insist."

"That's very kind of you. Thank you, we'd be delighted," Evelyn said.

"Splendid! Let's move to the house to eat," Thomas said, removing his apron and folding it.

He led them back into the house. A mud room opened into a bright interior with exposed wooden beams and a large open-plan area combining the dining and living room. Laura admired the space, her eyes landing on a beautiful stone fireplace that took up an entire wall. Handmade quilts draped over couches, and woven rugs softened hardwood floors. The place was inviting, with a rustic elegance that fit its owner.

"Please get comfortable while I take care of everything," Thomas said. "You're my guests, after all." He motioned for them to sit. "I'll bring dinner in just a moment."

"Would you like a hand?" Laura asked.

He shook his head with a smile. "No thank you Laura, but I appreciate the offer." He turned to the door leading outside. "I should settle Bailey in for the night." Thomas returned later with a tray, setting down plates of barbecued steak with blue-cheese butter, green beans, and potatoes tossed in parsley. "Here we are."

"Wow," Laura said, admiring the dish. "This looks amazing!"

Thomas smiled as he placed a bread basket on the table. "I hope you like the cheese. It's the Whitman Family Blue. It's made with Jersey cow's milk with hints of cracked black pepper."

Evelyn took a bite, savoring it before speaking. "This is divine. A fitting product of your impressive career."

"Nothing compared to my father and grandfather," he said, easing back in his chair.

Laura speared a slice of her steak. "Really?"

"My grandfather helped start the festival," Thomas said, sounding like he'd given this speech before but didn't mind repeating himself. "Both he and my father were cheesemakers, that being their sole focus throughout their entire lives. I'm the first to break from tradition...juggling multiple roles. The Whitman name means something in Vermont When people think of quality dairy in this state, they think of us." He traced the rim of his water glass, his expression thoughtful. "That kind of legacy...it's more than just business."

Laura nodded. "That sounds like an enormous responsibility."

"It is," Thomas said, "but it's also a privilege. Balancing tradition with change...that's my specialty."

Laura nodded. "As the head judge, it must be interesting to see how things have changed."

"Absolutely. Standards have developed significantly," Thomas said. "We now have much stricter criteria for texture, flavor, and creativity. Some producers always rise to the occasion."

Evelyn nodded. "Elderkin Cheese knows how to craft a winning wheel."

Thomas shifted to reach for a piece of bread. "Yes, they had quite the run."

"It's a shame Jeremy won't be here to see this year's results," Evelyn said, her mood sobering.

Thomas sighed. "Yes, it is."

"Was Jeremy someone you knew well?" Laura asked, cutting into her potatoes.

Thomas paused. "Not really. We only crossed paths during the festival. You know, the planning, and then the actual event."

"Did Jeremy ever strike you as someone with unresolved quarrels?" Evelyn asked, keeping her tone conversational. "The whole town seems shocked!"

Thomas set down his knife and fork and sipped his water. "Small towns and their gossip. This time, though...it isn't off base. He sure loved making things difficult." He turned to Laura. "You heard him going on at the tasting."

Laura nodded.

Thomas shrugged after taking up his cutlery for another mouthful. "As far as I know...he was just doing what he did best. Creating conflict where there didn't need to be any."

Laura was poised to ask another question, but decided against it. The mood had grown heavy, and she didn't want to dominate their dinner with talk of Jeremy's passing. Instead, she focused on her food, savoring the rich flavor.

"That was delicious, Thomas," Evelyn said once they'd finished, setting down her knife and fork with a satisfied sigh. "You're as talented in the kitchen as you are with cheese."

Thomas smiled. "Thank you. Cooking helps me unwind after a long day."

Laura was about to ask what his favorite thing to make was when something caught her eye. At the...bottom of the fireplace?

Thomas stood. "Who's ready for dessert?"

Laura exchanged a quick look with Evelyn. "You've already been so kind."

"It's no trouble!" Thomas said, gathering their empty plates. He gave a short, self-conscious laugh. "I had it prepared already. After cheese, sugar is my greatest weakness."

"I can hardly say no to a fellow sweet tooth. That'd be wonderful, thank you." Evelyn smiled.

Thomas nodded, disappearing into the kitchen and grinning as he shut the door behind him. Laura seized the opportunity and moved to the hearth. She blinked, not trusting her eyes. How strange. She shook her head before returning to her seat.

Evelyn stared at her. "What is it?"

Laura shrugged. "Just...thought I saw something."

Thomas returned with three large bowls. The smell of brown sugar and peaches filled the room. "Peach cobbler with vanilla ice cream."

"You need to share this recipe," Evelyn said, marveling at the dessert.

"I'll trade you for your Jook recipe," Thomas said, smiling.

Evelyn laughed. "You make a tempting offer."

Later, Laura leaned back, savoring the last bite of her dessert. "Absolutely delicious. Thank you."

Evelyn nodded. "My compliments to the chef."

Thomas chuckled. "Glad you enjoyed it. I can't tell you how nice it is to have company."

"Thank you for having us on such short notice! Let us at least help you clean up," Evelyn said, rising from her chair.

"No need, but thank you," Thomas said, and a laugh escaped him. "That's what dishwashers are for."

Evelyn and Laura laughed with him.

"We should be going," Laura said. "Thanks for having us."

Thomas walked them to the hallway. "My pleasure. You must visit the creamery sometime for a private tour."

"That sounds wonderful," Laura said, already envisioning it.

Thomas smiled, waving as they hurried toward the car. Laura guided her sedan down the long gravel driveway as a truck turned into the adjacent property.

Evelyn recognized the vehicle and waved. "Laura, could you roll down the window? It's Todd!"

Leaning out, Todd called over the rumble of his truck, "Evening! What are you doing this far out?"

"Visiting Thomas," Evelyn said. "We caught him while he was barbecuing, and he invited us for dinner." She gestured to Laura. "Todd, this is Laura, the new General Store café manager and my tenant and friend. Laura, this is Todd Miller, a local dairy farmer."

"Pleasure," he said. "And aren't you lucky? The man's cooking is something." He smiled. "Quiet out this way, isn't it? Not much happens on our side of the hill. I drove past the other night and the only thing doing something was Thomas' TV."

Laura tried not to look too interested. "You don't remember which night that was, do you? Just curious, you know, with everything going on."

Todd rubbed his chin. "Pretty sure it was Wednesday. Saw his car in the drive and him walking that dog of his earlier that evening. Then the lights and TV were on until about nine-ten." As he talked, his gaze drifted toward the boundary line between his property and Thomas'. His expression tightened.

"Thomas likes his routines, doesn't he?" Laura asked with a smile.

"Like you wouldn't believe," Todd said. "He always waves when he gets home, takes Bailey out at the same time." He chuckled. "The man's more reliable than my wall clock."

"It's lucky his car's still working," Laura said as she stored the information away. "I saw his motorcycle in pieces in his shed when he gave us a tour."

Todd gave a knowing nod. "He's been working on that bike forever. Should just take it to the shop."

Laura laughed. "He told me as much."

"It's been sitting like that for months," Todd said, his attention drawn back to the property line. "Speaking of fixing things, I have to continue working on my fences. Good seeing you, Evelyn. Nice meeting you, Laura."

"Good to see you too," Evelyn said, as Bailey's barking echoed in the distance.

Laura waved before rolling up the window, and he returned the gesture.

———————◆○◆———————

"Shall we take the scenic route back?" Evelyn suggested as they drove down a road. "You've not yet had the pleasure." Laura agreed, and Evelyn pointed to the upcoming fork. "Take a left here."

She turned, and they continued along a stretch of trees.

After several minutes of comfortable silence, Evelyn spoke up. "Thomas could give lessons in hosting. Not a single detail out of place." She pointed through the passenger window. "See there? That's the old Farley covered bridge. And there's the Dalton farmhouse. Five generations have lived there, though I hear the youngest boy wants to sell it. Look! That's the old sugar shack. Every spring, half the town would gather there for maple ice cream."

As Laura glanced in the direction Evelyn was pointing, something else caught her eye—a weathered entrance swallowed by undergrowth. "What's the story with that old gate?"

"Most of these properties have back entrances from the old days," Evelyn said, following her gaze. "Farmers needed multiple access points for their equipment. Half of them are forgotten now—nature reclaiming what they don't use." She pointed ahead. "Look, you can see Silver Springs from here."

They crested a small hill, and suddenly the first buildings of the town appeared below them. They descended toward the twinkling lights.

CHAPTER FOURTEEN

L aura unstacked the last few chairs, stepping back to survey the room. Everything was in place. The Summer Cheese Festival, though only a three-day event, took a mountain of planning and coordination. And this was where it all culminated: the final pre-festival meeting in the Silver Springs Town Hall. Involving not only the committee members, but all the volunteers, partners, and caterers.

All the last checks had to be completed before the proceedings began tomorrow. Her first Summer Cheese Festival. Laura didn't know what to feel.

The General Store had partnered with Victor and Larry from Beaumont Bistro, along with Colette from Chez Colette, to create a culinary experience befitting the festival's reputation. The bistro duo, known for their innovative flair, promised an unforgettable array of canapés featuring local cheeses and house-made charcuterie. Meanwhile, Colette's elegant touch ensured a sophisticated selection of French-inspired hors d'oeuvres, including her signature gougères and tarts. Jasmine had raved about the tangy quince tartlets from last year's event, which had been a crowd favorite. Laura hoped she'd get to try one.

She and Jasmine would serve refreshments and food during the events and assist Maggie. Eli, Jesse, and the others were left in charge of the store.

Alongside a few volunteers, Jasmine and Laura had set up for the first of many events in the Town Hall's biggest conference room—the heart of the festival. She checked her phone for perhaps the fifth time in the past half hour. Only fifteen minutes left until the meeting began.

She wasn't the only one with pre-festival jitters. Somewhere in between the chaos of preparation tasks, Alex had appeared in the space, occupying a chair at the back corner. He wore his attempt at 'dressing up'—an ironed instead of rumpled button-down shirt underneath navy overalls that, for once, weren't covered with signs of wear. He hunched over a notebook, scribbling with his fountain pen.

Laura approached, grateful for the distraction from the upcoming meeting—and maybe the chance to talk to Alex, too. She dropped into the seat beside him, offering a smile. "Mind if I join you for a moment? It's nice to pause before the whirlwind starts."

He startled and looked up, blinking from behind tortoiseshell glasses. "Oh, Laura. Good...morning."

Laura shifted in her seat. "I hope you haven't had any trouble. I saw a police car outside your place last night and I was a little worried."

Alex pushed his glasses up the bridge of his nose and waved off her concern with an unsteady hand. "Nothing to worry about. They were just asking questions." He paused, his eyes darting around the room. "About Jeremy. Just routine." He fiddled with the cap of his pen, then uncapped and recapped it several times. "All very standard."

She nodded. "That's a beautiful pen. Did you just get it?"

He gave her a jittery smile and looked down at it. "Thank you. Yes, I—needed a change. It was time anyway."

Laura smiled, nodded at him, and got up. Wait...his hands...they were clean. She couldn't recall the last time she'd seen them without streaks of ink.

Diana strode into the room, making a beeline for Thomas, who eyed her as she drew near. The two stood at the opposite end of the event area, engaged in a tense conversation. What could they be talking about?

The meeting was about to start when Maggie arrived, some of the crowd averting their gazes as she sat beside Laura and Jasmine in the front. Thomas checked his buzzing phone in the row ahead, relieved. Nearby, Diana whispered something to Alex, who responded with head shakes and nervous glances.

"Tell me if I'm imagining things," Jasmine murmured to Laura, "or is the committee about five seconds from spontaneous combustion?"

Laura nodded.

Rosalind approached the podium, clipboard in hand. She exchanged a subtle nod with Thomas and announced, "Welcome, everyone. Let's begin."

The meeting concluded with Rosalind thanking everyone for their time, asking the committee members to stay behind. Chairs scraped against the floor as people rose, buzzing with conversation and last-minute plans. Thomas got up from his seat and waited for the aisle to clear. He cast a glance at his phone, then moved through a gap in the crowd toward the front to join Rosalind.

In his haste, something slipped from his sports jacket, tumbling to the floor. A small green notebook, embossed with the initials T.W. Jasmine, who was close behind, bent to pick it up, calling his name. He spun, eyes wide, and took the notebook from her hands. She asked him a question, and he responded with a smile before hurrying away.

Steam spiraled from the large pot on the stovetop as Laura gave its contents a focused stir, the savory aroma wafting up to greet her. The industrial kitchen in the Town Hall, cavernous and bustling, was the heart of the last pre-festival activities. Stainless steel counters and shelves lined the walls, gleaming under the flickering fluorescent lights. Massive appliances hummed in unison, mixing bowls clanged, and the sound of knives chopping echoed from the far end where volunteers worked on last-minute prep.

Across from Laura, Jasmine chopped vegetables. The rasp of her knife against the cutting board was rhythmical, keeping time with the energy in the room.

Victor from Beaumont Bistro darted around in a flurry of activity. Larry, the bistro's front of house manager, worked nearby, polishing glasses and readying plates for service. Colette from Chez Colette, another of Silver Springs' upmarket restaurants, moved between several cooking stations, keeping watch over multiple pots and pans. Throughout the kitchen, staff members hustled about with purpose—some preparing ingredients, others operating the grill, a few stirring sauces or fetching supplies as needed. The team worked in synchronized motion.

Jasmine finished her pile of vegetables, only to have it whisked off by a line cook from Chez Colette, who replaced her empty board with another pile yet to be chopped. She heaved a sigh. "Here we go again."

Laura's face broke into a smile as Jasmine resumed her task.

"Thomas dropped his notebook earlier," she murmured to Laura. "I bent down to grab it and you'd think I snatched his wallet. The open page had names with numbers beside them. He said it was just cheese competition stuff, which seems strange, considering the judging hasn't even started."

Laura considered this as she added another sprinkling of herbs to the pot, stirring with renewed curiosity. Did that mean anything?

Maggie appeared in the kitchen doorway, her face ashen and her hands trembling. "Laura...Jasmine...can you come out here for a moment?"

Maggie led them to a small anteroom used for storing extra chairs. Once inside, she closed the door behind them and leaned against it.

"What's going on?" Jasmine asked, exchanging a worried glance with Laura.

Maggie took a shaky breath. "I thought you should know. There's a...situation developing."

Laura's pulse quickened. "Did something happen?"

"Elliott Harrington called Rosalind just before the meeting," Maggie said, her voice cracking. "He's the director of the Vermont Food & Wine Association."

Jasmine inhaled sharply. "That doesn't sound good."

"It's not," Maggie confirmed, slumping against the one unobstructed space of the wall, sliding down it to take a seat on the floor. "Of course, news of Jeremy's...passing has reached the Association. They're concerned about how it reflects on them."

"That feels misplaced, considering what's happened," Laura said. "A man has died!"

"To Harrington, that's a PR problem," Maggie murmured, her eyes welling with tears. "Rosalind said the Association is reconsidering their affiliation with the festival. And they just had to put the General Store's affiliation up for reconsideration too."

Laura sat beside Maggie. "I'm so sorry, Maggie. That's a lot to carry."

"The Association provides credibility with producers and access to their promotional channels. Without them..." Maggie let the sentence hang, unable to finish.

"What did Rosalind tell him?" Jasmine asked, her voice gentle as she joined them on the floor.

Maggie sighed. "She assured him everything was under control. It didn't seem to satisfy him. He's coming to evaluate 'the situation'."

"Did she say when?" Laura asked.

"Tomorrow," Maggie murmured. "Rosalind was furious about the short notice, but she had no choice but to agree. She's instructed everyone to be on their best behavior. No mention of the investigation, no gossip about Jeremy's death."

"That seems impossible," Jasmine said. "It's all anyone's talking about."

"Which is why she wanted us to know. We need to make sure the vendors and volunteers understand what's at stake." Maggie looked up at Laura, her eyes desperate. "If the Association pulls out, others will follow. If the festival gets canceled, I don't think the store can weather another blow."

"Let's make sure it never gets that far," Laura said. "We're going to make this festival one to remember. For all the right reasons."

A ghost of a smile touched Maggie's lips, and she squared her shoulders with visible effort. "Thank you."

———◆———

What felt like an eternity later, Laura peeked at the Town Hall's industrial kitchen wall clock. It was almost lunchtime.

Jasmine seemed to have read her mind. "Break time. I'm starving."

"I brought some almonds," Laura said, retrieving her bag. "Thought I'd just grab something quick here and—"

"Absolutely not!" Jasmine's eyebrows shot up. "We've been cooped up in this kitchen for hours. I need air that doesn't smell like onions and committee agendas." She hooked her arm through Laura's. "Besides, I need to go to the Post Office, and Yanni's place is next door. You haven't been to Wanderer Pantry yet, have you?"

Laura hesitated, shaking her head, then smiled. "I guess I can't say no to that. Count me in."

———◆———

Outside, the hazy, humid August sun beat down through scraggly clouds, casting Silver Springs in muted light as they made their way down Main Street.

"So, any progress with the...investigation?" Jasmine asked, tugging at her collar.

Laura sighed, lowering her voice. "I keep running into dead ends. No one's being fully honest."

"So it seems," Jasmine said.

One block down, they stopped where the Post Office occupied a neat brick building with a national flag flanking the entrance.

"I'll just be a minute," Jasmine said as they stepped inside. "I've got to post a letter to my mom."

As Jasmine headed for the counter, Laura lingered near the entrance where a rack of local newspapers stood, their headlines vying for attention. The bold print of the latest Maplewood Memo caught her eye. 'Murder Investigation

Narrows: General Store Co-Owner's Financial Woes Deepen.'

Laura's stomach clenched as she grabbed a copy and began reading: Anonymous sources claim Maggie Brook had been making regular payments to murder victim Jeremy Blackwood to suppress damaging information. These payments reportedly began after Blackwood's scathing review of her business eight years ago...

"All done!" Jasmine called, tucking her receipt into her pocket. Her smile faded. "What's wrong?"

Laura handed her the newspaper.

Jasmine's eyes widened as she scanned the headline. "This is ridiculous."

Laura sighed. "It's unfair. The press already has their mind made up."

"We need to do something," Jasmine said. "Before this gets any worse. But before that, we need some food. Shall we get some lunch from Yanni?"

———◆———

The bell above Wanderer Pantry's door jingled as they entered. Warmth and spices enveloped them—garlic, rosemary, and something citrusy Laura couldn't place. The small, hole-in-the-wall shop was arranged with a main counter and stone cookware dishes placed behind a glass display case. A little bench with bar stools stretched along one wall, and photos from all around the world decorated every spare inch.

Yanni broke into a wide smile and waved from behind the counter, his dark curls spilling over a light blue bandana tied around his forehead. "Jasmine! Laura! Perfect timing. You're going to like today's menu!"

He gestured toward a small chalkboard with 'Menu Of The Day' written at the top in big letters. Underneath had three sections: Sourdough Sandwich, Soup, and Cookie.

"Since you're new here, Laura, I'll explain how things work. It's a set lunch menu, a little different each day, and it changes with the seasons. It's always inspired by my travels."

Laura opened her mouth, but Yanni smiled, answering her question before she could ask it.

"I'm from Melbourne, Australia. I spent most of my twenties traveling."

Laura's eyes widened. "I'd love to hear the story behind that."

Yanni grinned. "Same as you, judging from the story you told at the Crafters Club. Looking for a change of pace, and found a lucky break. I love living here. So! Two lunch menus? To have here or takeaway?"

"It sounds perfect," Jasmine said. "And we'll have them here, please."

"Sure! I heard you're hard at work on the festival prep," Yanni said, laying out the ingredients for the sandwiches.

Laura nodded. "I can't believe it's almost here. I'm hoping it all goes smoothly."

"And let's hope we get through it all without another round of sensational gossip," Jasmine said, taking a seat at the bench.

Yanni's expression sobered as he spread butter on the bread before topping it with the fillings. "The rumors about Maggie? Bunch of nonsense. Not the profile of someone who'd...you know." He opened the lid of a stoneware dish and ladled liquid out into two waiting bowls. "Besides, if everyone who got a bad review from Jeremy Blackwood wanted him dead, half of New England would be suspects."

He presented their finished meals on two trays with a flourish.

"Here we are! Sandwiches with glazed ham, cheddar, and pear chutney, along with a chilled gazpacho soup. And of course, a lemon polenta cookie." He gave a rueful smile. "Still can't believe you folks don't call them biscuits."

Jasmine handed him some money with a chuckle as Laura's stomach growled in anticipation. They took their seats at the bench.

Laura made a noise of contentment as she took her first bite. "This is amazing, Yanni. Thank you."

"What did I tell you?" Jasmine said, grinning. They ate in comfortable silence for a moment before Jasmine sighed. "Have you seen today's issue of the Maplewood Memo?"

Yanni's forehead creased. "Yeah...anonymous source, huh? Convenient."

As they finished their meal, the conversation shifted to lighter topics—the festival schedule, Yanni's new preserving techniques, and Jasmine's letter-writing tradition.

"It started when I moved out of state for college," Jasmine said, sipping her water. "Mom and I have kept it up ever since. There's something about getting an actual letter."

Yanni and Jasmine continued chatting while Laura listened, savoring the last bites of her cookie.

When they stood to leave, Yanni wrapped two slices of walnut bread in brown paper. He pressed the package into Laura's hands. "For later. And Laura? Don't let these rumors distract you. The truth has a way of coming out in Silver Springs, whether people want it to or not."

CHAPTER FIFTEEN

T hat evening, after work, Laura and Evelyn had arranged to meet Rosalind at her home office. Before they did that...Evelyn had a little excursion planned.

By the time Laura had finished for the day, she'd wanted nothing more than to head straight home, wolf down some dinner, and go to bed early...but this investigation wouldn't solve itself. With fresh rumors swirling thanks to the day's Maplewood Memo issue, she had to do something before the situation got even more out of hand.

Laura was surprised when Evelyn directed her to a free parking space out the front of the Village Skein, the town's local yarn store. What other yarn could Evelyn need that wasn't in the stash she already had at her apartment?

It was a charming storefront with large bay windows displaying a rainbow of yarn and various tools. Handmade samples hung from the ceiling—a cascade of colorful shawls, sweaters, and blankets that formed a textile gallery. As they entered, indie folk music played in the background. Every surface held skeins of yarn in every imaginable color and texture.

Nell Mackenzie swept toward them, wearing a hand-knitted lacework tee in soft shades of purple and yellow, most likely her pattern and hand-dyed yarn.

Her otherwise brown hair, short with an undercut, had an asymmetrical long fringe dyed magenta. The color changed according to her whims, Evelyn had said.

"Evelyn!" she said. "Right on time. The new alpaca yarn just arrived."

"You never disappoint," Evelyn said. "Nell, this is Laura Evans. She's moved in above me and taken charge of the café at the General Store."

Nell's shrewd eyes assessed Laura. "Good to meet you. How can I help?"

"Laura's in need of some yarn," Evelyn said for her. Before Laura could get a word in edgeways, Evelyn turned to the younger woman, and said, "And don't even think about reaching for your wallet. It's already settled."

Laura looked back and forth between them. "I really appreciate it, but you don't have to—"

Evelyn dismissed the attempt to argue with a wave of her hand. "Nonsense! Let me get this for you."

Laura thanked her, reluctantly admitting defeat as she wandered off to investigate a display of hand dyed yarn, marveling at the subtle variations in color.

"Beautiful, isn't it?" said a young woman approaching from the storage room, arms full of yarn. "Not that I'm biased, of course, but those are Nell's."

"Laura, this is Katie Fowler," Nell said. "She keeps everything running smoothly here."

"Hi, Katie! Yes, I recognize you from the café," Laura said. "You're our morning regular."

"Best coffee in town," Katie confirmed, setting down her armload of yarn.

"How's Ruby, Katie?" Evelyn asked, scanning the room as if looking for someone else.

Katie smiled. "Well, I assume. She's not working today."

Another woman joined them—tall, with curly blonde hair and vintage-style glasses. She grinned, extending a hand to Laura. "Hi, I'm Rebecca. Welcome to yarn paradise."

"Or yarn purgatory, depending on how your current project is going," Katie said, making Laura laugh.

"How's the Crafters Club, Evelyn?" Nell asked.

Evelyn quirked a smile. "We keep busy."

"Now," Nell said, "let's find you some proper yarn for your next project, Laura. What do you want to make?"

"Maybe just a basic beanie?" Laura said. "Nothing fancy. Something to ease back in."

"We'll change that," Nell declared, leading her to a display of soft merino. "Every stitch tells a story. Might as well make it a good one."

⚬

Accompanied by Evelyn and a skein of new hand-dyed merino wool in a stunning deep indigo, Laura turned onto a tree-lined street where Rosalind's modest home sat. She swallowed her exhaustion as she parked, and they proceeded up the path to the front door. Evelyn knocked.

Rosalind answered, her hair falling from its bun, a frazzled look in her eyes. Her pearl necklace hung askew.

"Please, come in." Her voice was jittery as she ushered them into a room overrun with papers and accounting ledgers. She straightened a leaning stack of file folders. "I'm sorry for the mess. With the festival tomorrow, I'm behind on everything."

Evelyn had explained to Laura on the drive over that Rosalind worked as a bookkeeper for local businesses, in between managing all the festival responsibilities. The room's chaos matched Rosalind's flustered demeanor.

Evelyn smiled. "Thank you for making time for us, especially today. Would you mind if we sat?"

Rosalind nodded. "Of course. How may I help?"

Evelyn gave a grateful nod as she settled onto one of the wooden chairs, and Laura took the one beside her.

"We wanted to offer our help with any last-minute logistics," Laura said, keeping her voice light. "I can only imagine how stressful everything must be."

Rosalind's eyes flitted around the room. "Oh. I'm...managing..."

"It's rather a sizable undertaking, isn't it? But I know you're up to the task," Evelyn said.

"It's a gift you give the town, doing this year after year," Laura said.

Rosalind managed a quick smile.

Laura took a breath, careful not to sound too eager. "I hope it's alright to ask—do you know what's happening with the keynote?"

Rosalind stiffened. "Yes."

"Do you have a replacement in mind?" Laura asked.

Rosalind sat motionless, gripping the arm of her chair. "The keynote. Yes. That has been...an unforeseen complication. Unfortunately, I couldn't find anyone else. It's been...removed from the agenda." She let out an involuntary exhale.

"I imagine it's been a real challenge to reorganize," Laura said.

Rosalind's phone buzzed on her desk. She glanced at it, her face draining of color before she flipped it face-down. That was the third time it had vibrated, and each time Rosalind's reaction grew more pronounced.

"Is everything alright?" Laura asked.

"Fine," Rosalind said. "Just...festival business."

The phone buzzed again. Rosalind closed her eyes, as if steadying herself. When she reached for it, Laura glimpsed the screen—not a number but a name: 'Melissa.' Rosalind declined the call with a forceful jab and switched the phone to silent.

"Someone persistent," Evelyn noted.

"Yes, unfortunately." Rosalind's voice had a brittle quality. "One with no concept of boundaries."

Laura sighed. "That's rough timing with everything else going on."

Rosalind's posture softened. "Yes. Some people just don't...it's complicated. Old friendships sometimes come with old expectations that no longer fit."

"I get that," Laura said, nodding. She waited a few moments before asking her next question. "I never got to ask you about how your trip to Boston was. Did you get to eat some of our regional favorites?"

Boston. The word still conjured a mix of longing and relief. Her tiny former apartment in Jamaica Plain, the bustling Haymarket on a Saturday, the skyline from the Charles River Esplanade. So much of her life was rooted there, yet Silver Springs was slowly, surprisingly, feeling like home.

Rosalind shook her head. "I wish I'd had the time. It wasn't so much a trip. I was in the city meeting with potential sponsors for the festival." She smoothed her skirt with slow, deliberate movements. "It's another task that's been more than I bargained for." She sighed. "And yes, before you ask, I ran into Jeremy there." she seemed to realize what she was saying and snapped her mouth shut.

"You saw Jeremy there as well? Goodness, what are the chances?" Evelyn said.

Rosalind's gaze darted to a stack of papers on her desk and gave a distracted nod. "Indeed."

Laura seized the moment. "I've heard a few people wondering what his movements were like before it all happened."

Rosalind's eyes narrowed. "If you mean that ludicrous gossip, I pay no attention to idle rumors. Whatever Jeremy was doing in Boston was his own business." Her voice had taken on a brittle edge. "As was whatever he may have been...documenting."

Evelyn cleared her throat. "I apologize for the indelicacy, but there was talk...about lingerie found in his room. And something about a lovebite?"

"I beg your pardon?" Rosalind said, her eyes widening. "I wouldn't know anything about those personal matters."

"No, no," Evelyn said. "I wasn't suggesting—"

"It's unfortunate how things turned out," Rosalind said. "His reviews weren't getting the attention they once did. He'd been trying different tactics to maintain relevance in the industry." She straightened her pearl necklace with trembling fingers. "The festival has always strived to maintain a certain standard of professionalism. Ten years ago, a Jeremy Blackwood exposé could shake the foundations of the culinary world. His piece on counterfeit imported cheese brought down a major distributor. But lately? He'd been manufacturing controversy where there was none. And I suspect...what happened might've been part of it." She stood. "I have a full plate right now. I'm sure you understand."

Laura exchanged a quick glance with Evelyn before standing, too. "Of course, we didn't mean to take up so much of your time. You must have a million things to handle before tomorrow."

"...Indeed," Rosalind said.

Laura caught Evelyn's eye, about to leave, when Evelyn reached into her bag and produced a familiar green box from Layla's bakery.

"Here, I brought some cookies for you," she said, placing the container on a clear spot on the desk. "I had a feeling the next few days might call for reinforcements."

Rosalind blinked. "Thank you."

"Good night," Laura said, and as she passed, Rosalind's hands trembled.

They sped out of the house.

<hr>

They made it to the car and onto the road before exchanging a word. Rather than turning left at the intersection connecting the town to the outskirts, they turned right, heading back to the Morrison building. The final pre-festival event was in around an hour, just enough time to follow something up and reset before their next outing. Diana, her husband Lou, and their daughter Sara would host a tour of Mountain Valley Dairy. Evelyn and

Laura didn't want to miss it, and not just because they were interested in learning about the process.

"Now that struck a nerve," Evelyn said. "She leapt to her own defense before I could finish my sentence. I never even implied she was involved."

Laura nodded. "Did you see the way she reacted? Like she'd rehearsed it. And that comment. About Jeremy needing to stir things up."

Evelyn sighed. "Jeremy always did have a flair for the dramatic. His reviews held weight, but lately, fresher voices were eclipsing his."

"So you think there's truth to the underwear and lovebite story?" Laura slowed for a curve in the road.

"Difficult to know for certain," Evelyn said. "But if there's truth to it, and Jeremy was keeping records...someone with a reputation to protect might've found that inconvenient. Interesting how Rosalind admitted running into Jeremy, and how she hinted at knowing something about him. It's curious, isn't it? Jeremy's been part of these festivals for as long as I can recall. He took on the assistant judge role eight years back. Rosalind has been our director for twenty-five years, Thomas a judge for ten, and Alex has been helping since his thirties. Diana, of course, practically has curd running through her veins. And Maggie? Born and raised here. She started volunteering as a young woman."

Evelyn stared out the window at the passing houses and streetlights. "It puzzles me. Whoever's behind this had ample chances to be rid of Jeremy. So why act now?"

"Unless...it ties into whatever he was researching," Laura said. "Maybe this scandal was the final straw."

Evelyn nodded. "Perhaps. What do we know so far?"

Laura recalled the jumble of information. "Okay, so all the suspects were at that tasting. He said something provocative. They all had a reaction. Still...none of them seem like a killer..."

Evelyn nodded. "There's no better chance than tonight to keep an eye on things. Everyone will be out in full force. And we've got the festival. With you tucked behind the scenes and me mingling..."

"Part of me wonders if we're close...or way off?" Laura said, trying not to sound despondent but failing.

Evelyn didn't reply for several moments, but when she did, she looked Laura in the eye. "Losing heart is precisely what the killer would hope for. We mustn't hand them that victory. I can't promise we'll succeed, but I won't stop trying. And if you won't either..."

Laura nodded and offered a weak smile. "We're not done yet. Let's see it through."

<hr/>

Back at Evelyn's apartment, Laura hung up her phone with a frown.

"Everything alright?" Evelyn asked, preparing things for their next trip out that night.

"That was Daphne. She and I worked together at Hargroves," Laura said, settling into her chair. "I wanted to know if she'd heard anything about Jeremy's trip."

"Any luck?" Evelyn said.

"Yes, she was there with friends when he had dinner at Café Nouveau with a few people from the industry." Laura's brow furrowed. "Midway through, he left the table to talk to a woman he spotted across the room. Their conversation got heated."

"Did Daphne catch any details?" Evelyn asked.

"Not much, but she said Jeremy mentioned something about 'proof' and 'exposure.' The woman left in a huff. Jeremy came back to his seat, looking far too pleased with himself. And when I described Rosalind...Daphne said it was her." Laura frowned. "Odd, isn't it? Rosalind never mentioned he confronted her."

Arguing with her so publicly seemed strange, even for Jeremy. What had he talked to her about?

"That's true," Evelyn said, frowning. "However, she may simply have been embarrassed about causing a scene."

Laura pondered this. "Perhaps...but combine that with how uncomfortable she seemed...it doesn't sit right with me. That reminds me. Daphne also said she's not surprised there's been trouble ahead of the festival. Apparently, she has a friend who's a cheesemaker, and he refuses to enter anymore because he's convinced the results are rigged."

Evelyn looked up from her preparations. "That's...quite an accusation."

"That's what I thought," Laura said. "It makes you wonder."

———◦———

Groups of attendees chattered and laughed as they passed through the open farm gates. A new sign stood behind the fence, lit up by two floodlights, proclaiming: 'Welcome To Mountain Valley Dairy!' And beneath that, in smaller italicized text, read, 'Rooted In Tradition, Crafted with Care.'

It was darker than when they'd visited last, but something else seemed different. The fencing had a fresh coat of paint and the driveway was swept clean.

Warm light spilled from the farmhouse, where the visitors welcome area stood.

As they entered, the air-conditioned coolness was a sharp relief from the muggy night outside. Photographs of the farm and its history, along with framed certificates, adorned the walls. A large hand-drawn map of the property hung over the fireplace, unused at this time of year.

The space was clear of any furniture, making room for the crowd gathering inside. Many more people had turned up than Laura had expected. She recognized only a handful. Several festival attendees must've arrived early.

Right on schedule, Diana entered the room through a door at the back. At her heels was a tall man with a graying red beard who could only be her husband, Louis 'Lou' Cooper. Sara, their adult daughter, brought up the rear.

Diana raised her voice, drawing the crowd's attention. "Good evening and thank you for coming! My name is Diana Martinez, and with my husband Lou and our daughter Sara, we run Mountain Valley Dairy. It's one of the longest-running family dairies in the county." She beamed. "And tonight, you're getting a peek behind the scenes!"

The audience gave a smattering of polite applause.

"We're all about keeping the family legacy and our traditions alive," Diana continued, but she gave a self-deprecating smile. "It's hard work, especially when modern innovations are so tempting! But you can taste the difference." She indicated the side door, which a staff member had unlocked and held open. "Now everyone, what you've been waiting for. Follow us for the tour!"

Diana headed outside, followed by her daughter, husband, and the crowd. Laura and Evelyn lingered at the back, watching as attendees filed out. As the crowd thinned, Laura's eyes landed on one particular framed certificate in the back corner.

Evelyn looked about to follow the crowd, but Laura touched her arm. "Hang on a second. I think I see something." She walked over to investigate, the room now empty save the two of them.

"You'll need to hurry Laura, we're going to miss the tour," Evelyn said, glancing back at the open door.

Laura forged ahead, pointing to the framed certification. "Look at this! Diana didn't just study traditional cheese-making. She learned modern commercial techniques from a school in Wisconsin." Laura eyed the other certificates. "Here's one from the same school for Lou. They both learned to make cheese the modern way!"

Evelyn pushed her glasses up her nose and peered at the certificate. "This could mean a lot of things, Laura. They might've just taken this to further their education. It doesn't say they're using these techniques in production."

Laura frowned. "The way she reacts whenever someone brings up Jeremy's comments—it's more than frustration."

Evelyn conceded the point, but only just. "You're right, but we have to investigate further. And we should catch up, or we're going to be left behind."

CHAPTER SIXTEEN

At last, the day dawned. Friday, the Summer Cheese Festival's first day, Laura's first major event in Silver Springs, and her last chance to figure out what had happened in the stables. No pressure.

Her day had begun early and the first few hours had passed in a blur. In less than twenty minutes, the opening ceremony would begin. The scent of freshly baked bread from the adjacent kitchen mingled with the earthy aroma of cheese and the crisp pine garlands decorating the entryway.

Booths draped in white tablecloths lined the perimeter of the town hall's cavernous space. A mini fridge with the vendor's cheese sat on each table. All vendors were already there, preparing samples, checking displays, and chattering.

Strings of colorful bunting crisscrossed overhead, while the center front sported rows of chairs. The far end of the room accommodated the main stage: a modest affair with a simple wooden dais and a microphone. It drew the eye with its backdrop—a cheerful mural depicting everything from rolling pastures to cows and goats.

Children giggled around the base of the stage, darting between bales of hay arranged with milk pails and sprigs of greenery. Beside the stage, a long table promised refreshments.

Maggie had insisted Laura and Jasmine should have a small break to attend the opening ceremony. They'd done everything they'd needed to prepare for it and the cheese tasting, which would begin in one of the adjacent conference rooms as the second event of the day. Maggie had said since it was Laura's first festival, it would be great to witness the start. Laura appreciated the chance to rest—even if it was for only twenty minutes.

———◆○◆———

Not long now. Laura squeezed through the crowd. Jasmine waved, and Laura hurried to join her.

"I saved you a seat," Jasmine said, smiling and gesturing to an empty spot next to her.

"First festival jitters?"

"Is it that obvious?" Laura said with a laugh.

"Everyone gets them," Jasmine said. "In my first year, I mistook a Colby for a Cheddar. They still haven't let me forget it!"

Laura smiled and took a moment to breathe and observe. Every seat seemed filled, the crowd buzzing with excited conversation. As she turned in her chair, three familiar faces from the Maplewood Crafters Club waved at her from a row further back—Evelyn, Judith, and Martha. Two men accompanied them. One was a sleepy-looking man who had to be Judith's husband, Edward Lee. The other was a giant of a fellow. He whispered to Martha, before grinning and waving. Laura smiled. That must be Lawrence, Martha's husband. She returned the wave.

Thomas sat near the front with the other judges and festival committee members. Alex and Diana were a few seats across from him. Behind them, Maggie was next to Kathy, who was engaged in animated conversation with Larry and Colette, joined by Victor. He must've been persuaded out of the kitchen for once.

A stir near the entrance drew Laura's attention. A tall man in a tailored suit entered. His silver hair and commanding presence caused several committee members to straighten.

"That's him, Elliott Harrington," Jasmine murmured, noticing Laura's questioning gaze. "Vermont Food & Wine Association Director."

Harrington made his way through the crowd, nodding to those who greeted him. When he reached the front row, Thomas rose to offer a handshake. The Association Director accepted it with cool professionalism before taking a seat.

Three more distinguished-looking individuals entered the hall, making their way toward the front.

"Those are the guest judges," Jasmine said quietly, continuing her explanation of the who's who in the culinary world. "The woman with the red notebook is Claudia Alard, food writer from Boston. Very influential in New England culinary circles."

The woman surveyed the room, missing nothing.

"The man with the cravat is Professor Harvey Lín, who teaches Food Science at the Tremblay Institute Of Arts & Sciences," Jasmine continued. "And the older gentleman with the walking stick is Herbert Emerson. He's retired now, but his blue cheese won international awards for decades."

The audience hushed as Rosalind approached the podium on the stage, testing the microphone before speaking into it. "Welcome, everyone!"

The crowd burst into applause.

"I'm thrilled to see both familiar and new faces. Every year, we look forward to celebrating the wonderful creations of our talented local artisans."

A murmur of appreciation spread across the audience.

"Today marks the beginning of a weekend filled with fine local cheeses, and your participation makes this event possible," Rosalind continued. "We have a spectacular lineup of vendors for you this year, thanks to our hardworking festival committee." Rosalind flushed, her gaze flickering to the committee members. "But, of course, this year is different with the passing of our judge and friend, Jeremy Blackwood. His contributions to this festival were immeasurable, and his absence will be felt this weekend."

———◆———

The opening ceremony concluded, and Thomas approached to take the stage. That was their cue to prepare for the tasting. Jasmine and Laura rose too, heading down a row of chairs to the side of the hall.

Thomas' announcement trailed after them as they left. "Thank you, everyone, for joining us today. We're about to begin our cheese tasting session. Please make your way into the next room, as directed by our volunteers."

Chairs scraped against the hardwood floor. The once quiet space burst into conversations as people headed to the conference room. Laura and the others stood at the ready.

Around the perimeter, trays of tastings were on tables draped in crisp linens and adorned with signs featuring the vendor's name in elegant calligraphy. Small handwritten cards explained each cheese's origin and aging process, while wooden boards held artful accompaniments—honey, preserves, nuts, and sliced fruits.

In the room's center stood a simple podium facing the circular arrangement of round tables, each set with water glasses, crackers, and tasting note cards. Soft lighting from above cast a warm glow over the whites, golden yellows, and rustic rinds of the cheeses soon to be sampled.

"We do this every year, arranging the tastings in order of intensity," Jasmine said, appearing at Laura's side. "The fresh, mild varieties are at station one, and we work our way clockwise to the blues and washed rinds at the end." She smiled. "Like a good story. You build up to the dramatic conclusion."

"Did you just compare cheese tasting to narrative structure?" Laura asked, unable to suppress a grin.

"Hey, I double majored in creative writing and food science, you know," Jasmine said. "The way literature teaches you to see the world never leaves you."

The room filled with attendees finding their assigned tables. Thomas conferred with Diana near the podium, their heads bent over tasting notes.

Jasmine drew Laura's attention again, a tray of cheese in her hands. "Ready to serve? Don't forget to tell them a little something about what they're tasting! And don't worry, you'll be great!"

Laura smiled and nodded as she picked up her own tray of the first samples—a delicate fresh chèvre with a drizzle of local lavender honey.

Thomas tapped the microphone. The gentle conversations around the room hushed as he cleared his throat. "Welcome to our guided tasting. Today, we'll be taking your palates on a journey through the wonderful world of artisanal cheese, beginning with the most delicate flavors and progressing to the more robust varieties."

Diana stepped forward. "We recommend cleansing your palate between tastings with water and a plain cracker." She pointed to the items on each table. "And don't be afraid to make notes. There are no wrong answers in cheese appreciation."

Laura and the other servers delivered the first samples. The subtle, tangy aroma of fresh goats' cheese filled the air, mingling with the sweet scent of honey. Laura approached a table where Evelyn, Judith, and Martha sat with the latter two's husbands.

Lawrence's eyes lit up at the sight of the cheese. "Now this is what I call a proper Friday morning."

Martha smiled at Laura. "He's been talking about nothing else for days."

Laura laughed quietly and set down their plates. "Fresh chèvre from Elderkin Cheese. The goats are pasture-raised on the north side of the valley. The lavender honey comes from the farm next door."

Before she could move to the next table, Judith tugged on her shirtsleeve.

Judith leaned in, and said, "Evelyn talked to me about the former festival judge you wanted to contact. He's agreed to speak with you. I gave him your phone number, so forgive me for being presumptuous."

"No, it's okay, thank you," Laura said, feeling a thrum of anticipation. "I really appreciate that."

"Don't mention it," Judith said, patting Laura's forearm. "I hope he sheds some light on a few things."

As she headed back to get the next round of participants their plates, she caught snippets of Thomas's commentary, explaining how the cheese was made and what flavors to look for. A hush fell upon the room as people took their first tastes.

Jasmine came to stand next to her as they returned for the second round—a buttery Camembert paired with apple slices. She nodded toward the table, a giggle escaping. "Look at Evelyn. She's taking notes like she's a judge herself."

Laura glanced over to see Evelyn scribbling, her brow furrowed. Next to her, Lawrence had his eyes closed, lost in cheese-induced bliss.

With each round, the flavors became more pronounced. Laura enjoyed the rhythm of service, the quiet moments of concentration as Thomas or Diana spoke, followed by the hum of conversation as people shared their impressions. They reached the final pairing—a robust blue cheese with walnuts—and Thomas approached the podium one last time.

"And with that, we conclude our tasting. I hope you've discovered some new favorites today. Remember, all these cheeses are available for purchase at the vendor booths in the main hall."

As attendees rose from their tables, Laura caught Jasmine's eye across the room. Her colleague beamed and gave her a subtle thumbs-up, mouthing, "Well done."

Laura allowed herself a moment of pride, but as she began clearing plates, her mind drifted back to the mystery at the stables. Her festival investigative work had only just started.

CHAPTER SEVENTEEN

The structured tasting contrasted with the unrestrained enthusiasm of the main hall. Vendors spoke to customers, cheese samples appeared on toothpicks at every turn, and conversations overlapped in a cheerful cacophony. Laura found herself swept along with Jasmine toward the service entrance at the rear of the hall.

"We've got about an hour before lunch service," Maggie said as they entered the industrial kitchen. Victor supervised the salad preparation, while Colette arranged rows of artisanal bread loaves on cutting boards.

"General Store's famous salad and sandwich lunch," Jasmine said, slipping an apron over her head. "People look forward to it as much as the cheese."

This year's offering was a grilled cheese sandwich on Red Trillium Bakery's sourdough with caramelized onions, accompanied by a summer berry and mixed green salad with local chèvre and a vinaigrette.

Maggie handed Laura an apron. "You're on bread duty."

She took her place beside Colette, who nodded at her technique as she sliced the crusty sourdough into perfect portions.

"Nice knife skills," Colette remarked. "Not just front of house, then."

Laura smiled, nodding. "That's kind of you to say. My dad taught me. He believes a good meal starts with good bread."

"Is he French like me?" Colette asked with a grin.

Laura laughed and shook her head as she fell into the rhythm of the kitchen's organized chaos. Slice, arrange, pass to one volunteer who added a light spread of herb butter, then to another group of volunteers who assembled all the sandwiches. Meanwhile, Victor combined all the colorful ingredients for the salad while a staff member of his prepared Beaumont Bistro's signature vinaigrette.

Maggie clapped her hands for attention. "We'll set up lunch stations in the hall in about forty minutes."

Everyone turned toward her.

"Victor, Larry, and your staff, you'll handle salads," Maggie continued. "Colette and her people, sandwiches. Jasmine and Laura, you're with me on drinks. And volunteers, you're on floating duty. Please help wherever needed, we can't manage this without you!"

Laura nodded and continued slicing bread, pacing herself for the mountain of loaves still waiting. In the hall, the festival continued unabated. The cheese vendors were doing brisk business after the morning's tastings, and the excited chatter suggested people were already looking forward to lunch.

Later, Laura walked toward the lunch area, carrying a stack of plates. Three long tables stood waiting, covered in white tablecloths, adorned with shining silverware, embroidered napkins, and small vases of greenery.

"It's casual service," Maggie explained as they worked. "People help themselves, but we make sure nothing runs out and everyone finds what they need."

Laura glanced around the hall in between placing extra cutlery into containers. Rosalind and Thomas stood near a corner table, deep in conversation. Their expressions were serious, their voices too low to overhear. When Thomas noticed Laura looking, he straightened and offered a tight smile before turning back to Rosalind.

"They always get intense during festival weekend," Jasmine murmured, appearing at her side with a tray of water glasses. "Thomas takes the judging seriously."

"I imagine things might've...shifted a little without Jeremy here." Laura said.

Jasmine shrugged. "I suppose so. Different dynamics."

Laura nodded. The festival atmosphere provided the perfect cover for observing interactions and gathering impressions. Martha and Lawrence stood by one of the cheese booths. The latter gestured as he sampled something, lost in his own cheese-filled world. Martha caught Laura's eye and waved, pointing to her husband with a good-natured eye roll.

The final preparations took on a heightened energy—volunteers and staff wheeled out the sandwiches on their trays and the salads in their serving bowls, and positioned pitchers of water and iced tea on the drinks table.

"Remember," Maggie told Laura as they took their positions next to the drinks table, "keep things moving, smile a lot, and if anyone asks about the afternoon events, the schedule is posted by the door."

The lunch service began, and the hall filled with hungry festival-goers. Laura found herself in motion—helping with drinks, directing people to seating. Lawrence, Martha, and Evelyn approached, their plates already in hand.

Lawrence was recounting the morning's tasting to Evelyn. "—and then the blue cheese! Like nothing I've ever experienced. You should've tasted it!"

Evelyn let out a good-natured sigh as she poured herself a glass of iced water. "I was there, Lawrence."

Martha caught Laura's attention and smiled. "My husband, the cheese enthusiast. I convinced him to attend ten years ago and I almost regret it. I've created a monster."

"A happy monster," Lawrence said, helping himself to some iced tea. "This festival is a revelation, Laura. Always a revelation!"

The lunch service flowed, and the room resonated with the comfortable sounds of people enjoying food together. Laura found herself drawn into brief, friendly conversations as she worked—introducing herself to those she hadn't met, fielding questions about the afternoon's events, and pointing people toward vendor booths of interest.

Maggie crossed paths with Laura near the drinks table. "You're doing great! Keep it up."

━━━━◆○◆━━━━

The lunch crowd had dispersed, leaving only scattered crumbs, empty trays, and kitchen staff ready for their meal. After they'd cleaned the tables, stacked the industrial dishwasher high, and put away the mountains of dishes, Maggie turned to Laura and Jasmine.

"Now it's our turn to eat something." She gave an exhausted smile. "At last."

Victor had set aside salad portions and sandwiches for the staff and volunteers. Laura grabbed her meal and a glass of water, and slipped out to find a quiet corner.

The Vendors Hall hummed with activity. Attendees wandered from booth to booth, sampling cheeses, chatting with producers, and making purchases. Laura found an unoccupied chair against the wall. The sandwich burst with flavor, and Laura closed her eyes. Just five minutes of peace. That's all she needed.

"May I join you?"

Laura opened her eyes to find Evelyn standing before her.

"Of course." Laura gestured to the empty chair beside her.

Evelyn settled in. "You've been working hard. Is everything alright?"

Laura inclined her head with a tired smile.

Evelyn beamed. "I'm glad to see you're managing." Her voice lowered as she leaned in. "I passed the restrooms earlier and saw Alex on the phone. He said, 'I'll transfer the usual amount plus twenty percent for your silence on this. No one can connect us right now. It's too risky.' And 'I can't let this get out. It'll ruin me.' Rather brazen, wouldn't you say?"

Laura set down her fork. "That's...strange."

First the nervousness around his research materials, then the emails between him and Jeremy, and now paying someone hush money?

Evelyn caught her expression, frowning. "I don't like it. He doesn't strike me as the type, but we both know appearances can deceive."

"What if it's an act?" Laura said.

Her landlady let out a surprised huff of laughter. "If that's the case, he's far more cunning than he lets on." Evelyn glanced at the clock. "Your break's nearly over. I suggest you take a quick stroll through the vendor booths while you still can."

Laura finished her salad and sandwich, thanked Evelyn, and gathered her dishes.

The booths stretched before her. Evelyn was right. Since she had twenty minutes before returning to duty, why not explore? She wandered past displays of cheese in every form: wheels, wedges, blocks, crumbles. Some producers had elaborate setups with professional signage and uniformed staff. Others offered a more homespun approach—handwritten labels and checkered tablecloths.

"First time at our festival?" A woman with silver-streaked hair offered Laura a sample from a slate board.

"First time working it," Laura clarified, accepting the pale cheese.

"Welcome," the woman said. "I hope it's been an enjoyable experience so far, despite how hectic everything gets!" She grinned and shook her head. "I'm Helen Mercer, from Mercer Dairy." She gestured to a display of awards behind her. "It's wonderful to meet you."

"You too," Laura said. "I'm Laura Evans, Silver Springs General Store café manager." The cheese melted on her tongue—buttery, with a slight tang and unexpected sweetness at the finish. "That's incredible. What is it?"

"Our signature Alpine-style aged eighteen months." Helen beamed. "Tell me what you taste."

Laura described the flavors as best she could, enjoying Helen's enthusiastic nods. Thomas was across the hall. He moved with purpose, sampling cheeses and making notes in a small black notebook. It remained clutched in his left hand, angled away from curious eyes. As he sampled a crumbly blue cheese, he made a quick note.

"The judging isn't until tomorrow, right?" Laura asked.

"Official judging, yes." Helen's eyes followed Laura's gaze. "But the good judges do their homework. Especially Thomas."

Laura thanked Helen and continued her circuit of the hall. She paused at Elderkin Cheese, recognizing the chèvre from the morning's tasting.

A young man—sandy-haired, with a spattering of freckles—operated the booth. "Hi there! Would you like to try our new variety?"

"Yes, please." Laura accepted the small cube of cheese, letting it melt on her tongue. The creamy tang lingered. "This is delicious."

"Thank you," the man said, smiling. "I'm Clay Elderkin. The youngest of the bunch."

"Laura Evans." She returned his smile. "I manage the General Store café, but I've been helping with the catering."

"First festival?" he asked.

Laura nodded. "What's your farm like? I've heard wonderful things about Elderkin Cheese."

Clay's eyes lit up. "We've got a hillside property about twenty minutes from town. Beautiful views, especially at sunset. The real stars are our fifty goats, though. Each is named after a flower or herb." He grinned, leaning forward as if sharing a secret. "Daisy is my favorite. Temperamental, but her milk has the perfect fat content."

The judges made their rounds throughout the hall. Professor Lín analyzed samples at one booth, while Claudia Alard captivated vendors with animated commentary at another. Thomas tried cheeses with quiet focus. Most booths received polite attention and a select few earned longer visits. Herbert Emerson was in his element, complimenting every cheese he tasted, savoring each sample.

Laura checked her phone for the time, then excused herself from Clay's booth and went to the restroom. As Laura emerged, Rosalind stood in the main corridor, her phone buzzing—not a welcome interruption, judging by her expression. She ducked into a narrow service hallway, phone pressed to her ear.

On a split-second impulse, Laura followed, pressing against the wall until she reached the corner where Rosalind had disappeared. The unused-space was L-shaped, tucked away from the main hallway and hidden from public view. Storage doors lined one side, and Laura positioned herself where she hoped she wouldn't be seen.

"I told you not to call me during the festival." Rosalind said. "This is neither the time nor the place." A pause. "That situation is being handled. I've already taken care of what needed to be done."

Another pause, longer this time.

"You don't understand what's at stake here. If anyone connects me to what happened that night, everything I've built could collapse."

Laura pressed herself against the wall.

"It doesn't matter what he knew or what he threatened. It's over now."

The sound of approaching volunteers from the main hallway caused Laura to tense, but they passed by without turning down the service corridor.

"Listen, Melissa. You'll keep your mouth shut," Rosalind's voice was colder than Laura had ever heard it. "This has to end. Don't call me again."

Footsteps approached. Laura's heart raced as she scanned the hallway, spotting an empty food trolley draped with a cloth a few feet away. She darted toward it and ducked behind, pressing herself into the shadows between the trolley and the wall.

From her hiding place, Laura saw Rosalind emerge. The festival director squared her shoulders as she slipped her phone into her pocket, then patted her hair into place—reassembling her professional mask piece by piece.

Laura waited until the footsteps faded before emerging from behind the cart. She leaned against the wall. What situation had Rosalind 'handled'?

Taking a steadying breath, she checked her phone. Time to return to duty.

CHAPTER EIGHTEEN

The Summer Cheese Festival's 'Grazing Plates' dinner was the weekend's most expected culinary event. Beaumont Bistro, with its exposed brick walls and warm lighting, provided the perfect backdrop for the feast.

Colette swept past. "The rosemary crackers need more time to cool."

"Time is always the enemy," Victor replied, not looking up from the reduction he was stirring. "We do what we can."

Larry, clipboard in hand, appeared in the kitchen. "Five minutes until we open the doors. Are we ready?"

"We're always ready," Victor and Colette answered in unison, then exchanged surprised glances.

Laura prepared slices of aged cloth-bound cheddar alongside quince paste, positioning clusters of dried muscatels and walnuts beside them for balance. The festival's first day had been exhausting, but there was something energizing about this last event. It brought together everyone's efforts, a celebration before the competitive judging began tomorrow.

"Doors are open," a server announced, and the kitchen's pace quickened.

Laura finished the last board in her batch and handed it off to Jasmine, who added the final touch—delicate sprigs of micro herbs—before placing it on a tray for service.

Laughter and conversation buzzed through the dining room as Laura weaved between tables. Unlike the animated diners, Diana and Rosalind sat in silence. Diana fidgeted with her napkin corner, folding and unfolding it, while Rosalind stared at the wall opposite.

As Laura approached with their grazing board, Rosalind looked up with a tight smile. "Thank you, Laura."

Laura hesitated. "Everything all right?"

"Fine," Rosalind answered too quickly. "Just tired."

"Well, enjoy," Laura said, smiling, but her expression faded as she turned away.

The dinner progressed through its courses. Following the opening grazing boards came Colette's handcrafted ravioli filled with spinach and fresh chèvre in a brown butter sage sauce, topped with shavings of an aged Alpine-style cheese. For the final course, guests were treated to medallions of herb-crusted lamb paired with polenta infused with a local washed-rind cheese and caramelized shallots.

Throughout the service, the atmosphere grew convivial—at every table except Diana and Rosalind's, where the tension seemed to thicken with each passing course.

Laura and Jasmine collected empty plates and headed back to the kitchen.

"Did you notice Diana and Rosalind?" Jasmine asked in a hushed tone as they pushed through the swinging doors.

Laura set down her stack of plates. "They seemed tense."

"That's putting it mildly." Jasmine glanced over her shoulder. "Rosalind was whispering something to Diana, and Diana looked...horrified."

"What were they talking about?" Laura asked, keeping her voice low.

"I couldn't hear the first part, but Diana kept shaking her head and saying 'that's impossible' over and over." Jasmine deposited her plates beside Laura's.

"The dessert course is going out!" Victor called, interrupting their brief gathering.

As Laura distributed bowls, she couldn't help wondering: had Rosalind shared a piece of Jeremy's explosive revelation? And if so, what had Diana found so impossible to believe?

———◆———

Even late at night, after a busy day, the investigation didn't cease. Laura was getting ready for bed when her phone rang. Her mother? No, an unknown number. Could it be...?

"Hello? This is Laura Evans speaking."

There was a click, then a deep, measured voice. "Laura. Forgive the late hour, but my name is Lincoln Goddard.

Judith said you wanted to talk to me about Jeremy Blackwood's death. And...the festival."

It was him! She steadied herself.

"Yes, thank you so much for calling. I think Jeremy discovered something others wanted to keep quiet."

A sigh filtered through the phone. "I left that world behind for a good reason, Laura."

The line went quiet. Had it disconnected?

At last, he spoke again. "Last year, in what would've been my second time judging, I noticed patterns in the award results. I thought I was imagining things, but it became hard to ignore."

Laura's eyes widened. "What did you do?"

"I confronted Rosalind," he said. "She didn't believe me. Said I was undermining the festival's integrity with baseless accusations."

"And that led to the argument in the Town Hall?"

"Indeed. I thought others must've noticed, that they might've taken action...but I was mistaken. So I resigned. I refused to take part in a potentially corrupt system."

Laura hesitated before asking her next question. "Did...Jeremy contact you about this?"

"Yes," Lincoln said. "About two months ago. He wanted details. I was...reluctant, but he was persistent. I told him what I suspected—there was a pattern of favoritism. And I wouldn't put it past any of the committee members to be involved."

"That might've been what he was investigating," Laura said, half to herself. "Thank you for your help. I wanted to ask...would you be willing to tell Detective Sergeant Ramirez about the patterns you observed?"

Another long pause followed. "If it helps...I suppose."

After they hung up, Laura sat motionless. She had another lead. Her phone glowed with a new text, and she turned.

This time, it was her mother.

> "Coming to talk some sense to you in person. I've already booked my flight."

Outside, rain pelted against the windowpane, steady and insistent.

Laura typed a reply, backspaced, then tried again.

> "Don't come. I'm not leaving. Please cancel your flight."

She pressed send before she could second-guess herself. Her phone buzzed again immediately.

> "This isn't like you, Laura. I don't understand it. Who are you becoming?"

Laura gazed at the words. Who was she becoming? Her fingers hovered over the phone before typing:

> "Someone I'm proud of. Please cancel your flight. I'm staying."

She set the phone face-down and returned to her nightly routine.

CHAPTER NINETEEN

The next day, the Town Hall's Events Room buzzed as volunteers and staff prepared for Diana's live cheese-making demonstration.

"Is the milk supply here yet?" Jasmine called from where she arranged chairs in a semicircle facing the demonstration area.

"It just arrived," Laura replied, checking her list and holding open the door as two young men carried in large, insulated containers. Cheesecloth, strainers, thermometers, salt—all in their proper places. The scent of fresh herbs—mint, chives, and dill—drifted from bowls on a side table.

Diana entered, carrying a large canvas bag. She wore navy overalls, gumboots, and a black lightweight waterproof jacket. Laura's hand froze mid-motion as she stared at Diana's outerwear. That jacket.

The material looked identical to the scrap Ben had found caught in the hawthorn bush. Same color, same texture. And was that—a tiny tear near the pocket?

Diana unzipped her jacket and rolled up the sleeves, washing her hands at the sink before turning to inspect the setup. "Everything looks perfect." She unpacked tools from her bag—a curved cheese knife, small molds, and a digital pH meter.

There was a thin scratch along her jawline, concealed with makeup. Could it...be?

"Are you expecting a good turnout?" Jasmine asked, distributing tasting plates on a table behind the demo area.

"Should be full," Diana replied. "Fresh cheese demos are always popular. Everyone thinks they're getting a secret family recipe." She chuckled, though the sound held little humor. Her fingers lingered over the small tear on her jacket, not touching, and something flickered in her eyes—recognition? Worry?

Diana noticed Laura staring. "Is something wrong?"

"No, nothing," Laura said. "Just wondering where you got that jacket."

Diana's smile didn't reach her eyes. "I've had it for years. Can't even remember where I bought it. It's seen me through some...difficult situations."

Jasmine approached. "Anything else you need?"

"Just one thing," Diana said. "Can someone check if the cooler for storing finished samples is set at the right temperature?"

"I'll do it," Laura said.

As she adjusted the refrigerator settings, Laura's mind raced. The jacket was circumstantial at best—plenty of people owned similar outerwear—but combined with Diana's behavior last night and the rip...Laura glanced back. Diana now whispered with Rosalind. Both women looked serious, their conversation ending when they noticed Laura watching. At first glance, nothing in her demeanor suggested a woman harboring dark secrets, yet

Laura couldn't shake the feeling Diana knew more than she let on.

———◆———

On her way out the side entrance to fetch supplies for the event after Diana's demonstration—a cheese pairing workshop hosted by Herbert Emerson—she found her path blocked by a cluster of unfamiliar faces.

A woman with sharp features thrust a microphone toward her. "Excuse me! Are you an employee of the General Store? Can you comment on the allegations against Maggie Brook?"

Before Laura could respond, another voice cut in. "Is it true this is the second food critic to suffer after coming to Silver Springs?"

Laura blinked in confusion. "Second? What are you talking about?"

A man with a digital recorder stepped forward. "One critic's reputation was destroyed after visiting Silver Springs last year. Now another is dead. Coincidence?"

"I don't know what you're talking about," Laura said, maneuvering around them.

"So you're denying the pattern of food critics meeting unfortunate ends in Silver Springs?" a woman called out, her cameraman adjusting the focus on Laura's startled face.

The door opened again, and Thomas appeared beside her. "What on earth is going—" he cut himself off and his expression hardened. "This is a private event. Unless you have media credentials approved by the festival committee, I'll have to ask you to leave."

"Thomas Whitman!" The first reporter turned toward him. "As head judge, are you concerned about the festival's future, given these allegations?"

"The only threat to this festival," Thomas said, "is misrepresentation by opportunistic journalists looking for sensational headlines rather than facts." He gestured for Laura to follow him and guided her through the throng. "No further comments."

Once inside the storage room, Laura blinked a few times, recovering. "That was a lot."

"Vultures," Thomas muttered. His eyes softened. "I'm sorry you had to deal with that. What supplies do you need? Let me help."

"Thank you. I need five clean tablecloths for the pairing workshop Herbert Emerson is doing later," Laura said.

He nodded and began passing her the tablecloths from the higher shelves. "The story's gone national. They're spinning it like Silver Springs is a death trap for culinary journalists."

"That's ridiculous!" Laura said.

"It doesn't matter to them," Thomas said. "Rosalind's limiting press access, but they're persistent. Some are even approaching festival attendees for interviews." With a wry smile, he held the door open. "Let's go around the back this time. I wouldn't want you to have to face another ambush."

———————◆◇◆———————

An hour later, every seat was taken, and a standing crowd lined the back wall. They should've prepared more chairs! The audience watched as Diana worked her magic with milk and cultures.

"The key is maintaining the perfect temperature," Diana explained, stirring the warming milk. "Too hot, and the proteins break down incorrectly. Too cool, and they won't coagulate."

The demonstration continued. Diana narrated each step, from the initial curdling through to the cutting stage, then the gentle heating and stirring of curds to release whey.

"Now comes the draining," Diana said, pouring the mixture into cheesecloth-lined colanders. The whey drained away, leaving behind soft, white curds. "We'll add salt and herbs at this stage."

The audience murmured with appreciation as Diana worked herbs into portions of the fresh cheese, creating different flavor variations.

"And there we have it," Diana announced as she finished molding the final portion. "Fresh cheese, ready for tasting. While it's being served, are there questions?"

That was their cue. Laura and Jasmine gathered the small portions of herbed cheeses, plating them. As Laura handed them out, the audience began sampling, expressions of delight spreading across faces.

A man in the second row raised his hand. "How long does fresh cheese like this keep?"

"About a week in proper refrigeration," Diana replied. "Though it's best consumed within the first three to four days when the flavors are at their peak."

Laura nodded to herself as she handed out another tasting plate. The fresh cheeses she'd tried at the General Store had taught her the same—the flavors diminished after a few days.

An older woman near the front was next. "I've heard your family has been making cheese for generations using traditional methods. Could you tell us more about those techniques?"

Diana's smile faltered. "Yes...many generations." She then explained the methods she used.

The woman smiled. "How fascinating! And are these the methods you still use at Mountain Valley Dairy?"

Diana nodded. "Yes, that's right." Her eyes scanned the crowd. "Does anyone else have a question?"

"Do different breeds of goats produce different-tasting milk?" someone called out.

"Absolutely," Diana said, nodding. "Alpine breeds like Saanens produce a milder milk, while Nubians give a higher butterfat content that creates a richer cheese. We raise both on our farm."

"What's your favorite cheese you don't make yourself?" asked a teenager with bright blue hair.

Diana laughed. "That's like asking a parent to choose their favorite child! I'm lucky I only have one wonderful daughter. But I admire the clothbound cheddars from England. The complexity they achieve is remarkable."

As the demonstration concluded, attendees filed out, still discussing the cheese and the techniques they'd observed. Laura gathered empty tasting plates, watching as Diana cleaned her equipment, movements precise but somehow mechanical.

"That went well," Jasmine said, joining Laura.

Laura nodded, but her eyes remained on Diana and that waterproof black jacket.

CHAPTER TWENTY

E verything led up to this: the Summer Cheese Festival competition judging. Gone were the demonstration and tasting setups, replaced by a formal atmosphere. The room had a long mahogany table for the judges, each place marked with tasting sheets, palate cleansers, and water. Along the perimeter, smaller tables displayed the competing entries, each labeled by number.

Laura placed delicate water crackers on a silver tray, turning at the sound of the door opening. Thomas and Diana entered, followed by the panel of guest judges: Claudia Alard, the Boston food writer, her red notebook clutched in one hand and a sleek silver pen in the other; Professor Harvey Lín from the Tremblay Institute with his signature cravat; and Herbert Emerson, the retired cheesemaker, leaning on his walking stick.

Diana sat and arranged her tasting materials. She appeared on edge, though that wasn't new.

"The lighting is much improved from last year," Claudia said, opening her notebook to a fresh page.

Professor Lín approached one of the sample tables, bending to inhale the aroma of a nearby cheese without touching it. "The aging room conditions have been excellent this season."

"That's true," Diana said. "They must've maintained perfect humidity levels. You can tell from the rind development." She tried to smile, but her jaw was too tight.

Herbert settled into his assigned chair with a contented sigh. "Nothing like judging a good competition to make retirement worthwhile." He drank some water from his glass and frowned, nodding toward Laura. "Excuse me, please, young lady. Could I trouble you for another glass of water before we begin? This is a little too cold for my tastes. It risks dulling the palate."

Laura nodded and fetched him what he'd requested.

A small audience had gathered in the few rows of chairs set up a short distance from the judge's table.

Thomas surveyed the room with a critical eye before giving a nod of approval. "We'll begin with the fresh cheese." He turned to Laura, Jasmine, and the volunteers, sending Laura a subtle but kind smile. "Please ensure water and crackers are replenished between each category."

"And perhaps some apple slices for the stronger varieties," Professor Lín added, arranging his tasting sheets. "I find Granny Smith most effective for cleansing between the more robust samples."

"And pear too, please," Diana said. "It interferes less with the subtle notes in alpine-style cheeses."

Laura, Jasmine, and a few volunteers followed their instructions, bringing samples to the judges' table—fresh chèvre, ricotta, and delicate farmer's cheese.

Claudia removed her blazer and draped it over the back of her chair. "I'll need complete quiet during the evaluation. The subtleties of texture can be missed with distractions."

The judges worked in near silence with only their pens scratching as they took notes. Their expressions revealed nothing as they sampled each entry, cleansing their palates with water, a plain cracker, or some fruit. As the fresh cheese category concluded, there came a brief intermission while the next category was prepared. The aged cheddars would be judged next, followed by the bloomy rinds, then washed rinds, and the blue cheeses.

"The acidification level in the third sample was remarkable," Herbert commented to Thomas during the break. "Reminds me of what we achieved all those years ago with the spring milk."

"Indeed," Thomas replied, his voice low. "Though the balance wasn't there."

The second category began, with the judges now evaluating aged cheddars, their golden hues ranging from pale butter to deep orange. Claudia's pen moved across her notebook as she made detailed observations.

Alex pressed his back against the wall behind the small audience, his eyes squeezed shut, lips moving silently. When he caught Laura looking, he startled and hurried away.

The afternoon wore on.

"Final category," Jasmine muttered. "What a relief. My feet are killing me."

Herbert straightened in his chair as the blue cheeses were presented. Claudia's eyes widened at one particular sample, her pen pausing mid-note. Thomas, too, fixated on this entry, labeled as number thirty-seven. He tasted it twice, his expression unreadable. Professor Lín made a small, appreciative sound, covered by a discreet cough.

"The results will be tabulated and announced at tomorrow's closing ceremony," Thomas declared, standing.

The judges gathered their notes, shaking hands before departing. Claudia tucked her notebook into a case, while Professor Lín conversed with Herbert about enzymatic breakdowns in aged varieties on their way out. Thomas remained at the table, organizing the scoring sheets into a portfolio.

"Thomas?" Laura said. "Would you like more water before we clear everything?"

"No thanks, Laura, but I appreciate it." He secured the portfolio with a small strap, smiling. "You all did a wonderful job today. Please tell Maggie and Jasmine thank you from me."

Laura nodded. "Of course. It was a fascinating process to watch."

Thomas let out a small huff of laughter. "Now, really, Laura, I appreciate you saying so, but it was more than a little...repetitive." He grinned. "Another judge might make a big thing of the 'rigor' involved...but I'm just sitting there and tasting cheese, for goodness' sake, not performing strenuous activity."

Laura didn't know whether to join in his merriment or smile politely. "Still...I've never seen something like it before. It was an interesting experience."

Thomas nodded. "I'm glad you appreciate it. It's not just about personal taste. There are objective standards of excellence." He patted the portfolio. "That's why documentation is so crucial."

"Will the results be close this year?" Laura asked, gathering empty water glasses.

Thomas smiled. "There were some...unexpected standouts. Quality speaks for itself." With a friendly nod, he left the room, portfolio tucked under his arm.

Jasmine approached, carrying a tray of leftover crackers and cheese remnants. "Two hours of sniffing and squinting at dairy products. This is what peak performance looks like."

Laura smiled, but her mind was elsewhere.

CHAPTER
TWENTY-ONE

F unny how for events like these there were weeks of
build-up, only for the occasion itself to fly by. Already
it was late Saturday afternoon, with the second day of the
festival over. It had ended earlier than the previous day, like
it did every year, to provide a break for the volunteers and
staff before the dinner later that evening, and also to give a
chance for the long-weekend vacationers to see the town.

All attendees had exited the building, leaving it strangely
empty, save for the flurry of activity setting up the main
hall for tomorrow. Laura helped a group of volunteers
maneuver tables and chairs for the next day's events, her
arms feeling like jelly after the last several hours. Someone
had hijacked the sound system setup for the main stage,
and classic rock crackled through the speaker. Just the
motivation they all needed.

The sudden sound of Maggie's voice caught Laura's
attention from the adjacent hallway.

"What do you mean you're pulling the contract?"
Maggie's voice carried, despite her apparent attempt to
keep it down.

Laura hadn't intended to eavesdrop, but she couldn't
avoid hearing the conversation.

"You've been with us for years!" Maggie continued, her voice rising. "Uncertainty around the business? That's..." There was a pause. "I understand, but these are just rumors! Nothing has been proven! Such short notice, too. Couldn't you at least have—"

Maggie let out a heavy sigh. They must've hung up on her. Laura continued her task as footsteps approached.

Maggie entered the main hall, a bundle of frantic energy. Her eyes widened. "Laura. I—"

Is everything okay?" Laura asked.

Maggie's shoulders slumped, and she looked embarrassed before resignation settled on her face. "That was Hyland Farms on the phone. They're pulling their contract."

"What? Why?" Laura asked, trying to feign ignorance.

Maggie sighed. "They're citing 'uncertainty' around the business. And you know what they mean by that."

It had to be the rumors. But really? They'd back out with only that as a motivator? The police still hadn't said anything either way!

Maggie rubbed her temples. "I'm sorry you heard all that."

"No, I should be the one apologizing. I'm sorry I overheard the last part of the conversation."

Maggie attempted a wan smile. "Not your fault. I wasn't taking the call anywhere private."

"There has to be some way to fix this," Laura said.

"Thank you," Maggie murmured. "Let's get the festival out of the way first."

———————◆◇◆———————

Laura surveyed the tidied-up space one last time, exhaustion settling into her muscles. Alex sat alone in the back corner, staring at a pile of papers.

"Alex?" she said as she approached. "Are you alright?"

He looked up with red-rimmed eyes. "I've made a mess of things. I keep telling myself I did what I had to, but..."

Laura's heart thudded. Was he...the one? She motioned for him to go on.

"Jeremy knew. I can't stop thinking if I'd been honest from the beginning...how do you live with yourself?" He stood abruptly. "I'm sorry. I shouldn't burden you with this."

He left without a backwards glance. Was he...referring to whatever secret he carried, or could he have...she shuddered. She needed answers. Proof. Neither of which she had. With a sigh, she gathered her things and walked toward the Town Hall's side entrance. She stepped outside, letting the door swing closed behind her.

"Heading home, Laura?"

Laura startled at the voice.

Ramirez appeared from around the corner, standing a few paces in front.

"Goodness, Detective Sergeant. You gave me a fright!" She remembered her manners and the question. "And, good evening. Yes, I've just finished up."

"Mind if I walk with you?" Ramirez fell into step beside her without waiting for an answer. They crossed the

Village Green. "I understand you've been asking questions around town about Jeremy Blackwood's death."

Laura swallowed. "Maggie didn't kill Jeremy. Someone is framing her! If I don't do something—"

"That's my job," Ramirez interrupted. "Amateur investigations can compromise evidence and tip off suspects."

"Maggie is losing suppliers because of these rumors," Laura said. "Hyland Farms just pulled their contract today after years of partnership."

They reached the entrance to the Morrison Building.

Ramirez stopped, turning to face Laura. "I understand your loyalty to Maggie. And if she's innocent, I want to prove that properly, through official channels. Your questions are making my job harder."

Laura met the other woman's gaze. "I'm just trying to find the truth."

"So am I," Ramirez said. "If you keep poking around, you might push the killer to cover their tracks, or worse, put yourself in danger. I need your word, Laura. No more unofficial investigating."

"I just want to protect Maggie and the store!" Laura said.

"I know." Ramirez' expression softened. "And the best way to do that is to let me do my job."

"Remember, no playing detective."

Laura met her eyes. "I understand what you're saying."

Ramirez' lips pressed into a thin line, but she didn't push further.

—◆◇◆—

Only when the chopping was done and the platters placed did Laura remember to look around—and realize she was somewhere beautiful.

Chez Colette had a reputation as one of the best gourmet dining experiences this side of Vermont, and as she examined the interior, she could see why. The restaurant exuded French provincial charm—ivory walls adorned with copper cookware and framed botanical prints, each table draped in crisp linen. Delicate chandeliers with amber glass shades cast a honeyed glow over the dining room.

The marble-topped bar along one wall displayed an impressive collection of wines, and the open kitchen concept allowed diners to glimpse Colette orchestrating her culinary magic.

"What do you think?" Colette appeared beside her.

Laura smiled. "It's gorgeous."

Colette nodded like that was the only appropriate response.

Laura's eyes drifted to the large blackboard affixed to the wall where Colette had written the menu.

"For tonight, I've created something special," Colette had explained earlier when Laura had arrived. "French classics with Vermont's character."

For the appetizer, an heirloom tomato and goats' cheese tart with micro herbs. And for the main, people could choose between cider-braised pork shoulder with vegetable gratin, or wild mushroom and leek vol-au-vent with asparagus. Strawberry and rhubarb clafoutis with crème anglaise would be the dessert.

Later, the dining room filled with festival attendees, eager for more of Colette's cooking.

Martha and Lawrence sat at a six-top with Judith, Edward, and Evelyn. The space hummed with conversation as Laura moved between tables, pouring wine and delivering dishes.

"That smells divine," Evelyn said, as Laura placed a plate in front of her. "Colette's worked her magic, I see."

"I'll tell her," Laura smiled, pausing for a moment. "Are you enjoying the festival?"

"Immensely." Evelyn lowered her voice. "And I've kept watch. Earlier, before the judging began, I spotted Diana swapping label cards between two cheeses. She thought no one was watching, moved number thirty-seven onto a different sample. Then Thomas came by and nearly scared her out of her shoes."

Laura's eyes widened. "You're certain?"

Evelyn nodded. "I may require spectacles for fine print, but I've never had trouble seeing across a room. Diana looked about, then made the switch so fast you would've missed it in a blink. But I didn't blink."

Laura frowned. "That's...concerning."

With a friendly but distracted goodbye, she continued her rounds. Why would Diana switch the labels?

"Excuse me," called an older gentleman from a nearby table. "Could we trouble you for some more bread?"

"Of course," Laura replied, composing herself. "I'll bring it right away."

She retrieved a fresh basket of bread and delivered it to the table, where the man sat with his wife.

"This is our fifteenth festival," the woman said. "And I must say, Colette has outdone herself this year."

Laura smiled. "I'll pass along your compliments."

She excused herself and continued working, but Diana's actions lingered in her mind. As she poured wine at a table near the window, she caught sight of Diana, sitting with her husband and daughter, laughing at something Sara had said. She appeared at ease, a stark contrast from her meal with Rosalind.

"Is this your first festival?" asked a middle-aged woman at the table, noticing Laura's momentary distraction.

"Yes," Laura said with a smile. "It's been quite an experience."

"Always is," the woman said. "I've been coming for twelve years, and there's never been a dull one. This year's been more...eventful than most. Some producers would do anything to get an award. Anything."

Two people in their early thirties at the next table caught Laura's eye, so she excused herself and went over.

The woman grinned at her. "Is that a Boston accent?"

Laura smiled. "It is, yes. Are you from there too?"

The man nodded. "We drove up from Boston just for the festival, and it was worth it."

"I'm so glad to hear that! It's my first time working at the event, and it's been amazing, so I can see why you've come all this way."

The evening continued, the dining room's energy shifting from the focused appreciation of the meal to relaxed satisfaction.

Colette emerged from the kitchen to make her rounds, accepting compliments with gracious nods. When she reached Laura, she smiled. "You did well tonight. Good rhythm, good presence. Important qualities in service and in life."

Laura smiled. "Thank you."

———————————◆○◆———————————

Later, when the guests had gone home, Colette, Victor, Larry, and all their respective staff sat with plates of their own at the largest table in the dining room. Laura and Jasmine joined them. The heirloom tomato and goats' cheese tart's complex flavors unfolded one after another.

"I could get used to this," Jasmine said, savoring a bite of her tart. "It's time I started putting in more effort for my own dinners instead of just slight variations on sauteed vegetables and beans."

Laura laughed. "What's your specialty? Let me guess. Beans with carrots on Monday, beans with zucchini on Tuesday..."

"Don't forget Wednesday's incredible offering. Beans with carrots and zucchini," Jasmine replied with a grin, reaching for her wineglass. "My culinary adventures know no bounds."

One of Larry and Victor's staff members, a tall man with salt-and-pepper hair sitting next to Jasmine, leaned forward. "You know, my grandmother said you can tell everything about a person by how they treat ingredients."

"And what does my treatment of beans say about me?" Jasmine asked, grinning.

"That you need cooking lessons," he replied.

Jasmine guffawed.

Victor, at the head of the table, raised his glass. "To everyone here who made tonight a success. The festival may be demanding, but moments like these make it worthwhile."

"Hear, hear," Larry agreed, clinking glasses with a server beside him. "Though I had my doubts when that couple at table twelve salted everything before even tasting it."

Victor pressed a hand to his heart. "Each premature seasoning is a tiny death for my soul."

Colette rolled her eyes but couldn't suppress her smile. "So dramatic, Victor. The customer is the one in charge, even when they have questionable taste."

"Says the woman who once refused to serve a customer who asked for ketchup with her soufflé," Larry teased, ducking when Colette threw a napkin at him.

The warm glow of the hanging lamps cast a golden hue over the table as one server recounted their most memorable customer interactions from the evening. Laura glanced around, taking in the scene—the hum of conversation punctuated by laughter, the clink of silverware, the way everyone had loosened collars and rolled-up sleeves now that the formal part of the evening was over.

Colette rose to fetch a tray of small chocolate confections from the kitchen. "A final indulgence before we tackle the clean-up."

Laura bit into one, closing her eyes as the rich ganache center met her tongue. She'd savor it while she could before facing the mountain of dishes awaiting them in the kitchen.

———◆◇◆———

The stairs to Evelyn's apartment creaked beneath Laura's tired feet.

"Just in time," Evelyn said, welcoming her inside. "Sit before you fall over."

Laura settled into an armchair and closed her eyes for a moment.

Evelyn returned with two steaming mugs, handing one to Laura with a smile. "Some lemon balm tea."

"Thank you very much." She smiled and cradled the mug between her palms, taking small sips.

"Detective Sergeant Ramirez caught me outside the Town Hall," Laura said after a long moment of silence. "She knows we've been investigating."

Evelyn's eyebrows furrowed. "I suspected that would happen."

"She warned me off. Said I could compromise evidence or..." Laura paused, "put myself in danger."

"It's a sensible concern to have," Evelyn said, settling deeper into her chair. Oscar jumped onto her lap, kneading, before curling into a ball.

"She says we should stop," Laura said, staring into her mug. "Let her handle it."

Evelyn studied her over the rim of her glasses. "Is that what you want to do?"

"No!" Laura ran a finger around the edge of her mug. "What if we don't solve this in time? Tomorrow's the festival's last day. The awards ceremony."

Her last chance to solve this. Before the Vermont Food & Wine Association made their irreversible decision. Had she left it too late? Would her...mother be right after all? Her phone lit up, and she jumped. Talk about timing. Except it wasn't her mother. It was Connor.

> "Mom's worried. You know what you're doing?"

Did she? Could she say yes? When she met Evelyn's gaze, she didn't see judgement, disappointment, or expectation. Just...hope. Warmth. Encouragement. Exactly what she needed right now.

The older woman's eyes twinkled. "And we'll both be there, won't we? Just two observant members of the community. Noticing things others miss."

"You're right. I can't give up now." Laura replied. She knew how to respond to Connor.

So, she typed:

> "I do. I've got this."

He sent a thumbs up emoji. Her youngest brother trusted her. She just had to trust herself. They might need to be more subtle in their approach, but she wasn't ready to abandon Maggie to fate. Not yet.

CHAPTER
TWENTY-TWO

S unday. The festival's final day, featuring one of the
most fun and anticipated events: Cheese Trivia.

At the front of the main hall, neat rows of tables faced
the central podium in a semi-circle, each with four chairs.
Behind the podium, a projector screen had been set up.

A crowd gathered, lingering around the edges, eager to
start. Evelyn stood toward the back.

Laura headed over. "Morning, Evelyn!"

Evelyn turned around and beamed. "Laura, there you
are! I hope you've come prepared. The cheese trivia contest
is serious business for some people." She nodded toward
Martha, who was setting up a whiteboard for tracking
scores, her reading glasses perched on the end of her nose.

Jasmine arrived, looking more relaxed than she had all
weekend. "Generous of Maggie, isn't it? Giving us the
hour off to take part."

"I'm here!" Ben said, appearing from nowhere. "Prepare
to be impressed by my cheese knowledge."

They jumped and turned to stare at him. Jasmine was
the first to speak. "Shouldn't you be...working?"

He shrugged, grinning, and produced a checklist in his
spiky handwriting. All items were marked off. "Everything

for this morning is done and dusted. I have a few hours, so I figured I'd apply for the fourth spot on your team."

Jasmine scoffed. "You? Good at trivia? The last time we played at Jesse's birthday, you thought the Magna Carta was a luxury sports car."

Ben drew himself up. "A classic bluff! Lower everyone's expectations, then get them when they least expect it."

"I remember you referring to Gouda as 'that yellow one from the land of the windmills' last festival," Jasmine retorted, crossing her arms.

"I was...jogging my memory!" Ben protested. "And clearly, it worked last time."

Evelyn raised a hand. "Ben joining the team won't hurt."

Ben beamed, shooting Jasmine a smug look. "See? Evelyn appreciates my cheese prowess."

Jasmine rolled her eyes so far back they might've disappeared into her skull.

Laura hid a smile, glancing around as the room filled. Diana entered with Sara and two others: a young woman and a man—employees from Mountain Valley Dairy, Laura guessed. Thomas settled near the back with a few men while Alex hovered by the refreshment table.

"Attention, everyone!" Rosalind said. "We'll begin the cheese trivia competition in five minutes. Please form your teams, four members maximum, and choose a table."

"Shall we sit?" Laura asked, looking between Jasmine, Ben, and Evelyn.

"Absolutely," Evelyn agreed.

They claimed a table near the center of the room as Diana organized her team at a table to their right. The cheesemaker appeared more composed today.

"We need a team name," Ben said.

"The Cheese Geniuses?" Jasmine suggested.

Laura pondered, and Ben groaned. "Please, no."

Ben's eyes lit up, and he slammed his fist on the table. "What about The Big Cheeses?"

Laura muffled a laugh, and Jasmine snorted.

Evelyn tapped her chin. "How about The Cultured Club?"

They all nodded, though Ben looked rather dejected.

Martha approached their table with a clipboard. "Team name?" she asked, pen poised.

Laura told her.

Martha's eyes crinkled. "Clever. Evelyn's choice, no doubt." She noted it and moved on.

"The Big Cheeses was better..." Ben muttered.

The buzz of conversation died down as Rosalind returned to the podium. "Welcome to our annual cheese trivia competition! I'm delighted to see so many knowledgeable faces. Martha Henderson will keep score. The rules are simple: each question will be displayed on the screen behind me and distributed on paper by our volunteers. You'll have two minutes to discuss and write your answer. Please designate a scribe for your team."

"I shall be the scribe!" Ben said.

Jasmine harrumphed, and a nearby participant shushed her, thinking better of it as Jasmine shot them a glare.

"Each correct answer earns ten points," Rosalind continued. "The team with the highest score after twenty questions wins this year's Golden Cheese Wheel trophy."

Ben gave a dramatic gasp. "The Golden Cheese Wheel! Second year in a row, let's go."

Laura stifled a laugh.

"Our wonderful volunteers will collect your answer sheets after each round," Rosalind said, gesturing to several people standing close by. "Let's begin."

The projector flickered to life, displaying the first question: "In cheese-making, what's the purpose of rennet?"

A group of volunteers handed each table a printout of the question and an answer sheet. Laura's group huddled together, whispering answers as Ben jotted them down. They held their own, though Diana's group—the On Our Whey To Win team—took the lead. Laura enjoyed the challenge, the camaraderie, and the laughter when Martha announced a creative wrong answer.

By question fifteen, the scores were tight. The Cultured Club trailed Diana's team by just five points.

"Question sixteen," Rosalind announced, as the projector displayed: 'What innovation in cheese-making, introduced in the mid-twentieth century, reduced aging time by accelerating the development of flavor and texture?'

The volunteers distributed the question sheets. Diana leaned forward, whispering to her team. When they finished conferring, she took the pen from her designated scribe and wrote the answer herself. When the two minutes ended, the volunteers collected the answer sheets. Martha and Rosalind conferred, checking responses against the answer key.

"On Our Whey To Win has answered correctly," Rosalind said. "Using industrialized starter cultures, controlled temperature, and humidity chambers. These allowed cheesemakers to standardize production and shorten aging periods. Ten points."

Anticipation heightened in the room. Around them, the other dozen teams huddled at their tables. Ben straightened in his chair.

"Question seventeen," Rosalind announced. "Which famous French cheese is ripened in caves and washed with brandy?"

A murmur rippled through the room as teams bent their heads together. At a window table, a team erupted into hushed but intense debate. Three tables over, a quartet of older gentlemen who'd introduced themselves as 'The Whey-ward Seniors' scribbled their answer.

Ben let out a gasp. "I know this one."

Jasmine offered him a skeptical look.

"Trust me," Ben said. "It's Roquefort."

"That's a blue cheese," Evelyn said. "And it's not washed with brandy."

"It's Époisses de Bourgogne!" Jasmine said.

Ben frowned but wrote the answer, muttering something about "showing off" that made Jasmine stifle a laugh.

When the volunteers collected their sheets, Diana's team were all smiles. Behind them, at the 'Say Cheese!' table, a woman snatched their answer sheet back from the volunteer for a last-second correction, causing a ripple of laughter.

"Question seventeen," Rosalind said after the sheets were tallied. "The Cultured Club has answered correctly: 'Époisses de Bourgogne.' This distinctive washed-rind cheese develops its pungent aroma and complex flavor from regular bathing in Marc de Bourgogne, a brandy made from grape pomace. Also correct were On Our

Whey To Win, Cheese Queens, and The Whey-ward
Seniors. Ten points goes to each."

Ben pumped his fist, prompting Jasmine to roll her eyes.
At the Cheese Queens' table, four women clinked their
water glasses in celebration. Several teams were bunched
in the middle, with a few stragglers at the bottom.

"Question eighteen," Rosalind continued. "What's the
name for the rind on cheeses like Brie and Camembert,
and what causes it to form?"

Ben leaned forward, his expression thoughtful for once.
"That's a bloomy rind. Penicillium candidum if you're
feeling science-y. Or 'the good mold' if you're me."

Without waiting for the others to react, he wrote their
answer. At the table in front of them, someone whispered
"white mold", followed by a heated debate among their
team members. Laura glanced toward Diana's table
again. Diana gesticulated as her employees listened. The
Whey-ward Seniors' answer sheet was already complete.

After the volunteers collected the guesses, Rosalind
announced: "Question eighteen. Several teams have
answered correctly! The white rind on Brie and
Camembert is called a 'bloomy rind,' formed by the
Penicillium candidum or Penicillium camemberti mold
cultures. The Cultured Club, On Our Whey To Win, The
Whey-ward Seniors, Curds of Wisdom, and Say Cheese all
get ten points!"

"We're still in the race," Jasmine murmured.

"Question nineteen," Rosalind announced. "In Alpine
cheesemaking, what's 'transhumance' and how does it
affect cheese production?"

Puzzled looks passed between several teams. The Cheese
Louise crew looked bewildered, while the Cheese Queens

put their heads together. The Cultured Club huddled closer.

Evelyn pursed her lips, thinking. "It describes the seasonal migration of livestock—ascending into the mountain pastures each summer, descending to the valleys when the frost returns."

Jasmine nodded. "And it affects the cheese because the different pastures at different elevations have unique alpine flowers and grasses, which influence the milk's flavor."

"That makes sense," Laura said.

Ben jotted down their answer, his tongue poking out in concentration. The Whey-ward Seniors, less confident than before, submitted their answer just in time.

"Question nineteen," Rosalind said after collecting the sheets. "This was a challenging one! Only four teams got it right. Transhumance...is the practice of moving livestock to higher elevations during summer months and back to valleys in winter. The diverse flora at different elevations imparts unique seasonal characteristics to the milk and resulting cheese.' Ten points to The Cultured Club, On Our Whey To Win, Cheese Queens, and Curds of Wisdom."

The Whey-ward Seniors groaned. The room buzzed as Martha updated the scoreboard, which showed Laura's team tied with Diana's for first place.

"Final question," Rosalind declared, as the projector showed: "What cheese is made from the milk of water buffalo?"

Laura's team huddled together, deciding on their answer as Ben wrote it down. After the volunteers gathered the last round of answers, Martha tallied the final scores and whispered to Rosalind.

"The results are in!" Rosalind announced. "We have a tie for first place! Both The Cultured Club and On Our Whey To Win finished with one hundred and eighty points."

Ben launched himself upward, nearly knocking over his chair. "Nailed it!" He shot a look at Jasmine, who rolled her eyes despite her smile. "How could you ever have doubted me?"

"I have some reason to," Jasmine said with a smirk, "as we weren't the only winners today."

Ben's triumphant expression faltered. "Let's just...ignore that part."

"Sure, rewrite the rules so they better fit your worldview," Jasmine said, but she was grinning.

Laura chuckled.

"Since we have a tie," Rosalind said, "I'm pleased to present both teams with our Golden Cheese Wheel trophy!" She ushered them all to the stage.

Diana reached for it at the same time as Ben. He stared at her for a few seconds, frozen.

"Shall we?" Diana asked.

Ben grinned and together, they held up the trophy as the crowd applauded.

"Unfortunately," Rosalind said with a hint of a smile, "You'll have to decide who gets to take it home."

Ben dropped into an exaggerated fighting stance. "Bring it on!"

Diana held her hands up in surrender. "Oh no! What'll I do? He's too fierce." She rolled her eyes, but there was the barest hint of a smile there. "You can have it, Ben. It seems I'm no match for such intimidating cheese expertise."

Ben straightened, his chest puffing out. "Really? I mean, of course! Victory is mine—wait, ours!"

Laura couldn't help but smile as the crowd laughed and clapped.

———◆———

The Silver Springs Historical Society's reading room was an ideal spot for investigating. Laura settled at a polished oak corner table, her lunch—a thrown-together sandwich—wrapped and forgotten beside her phone. She'd slipped away during her break, drawn by a hunch that needed investigating.

The library had digitized the town archives years ago, including decades of Summer Cheese Festival records. Valeria 'Val' Del Solar, a historical society volunteer, had directed her to the dedicated terminal with a smile.

"Researching the Cheese festival?" Val had asked.

Laura had nodded, not meeting her eyes. "Just curious about the festival's history."

Now she scrolled through past festival ephemera. The system was intuitive—each year's festival cataloged with photographs, articles, and official records. She started with the most recent five years, jotting down her notes. As minutes ticked by, a pattern emerged, subtle at first, then unmistakable. Laura leaned closer to the screen, her heartbeat quickening. She expanded her search to ten years back.

It couldn't be a coincidence.

Laura glanced at her phone and stifled a gasp. Her break ended in twenty minutes. She needed to find Jasmine and Evelyn.

Val looked up from the front desk. "Find what you were looking for?"

Laura paused, clutching her notes. "I might have found more than I expected."

———◆———

Five minutes later, Laura sat in a small library meeting room with the door closed, all the evidence organized on her phone in her notes app. A timeline, suspect information, images, screenshots of newspaper articles, and snippets from their interviews.

Evelyn sat across from her frowning. Jasmine's eyes were wide.

"We're missing something," Laura said, rubbing her temples. "All these pieces, but the picture still isn't clear."

Evelyn nodded. "Let's walk through it once more. What facts do we have?"

"Jeremy knew someone's secret," Laura said. "Eli overheard him on the phone threatening them. He had 'explosive findings' he planned to reveal during his keynote."

"And yet, they all had something to hide, didn't they?" Jasmine asked.

Laura stood, pacing. "But which secret was worth killing for?"

Evelyn pursed her lips. "What if the secret wasn't the end of it? What if someone's guarding something far more consequential?"

Laura stopped pacing. The pieces were aligning.

"The alibi seemed perfect," she murmured, reaching for her phone. She searched through her notes to find a conversation she'd had days earlier. The casual mention had seemed insignificant, but now it stood out in stark relief. "It's all connected. It's—" Her voice faltered as the realization hit her. She sank into a chair.

Evelyn's eyes widened. "Good grief, Laura. You don't mean—"

"Yes," Laura said, rocking back and forth. "It has to be."

Jasmine's face fell. "Are you sure?"

"I wish it weren't true." Laura's voice caught. "I kept hoping I was wrong."

Evelyn reached across the table to squeeze Laura's hand. "That's what makes this so difficult. Accusing a respected figure in public."

Laura glanced at the notes on her phone. "What choice do I have?"

Evelyn was silent for several long moments. "We'll call the Detective Sergeant and explain everything."

Laura picked up her festival program, flipping to the list of events, reading through what was left. In only a few hours, she'd do what Jeremy couldn't.

CHAPTER
TWENTY-THREE

T his was it, the awards ceremony. The main area of the Town Hall was packed, a sea of excited faces filling the rows of chairs that faced the stage.

Laura stood at the back, surveying the crowd, her heart ramming against her ribs. Her gaze traveled over the attendees—Martha and Lawrence sitting near the front, Judith and Edward beside them with Evelyn, who waved when she caught Laura's eye.

"Nervous?" Jasmine appeared beside her, holding two cups of water.

Laura accepted one. "Thank you. Is it that obvious?"

"Only to those of us who know you," Jasmine said, squeezing her arm. "You've got this. We're all with you. Even Ramirez." She gestured to where the Detective Sergeant stood near a side entrance, her expression unreadable.

Laura nodded, taking a deep breath.

In the front row, the judges' panel waited.

Diana sat ramrod straight, while Thomas, beside her, flipped through his notes. On his other side, Claudia had her ever-present red notebook open, pen already poised. Just beyond her, Professor Lín exchanged a few low words with Herbert, who had propped his walking stick against the leg of his chair. The five people presented a formidable panel—each bringing years of expertise to the competition, their decisions about to be revealed to the public.

Alex hovered near one of the side doors, fidgeting with his fountain pen. Rosalind stood near the stage steps, consulting her clipboard. Maggie and Kathy had just arrived—Kathy's arm snug around Maggie's shoulders. Exhaustion clung to Maggie's face, the strain of the past days etched in the dark circles beneath her eyes. A pang twisted in Laura's chest, but lessened as Maggie locked eyes with her, giving her a brief nod.

As Rosalind ascended the stage steps and stood beside the podium, a hush fell over the crowd.

"Good afternoon, everyone," Rosalind began. "Welcome to the closing ceremony of this year's Summer Cheese Festival. I'd like to begin by thanking our dedicated committee members, our wonderful vendors, and all the volunteers who've made this weekend possible."

The audience responded with enthusiastic applause.

"Despite the unfortunate circumstances we've faced," Rosalind continued, her expression sobering, "the festival has been a remarkable success." She gestured toward the judges' table. "I'd like to thank our esteemed panel for their expertise and diligence."

All five judges nodded, the portfolio of results resting on the table before them.

"And now," Rosalind said, "it's time to announce this year's winners. Thomas, would you do the honors?"

Thomas rose from his seat and made his way to the podium. "Thank you, Rosalind. It's my privilege to present the results."

The room fell silent as he arranged his notes, the rustling of paper amplified in the expectant hush.

"Welcome, everyone, to the culmination of our Summer Cheese Festival," he paused, surveying the audience with a smile. "This year's festival has been a testament to the extraordinary spirit of our community. Despite the...difficult times we've been through, you've all rallied together to showcase the very best of what our region offers. The art of cheese-making continues to inspire us all, connecting us to our agricultural heritage while embracing innovation. I've had the privilege of judging this festival for a decade now, and I can say the quality of entries this year has been nothing short of exceptional. Our producers have outdone themselves in every category."

"Before I announce the winners, there are a few speeches to come. First, I'd like to acknowledge my fellow judges for their expertise, the caterers for their delicious food and hard work, and of course, a special thank you to the festival committee members. And last, but never the least, the wonderful Rosalind Prescott, our festival director, whose tireless efforts ensure this event's continued success." He raised his water glass in a toast. "To another successful Summer Cheese Festival."

The audience burst into enthusiastic applause.

Rosalind stood. "Now, a longtime festival committee member and woman who helped with all the delicious food will say a few words. Maggie Brook, please come to the front."

Confusion filled the room as Maggie made her way to the podium. She looked back at Laura with an imperceptible nod. Laura took a deep breath and followed her boss toward the front.

"What's she doing?" a voice muttered as Laura passed. "Why are they letting her say a few words?"

"This shouldn't be part of the program!" someone else murmured. "She's been suspected of...you know."

Laura caught sight of Evelyn, who gave her a nod. Martha and Lawrence exchanged puzzled glances. Maggie made her speech, her voice stronger than it had been in days.

"And now, I'd like to introduce Laura Evans, who has something important to share with all of you." She stepped aside, gesturing for Laura to approach the microphone.

Another murmur of bewilderment rippled through the crowd. Laura's legs almost refused to move, and for a terrible moment, she feared her voice would fail her. She gripped the edges of the podium, steadying herself. If she could handle a sudden visit from the Mayor of Boston with a kitchen in meltdown, she could handle this. This was for Maggie, for Silver Springs.

Her eyes swept across the room, noting reactions—Diana's tense posture, Alex's nervous fidgeting, Rosalind's frozen smile from where she stood a few steps away from Laura.

"I came to Silver Springs looking for a new start," Laura began, her voice steady despite her racing pulse. "Instead, I found myself surrounded by a murder investigation. But as I soon discovered, it goes deeper than that. It involves years of deception that culminated in Jeremy Blackwood's murder. While examining the festival's archives, I noticed a pattern in the winners over the past decade. Certain producers consistently took home awards, regardless of changing judges or competition. This seemed...unusual."

The room had gone still. Diana stiffened.

"Detective Sergeant Ramirez and her team confirmed what I'd suspected. Corruption. A system of kickbacks for favorable judging."

Gasps rippled through the audience.

"Jeremy Blackwood discovered this scheme," Laura continued. "And he began blackmailing someone. A few days before his death, Jeremy was overheard on the phone. He was increasing his demands, putting pressure on the murderer. Then came the pre-festival tasting at the General Store stables. Jeremy alluded to surprising discoveries he intended to reveal at his keynote speech. That night, someone lured Jeremy to the stables, claiming they would pay what was demanded. But they had no intention of paying. At first, their alibi seemed perfect. Their television was on, their car remained in the driveway, and their motorcycle was out of commission. That was all true. But sometimes...it's the person you least expect. How could you... Thomas?"

Laura's voice caught as she said his name. She had to force herself to look straight at him as his eyes widened in horror. The pleasant conversations, the peach cobbler and vanilla ice cream, his kindness...to think he'd been hiding such dreadful secrets, all this time.

"Oh my heavens," someone gasped.

"Thomas? It can't be..."

"It's a mistake!"

"Thomas knew Maggie and Kathy would be away that night," Laura said. "They'd talked about it at the festival meeting. Maggie's friend's birthday celebration in Burlington, Kathy's dinner in Montpelier. No one would hear or notice anything. Jeremy had been threatening him for weeks about those kickbacks, recording everything and demanding cash for silence. He said he'd expose everything at his keynote speech if Thomas didn't pay."

"So they met at the stables. Thomas knew there were no cameras because Maggie couldn't afford to install them yet. And Jeremy was staying at the Quartermark Inn, just a short walk away. Thomas turned on his TV and left his car in the driveway. Then he snuck out the back wearing dark clothes, using the hiking trails behind his property to head into town. They go past Alex's place, and if anyone saw Thomas walking past, they might think it was Alex. After he pushed Jeremy over the mezzanine railing, he took Jeremy's notebook. Then he planted those 'consulting fee' records in Jeremy's bag to make it look like Maggie was paying him. Thomas knew about her cash withdrawals from the credit union. He'd seen her making them when he was there and took the opportunity to frame her. He didn't know she was saving for Kathy's anniversary gift. But I think Thomas' motivation wasn't just about the money. Thomas' grandfather helped start this festival. Whitman Family Creamery is renowned throughout New England. Jeremy could've, at any moment, ruined Thomas by revealing his secret. So he killed Jeremy to protect his reputation, as if that was worth more than a human life."

"He burned Jeremy's notebook in his fireplace." Laura said. "But he missed something."

Ramirez emerged from the side entrance, her presence commanding attention as she moved forward. "When I questioned Laura, she said she'd spoken with Todd Miller one night, and he claimed he'd driven past Thomas's house and seen his TV on. He told me as much too. Yet he failed to mention he'd been farming Thomas' land illegally for years, getting government subsidies for it. When I asked him about this, he said Thomas threatened to sue him unless Todd backed up his story."

Murmurs swept through the crowd.

"Laura also remembered thinking she'd seen something in Thomas' fireplace," Ramirez continued. "My officers' search confirmed her suspicions. There, they found the silver cheese wheel bookmark from Jeremy's notebook."

She produced a small evidence bag containing the pendant, then held up another, this one containing a scrap of black fabric.

"This ends now, Thomas. Lab analysis found pet hairs on this scrap. Just a matter of extracting the DNA profile, cross-referencing it with local adoption records...these hairs belong to your dog, Bailey. We also have testimonials from three producers who paid you kickbacks over the past two years. And we know about your creamery's financial troubles."

Thomas lunged for the side exit, but two uniformed officers blocked his path.

"No!" he shouted, his voice breaking. "You don't understand! My family built this town's reputation! Everything I did was to protect that legacy!"

"Thomas Whitman," Ramirez continued, "you're under arrest for the murder of Jeremy Blackwood."

As the officers moved to handcuff him, Thomas's shoulders slumped in defeat.

"He was going to ruin everything. Decades of work, my family's legacy. All of it would have been destroyed."

A lump formed in Laura's throat. The man she thought she'd come to know—so kind and affable—reduced to this. Part of her wanted to look away, but she made herself bear witness. Ramirez recited his rights as he was led away, the stunned audience watching in silence.

As Thomas passed near her, their eyes met for only a second. Yet it was enough to see the profound remorse, like he'd only just realized the terrible consequences of what he'd done.

Maggie stepped forward, facing Laura, tears in her eyes. "Thank you."

Kathy made her way through the crowd. When she reached Maggie, she stood beside her, their shoulders touching. Maggie exhaled, as if able to breathe again. Kathy didn't speak—she didn't need to.

Rosalind stood frozen by the podium, her clipboard fallen to the floor, face paler than Laura had ever seen it. "If only I'd listened…"

Alex pushed through the stunned crowd, his face streaked with tears. He reached Laura. "I have to—" he started, his voice cracking. "I need to say something. Please—I can't stay silent anymore."

She had a feeling of what he intended to say, but she nodded.

"I lied. You've just…shown some secrets destroy everything they touch. I've been taking credit for work that wasn't mine. Jeremy knew, and I was terrified he'd expose me. I never hurt him—I would never—but I was a coward.

And I can't be one anymore. Whatever the consequences." For the first time in perhaps years, the man gave a resolute nod, before walking away.

In the chaos that followed, Laura slipped away from the stage, overwhelmed by the enormity of what'd just transpired. Her fingers trembled around her water glass as she took a shaky sip. She'd moved to Silver Springs for a quiet life managing a café. She never imagined she would uncover fraud and help solve a murder.

Thomas' pleasant demeanor, the dinner, the genuine passion with which he'd spoken about cheesemaking. How much of that man had been real? Had Bailey noticed something amiss? Could dogs sense the darkness in their owners?

She would never know.

Maggie embraced Kathy, holding her close. Laura had made the right choice. Silver Springs had welcomed her. It was her home now, and she would do what she could to protect it.

CHAPTER TWENTY-FOUR

L aura arrived at work as dawn broke, the pale light casting long shadows across the empty café. She enjoyed these quiet moments before the morning rush—time to think, to plan, to breathe.

Someone knocked at the back door. Laura went to open it, and Ben ducked in, a toolbox in one hand and measurements scribbled on a crumpled piece of paper in the other.

"Morning, detective!" he called, setting down his toolbox with a metallic clunk.

"I'm a café manager, not a detective," Laura said, unable to stop a smile from escaping.

"Could've fooled me," Ben said. "Maggie's got me reinforcing those old heritage fences today."

"Shall I get you a drink?" Laura asked. "A lactose-free decaf caramel latte, right?"

"The correct term for that abomination is dessert with an identity crisis," Kathy said upon entering the café, carrying a crate of the latest delivery of summer vegetables, a wry grin on her face. "Morning, Ben and Laura." She turned to the young man. "Need anything before you start?"

Ben blinked. "Good morning to you too, Kathy. I'm okay, thanks." He turned to Laura with a faint smirk. "One of what she said please. Hold the judgment."

Laura laughed as she prepared his requested drink.

"Alright, Laura?" Kathy asked as she began placing the produce in the retail space.

"All good," Laura said.

Kathy nodded as she left.

Ben turned his attention toward a stack of boxes Laura had been unpacking, continuing the task. Laura watched with a bemused smile as she set up the display counter.

Ben grinned. "So. Who would've thought? Our town hero!"

"I just pieced a few things together!" Laura said with a shake of her head.

"The real hero is the one who found that fabric scrap in the hawthorn bush, right?" He dissolved into laughter, his eyes twinkling. "I'm kidding! Seriously, that was some impressive detective work."

"It wouldn't have been possible without everyone's help," Laura said. "Including yours."

Ben shrugged, arranging the last box on the shelf. "All in a day's work." He picked up his toolbox, then paused. "Hey, if you ever need any help in the future, not that anything will happen, of course, one murder's plenty, but if you do, let me know." A mischievous grin lit up his face. "I'll have to add 'Professional Evidence Finder' right under 'Handyman' on my business card."

Laura laughed. "I'll keep that in mind."

Ben nodded and headed out the back door.

Jasmine strode in, a folded copy of the Maplewood Memo clutched in her hand. "You won't believe this. Wait—you might, but..."

Laura's stomach gave a familiar lurch. "What is it now?"

Jasmine slapped the newspaper onto the counter. "Front page. You need to read this."

Laura eyed the paper. She'd had her fill of newspapers and their speculative headlines.

"No, Laura, you really do."

She unfolded the paper, turning it so the bold headline screamed up at Laura: 'Festival Fraud Exposed! Whitman's Web Of Kickbacks Unravels & Committee Pledges Reform.'

Laura's breath caught. Her fingers, of their own accord, reached out, drawing the newspaper closer. The small print swam before resolving into stark, undeniable words.

'Years of inflated vendor fees...' Her gaze jumped down the column. '...consulting services with no discernible output...a meticulously maintained façade masking significant profit skimming.'

Thomas's jovial laugh, his kind eyes...the disconnect made her stomach clench.

Further down, the article shifted: 'The Festival Committee announced an immediate and thorough audit...' Good. '...full restitution for all verifiable discrepancies. Rosalind Prescott, the festival committee chair, spoke to us about her regret in allowing this to happen. She apologized for not believing concerns when they were raised and promised to take steps to ensure everything is properly audited, recognizing the error of her ways in taking on too much responsibility and not sharing the load. She anticipates a bright future for the festival.'

A small, tight knot in her chest loosened. The truth, however painful, was out at last.

———————◆———————

Laura climbed the Morrison Building stairs to the second floor on Monday evening, a spring in her step that had been missing for days. She cradled a plate of lemon-thyme shortbread cookies—her first solo attempt in the General Store's kitchen. As she reached the landing, the door swung open before she could knock.

Evelyn stood there, beaming. "Right on time! Come in, come in."

The living room buzzed with activity. Judith and Martha had claimed their usual spots, their projects already spread out before them. Fran sat cross-legged on the floor, stitching her miniature bird in-progress onto the fabric. Marcela's nimble fingers worked away at her cross-stitch, a half-finished page from her latest coloring book peeked out from her project bag. Yanni's amigurumi moose now sported tiny antlers, while Christopher's pencil flew across his sketchpad. Everyone looked up at their entrance, and the room erupted into chatter.

"She's here!" Judith said, bouncing in her seat.

"Laura!" Martha exclaimed, setting down her crochet with haste. "We've been waiting for you!"

"The woman of the hour," Christopher announced with a theatrical bow from his corner.

Fran, typically focused solely on her embroidery, looked up. "Now we can get some answers!"

"Give her some space to breathe," Evelyn chuckled, guiding Laura further into the space as the group reluctantly settled back.

"I brought cookies," Laura said, holding up her plate.

"Perfect!" Evelyn took it and placed it on the dining room sideboard, already laden with containers.

"I hope they taste as good as they smell," Laura replied. "I used fresh thyme from Tracy's delivery."

Oscar padded over, winding himself around her ankles in greeting. Even Monty deigned to acknowledge her with a slow blink from his perch on the windowsill.

Jasmine arrived moments later, let in by Evelyn, her knitting bag bulging with blue yarn. "Sorry I'm late!" She threw herself at Laura, giving her a big hug before settling into a vacant chair beside her. "Ready to recount how you saved Maggie's reputation and her business?"

"We want to hear everything," Yanni said. "Every detail!"

"Please," Marcela added, leaning forward. "Tell us what happened. From the beginning."

Laura glanced at Evelyn, who nodded. So she began, settling into her chair.

When she finished her retelling of what transpired the day before, plus everything she, Evelyn, and Jasmine had discovered during their investigation, the room remained silent for a moment.

"Remarkable," Yanni said.

"The cheese wheel bookmark!" Judith said, clasping her hands together. The cryptogram she'd been working on had lain forgotten the entire time Laura had been talking. "Such a tiny detail to catch. That was brilliant, Laura."

"And let's not forget Evelyn's sharp eyes," Martha said, smiling at her friend. "That woman spots suspicious things from a mile off."

"I still can't believe it was Thomas," Christopher said, his usual cheerful demeanor subdued. "I've known him for fifteen years. Never suspected a thing."

"He got what was coming to him, the snake in the grass," Fran said.

"When you stood up at that podium," Martha said to Laura, "I've never seen such bravery."

Laura ducked her head, smiling. "I couldn't have done it without Evelyn. Her wisdom and experience guided me through the entire investigation."

Evelyn beamed.

Laura turned to the woman sitting beside her. "And without Jasmine, I never would've known what leads to follow. The information she provided...none of the pieces would've come together otherwise."

Jasmine grinned. "Always happy to help."

Marcela nodded. "The whole town would still be gossiping about Maggie if you all hadn't investigated."

"Speaking of Maggie," Martha said, "how is she doing?"

Laura smiled. "Much better. Hyland Farms called this morning to apologize. They want to renew their contract."

Marcela nodded. "Good. Small businesses need to support each other, not run at the first sign of trouble."

Martha cleared her throat, drawing everyone's attention. "Laura, we all heard your speech, and your explanation just now...but we're curious about a few...loose ends. For starters, whatever happened with Diana and her so-called 'ancient' family recipe?"

Laura sighed. "It turns out the recipe isn't as old as she said it was." She looped yarn around her hook as she continued. "Her mother developed it, but somewhere along the way, the family started marketing it as an 'old-world tradition.' Diana said she's relieved it's out in the open. She's proud of the cheese's quality, regardless of its origin story."

"That's something, at least," Judith said with a nod.

"And Alex?" Fran asked. "You said he seemed nervous at the festival."

"With good reason," Laura replied. "He admitted to copying marketing materials from obscure European festivals and passing them off as his own."

"I knew it!" Judith exclaimed. "His 'genius reputation' always seemed suspicious to me."

Martha raised an eyebrow. "Now Judith, we shouldn't be so quick to judge. Yes, what he did was wrong, but he doesn't appear as having done so out of malice."

Laura nodded. "He'd been in a tough spot for months. Completely blocked with his work, isolating himself, and all that pressure to live up to his reputation. He'd been wrestling with himself since the murder. He said seeing what keeping secrets had done to Thomas...he realized he needed to come clean before it was too late."

"How is he handling it now?" Evelyn asked.

"It's been hard," Laura said. "He's lost some clients, but he told me yesterday he's starting fresh, taking on smaller projects and being transparent about his process."

Yanni nodded. "There's something to be said for that kind of courage."

"And he's been volunteering at the Good Neighborhood Guild community center," Laura added.

"Teaching design to adults returning to education. He said he wants to build something real this time."

Martha made a cross between a disapproving and pleased noise. "Let's hope it continues. Wait...I've never seen him without that notebook and fountain pen of his, did he make those inky fingerprints?"

"Yes. Jeremy cornered him after the tasting," Laura replied. "Showed Alex he had evidence in his messenger bag. Alex panicked and tried to grab it, leaving blue ink fingerprints from his fountain pen."

"And the phone call I overheard at the festival?" Evelyn added, for everyone else's benefit.

Laura nodded. "He was talking to a graphic designer he'd hired to do some of his work. He was paying them extra to keep quiet about it."

Christopher glanced up from his sketching. "Is he going to lose his position on the committee?"

Laura shook her head. "No, he's promised to create original work from now on. Rosalind believes in second chances."

"Speaking of Rosalind..." Judith leaned forward, eyes gleaming with interest, "there was something going on with her. I could tell."

Laura hesitated, then nodded. "Now, can you all promise to keep this to yourselves? For Rosalind's sake?"

The older woman, for once, acquiesced. "Of course, Laura. My lips are sealed."

"They had...a brief affair a few weeks before his death."

Everyone's eyes widened.

"Goodness," Judith murmured. "No wonder she looked so stressed."

Martha elbowed her. "What did you just say?"

Judith had the grace to look downcast. "I meant...I won't say anything more on the matter."

The group laughed and even Judith had to smile.

Laura's expression sobered. "And Rosalind's been under so much pressure lately. Melissa, her ex-partner, found out about the affair and kept threatening to expose it."

Judith raised an eyebrow. "It would seem there's a reason she's an 'ex'."

Fran nodded, muttering something about disrespectful former lovers.

Martha sighed. "I hope, one day, she finds someone who treats her well."

Jasmine made a noise of agreement, then her expression shifted. "I feel so bad for Maggie, too. All that suspicion for nothing."

"Indeed. So, what about the cash withdrawals from her account?" Evelyn prompted.

"It was Kathy's anniversary gift, not payments to Jeremy Blackwood," Laura said, smiling at the memory of Maggie's sheepish confession. "She was buying a rare antique architectural drafting set. She withdrew the cash in small amounts so Kathy wouldn't notice."

"The important thing," Laura continued, "is every cent of the profit the business makes is going toward paying off their debts. Maggie's gift to Kathy came from her savings account. Kathy helped clear things up too—she pointed out how the 'consulting fees' didn't seem to match the 'consulting arrangements.' I'm guessing Detective Sergeant Ramirez compared the real numbers to what Maggie was supposedly paying him and came to the same conclusion. And those final notice bills I saw in her office? They'd actually already been paid. Maggie just hadn't gotten around to processing them through her filing system yet."

Evelyn nodded. "That sounds so much like Maggie, struggling with delegating. I'm so glad she hired you."

Laura smiled. "Speaking of that...Kathy convinced her to get an accountant to help manage the business."

"About time," Judith said. "That woman tries to do everything herself."

"What about the blueprint?" Jasmine asked. "The one with the stables circled in red?"

"Security camera plans," Laura said. "Maggie was planning to install them throughout the store, if only she'd gotten around to it sooner..."

"And Diana's suspicious phone call?" Judith asked.

Laura nodded. "She was talking about a difficult client she'd been trying to get rid of for months. She wanted to redirect that energy into expanding distribution for Mountain Valley Dairy."

"So her jacket looking like the scrap you found...?" Fran began.

"Just a coincidence," Laura said.

"And her reaction at the cheese trivia?" Martha asked.

"She was embarrassed about answering the modern techniques question too easily when she's supposed to be the traditional methods expert," Laura explained. "She worried it would make her look hypocritical."

"What about when Evelyn saw her switching those labels during the judging?" Christopher asked, looking up from his sketch.

Laura nodded. "A volunteer had accidentally misplaced the entry cards earlier that morning. Diana noticed her cheese was labeled incorrectly and was just putting it right."

"So she wasn't trying to cheat?" Judith asked, eyebrows raised.

"Not at all," Laura said. "Just fixing someone else's mistake."

"What'll happen to Thomas' creamery now?" Yanni asked, his brow furrowed with concern.

"Diana and Lou are acquiring it," Laura said. "They're keeping all the employees on, and they're even taking in Bailey. They're also getting Todd Miller's dairy farm—he was arrested for providing that false alibi and it turns out he had his own legal troubles brewing. And Thomas threatened to sue him over building on the property line if he didn't comply. Apparently he'd been cutting corners on regulations for months, and when the authorities dug deeper after his false testimony..." Laura shrugged. "They found enough violations to shut him down."

"Todd was so desperate to avoid more legal trouble he was willing to lie...for that?" Yanni asked. "What a mess."

"Indeed. And that poor dog." Judith sighed. "Not his fault his owner was a murderer."

Laura nodded, feeling a sudden tightness in her chest. The image of Bailey—his warm brown eyes and enthusiastic tail wags when she'd visited Thomas' property—flashed in her mind.

"Diana said Bailey's already bonding with their farm dogs," Laura said. She looked down at her hands. "I was worried about what would happen to him. It's good to know he'll have a home with people who'll care for him."

She blinked, surprised by the tears that threatened to fall from the corners of her eyes. It wasn't just about the dog.

It was everything—the betrayal and the stress of the last few weeks. Jasmine placed a hand on Laura's shoulder.

"Good to hear," Christopher nodded. "I wonder if Bailey noticed anything suspicious about Thomas? I've always believed dogs have better judgment than humans."

"You would say that, O'Reilly," Fran said, not looking up from her embroidery.

"I still think Christopher suits him better," Marcela said, threading a new color into her needle.

Yanni chuckled. "I'm sticking with Chris."

Martha shook her head. "It's Kit to me and always will be."

"What about you, Laura?" Christopher asked with a twinkle in his eye. "Have you decided what amalgamation of my name you'll be using?"

Laura paused. "What would you prefer me to call you?"

Christopher laughed. "So considerate! Christopher is fine."

Evelyn set down her knitting. "With that settled, perhaps it's time we welcome Laura into our club."

"What?" Laura asked.

Evelyn smiled, her eyes twinkling. "The Maplewood Crafters Club isn't just about crafting. For over thirty-five years, we've been Silver Springs' secret helpers."

"We do more than gossip and craft," Martha added. "Though we do plenty of both."

Judith nodded. "When someone in town needs help, we step in."

"Like when Clyde Hastings' son needed college tuition," Fran said. "We organized that 'spontaneous' town auction of handcrafted items."

"Or when the Willowers' roof collapsed last winter," Christopher added. "We arranged the repair crew and supplies, all anonymous donations."

"Even your Gran was part of it," Evelyn said.

Laura's eyes widened. "She knew about this?"

"Of course." Evelyn smiled. "She said you had a knack for noticing things others missed. A gift for seeing the truth behind people's words. And, most importantly, a kind heart. She thought you'd fit right in."

"And she was right," Jasmine said.

"So," Evelyn said, raising her glass, "to Laura, our newest member. Welcome to the Maplewood Crafters Club! May your crafting improve and your kindness continue to shine."

"Here's to Laura!" they echoed, glasses clinking.

Jasmine pulled out her phone. "Now to add you to the group chat."

"Oh no," Christopher said in mock seriousness. "You don't know what you're getting yourself into."

The room settled into a comfortable rhythm—the soft click of needles, the rustle of paper and snacks. Laura resumed her crochet, finding comfort in the familiar motions.

<hr />

The last members of the Crafters Club had departed, leaving behind the comfortable clutter of an early evening well spent. Laura helped Evelyn stack the dishwasher, which thankfully was a lot less full than the dishwashers at the festival.

"You don't have to help clean up," Evelyn said.

"I'm happy to." Laura smiled.

Evelyn switched on the kettle. "Your lemon-thyme shortbread was a success! Even Judith was impressed, and she claims to have the most discerning palate in three counties."

Laura smiled. "It was just a novelty. Next week, they'll be expecting something more impressive."

"That's the burden of talent," Evelyn teased, selecting two mugs from her eclectic collection. "Stay for one more cup? It's still early."

Once the tea had brewed, they settled in the living room. Oscar claimed Laura's lap, while Monty sat on the arm of the couch across from her. "I got a call from my mother today," Laura said after a comfortable silence had settled between them. "She saw the news about Thomas."

"Oh?" Evelyn's eyebrow arched. "What did she have to say about her daughter, the amateur detective?"

"She was...surprised." Laura smiled, remembering her mother's uncharacteristic speechlessness. "She's having trouble reconciling the Boston Laura she knew with the Silver Springs Laura, who helped solve a murder."

"And which Laura do you prefer?" Evelyn asked, her eyes twinkling.

Laura considered the question, stroking Oscar's soft fur as he purred. "This one."

Evelyn nodded. "I've found that's often true. We don't become different people when we change locations—we just discover new facets of who we've always been."

Laura sipped her tea, nodding. "When I first arrived, I thought I was just escaping from the disappointment at

Hargroves, from the life I'd planned falling apart. I never expected to find..."

"A community?" Evelyn suggested.

"That." Laura met her friend's gaze. "Thank you. For welcoming me."

A package had arrived yesterday—delivered to the General Store with Laura's name. Inside, she'd found a handcrafted ceramic planter, painted in blues and greens that matched her apartment's color scheme. The note, in her mother's precise handwriting, had read: 'For your new home. Hope you like it. Mom.' Her mother might never understand why Laura had chosen Silver Springs over Boston, but the gesture was a start.

Evelyn reached over to pat Laura's hand. "Silver Springs is better for having you in it."

The mantel clock chimed, marking the hour.

"I'm going to enjoy being part of the next Crafters Club project," Laura said. "Whatever it might be."

Evelyn smiled. "I thought you might say that."

———◆———

Tuesday afternoon brought some much-needed relief from the bright sun. Laura stepped outside the General Store. She'd forgotten a book she'd borrowed from the library at home—the new mystery she'd been dying to finish during her lunch break—and walked back to the Morrison Building to retrieve it.

As she descended the store steps, she collided with Vernon Reed, a long-time apple farmer and supplier for the General Store. He was so engrossed in a heated phone conversation, he didn't seem to notice her.

"I don't care," Vernon hissed. "We all know the truth."

Laura paused and bent down, pretending to tie her shoelace.

"We all know," Vernon continued, his voice rising. "Who deserves the legacy!" He glanced up, at last seeing Laura, and lowered his voice. "We'll discuss this later," he muttered into the phone before pocketing it.

"Good morning. Is everything okay?" Laura asked as she straightened.

Vernon forced a smile. "Just a small disagreement. Nothing to worry about." He searched for a change of subject. "Apple picking season will be here before we know it."

Laura nodded. "I'm looking forward to experiencing it."

"It's something special, alright," Vernon agreed, his eyes distant. "Been part of my family for generations." His expression darkened before he smiled again. "I'd better be off. Have a good day...Laura, isn't it?"

Laura nodded and so did he, turning and heading off in the opposite direction as she continued toward the Morrison Building.

Whatever was happening at Goldenleaf Apple Farm, Laura was sure the Maplewood Crafters Club would soon discuss it over their projects. After all, every town had its secrets—and Silver Springs' newest resident was getting good at uncovering them.

THE END

———————◆O◆———————

Get your surprise reader bonuses here:
__cozycozies.com/pages/ss1thanks__

Thanks for reading. I hope you enjoyed it.

THANKS FOR READING!

I hope you enjoyed reading! I have something extra for you if you're willing to leave a review...

You know how in your favorite cozies, neighbors help neighbors without expecting anything in return? I have a small favor to ask that won't cost you a penny, but could make all the difference to a fellow reader you've never met.

Here's another mystery that needs solving...

How can we help more readers discover cozy mysteries that bring them joy, comfort, and a relaxing escape from everyday worries?

I'll give you a few moments to think...

The solution? Your review!

Just like how the smallest clues matter most, your few words about this book could be the clue that leads another reader to their new favorite series.

Your review takes less than a minute but lasts forever.

- If you're reading this on your Kindle, just scroll to the bottom and tap "Rate and Review."

- If you're listening on Audible, tap those three dots in the top right corner and select "Rate & Review."

For all other places on the internet, I've put together a page of handy links! Visit **cozycozies.com/pages/ss1review**

Or, scan the QR code with your phone's camera below!

Once you're done, email me: jodie@cozycozies.com and tell me where you wrote it. I'll send your VIP bonuses!

If helping another book lover sounds like something you'd do, then you're exactly the kind of reader I write for. Welcome to our cozy community! I'm so grateful you took this journey with me, and I can't wait to share future books with you.

Your review, a true act of kindness, would mean the world to me and help so many others find their next favorite escape. From my writing nook, I'm sending you all the coziest reading vibes, and wishing you many delightful mysteries to unravel.

Have a wonderful day!

Cheers Jodie

P.S. If you'd like to receive exclusive short stories and bonuses, plus printable puzzles, discounts, and more...sign up for my newsletter at cozycozies.com/pages/newsletter.

P.P.S You can find all my books in all formats on your favorite online store. You can also get my books, special editions, and bundles directly from me at cozycozies.com.

ACKNOWLEDGEMENTS

W riting a cozy mystery isn't a solitary endeavor, and I'm so grateful to everyone who helped bring this story to life!

First, my heartfelt thanks to my editors, Zach and Cameron, whose sharp eyes and gentle guidance helped me untangle plot threads and polish every clue.

Special appreciation goes to my family for their understanding. They never complained about me testing dialogue on them, helping me fix plot holes, or working out red herrings and alibis! Thank you for your endless patience.

Finally, to the cozy mystery authors who inspired me. Thank you for proving that mysteries with heart, community, delicious food, crafting, and cats are delightful to read and write.

AUTHOR'S NOTE

When I first envisioned Silver Springs, I'd fallen in love with Vermont during a chance encounter with a video featuring the state's gorgeous scenery.

I knew this picturesque place would be the perfect backdrop for mysteries that unfold at a gentler pace. There, nestled in the green mountains: a small New England town where everyone knows everyone—and their secrets.

Laura embodies the curious spirit we all have when we notice something doesn't quite add up in our community. Silver Springs is the place where a morning coffee at the local café can reveal surprising clues, and where neighbors care about each other. (Even when they frustrate each other!)

Writing these mysteries has been my way of exploring how ordinary people can do extraordinary things when their community is threatened. I've spent countless hours researching small-town Vermont life, and I've learned so many wonderful things.

I hope you enjoyed the story! What did you like best in the book? And what are your favorite cozy mysteries? I'd love to hear from you. You can find me at <u>cozycozies.com</u>.

I really enjoy it when readers email me to say hello. The lovely folks who read my books are my kind of people!

I'm so lucky to have such a wonderful community. Which is why I'd like to introduce...It's The Cozy Life For Us!

It's a discussion group for people who love all things cozy (mysteries, puzzles, fiber arts, books, food) to share what we've been enjoying, reading, or making. There are also lots of member-only bonuses.

Visit skool.com/cozy to join the cozy fun!

Character Compendium

- **Alexander 'Alex' Caldwell**: The festival's marketing manager.

- **Alice**: Maggie's college friend who lives in Burlington.

- **Anton Reynolds**: The General Store's chef.

- **Bailey**: Thomas' black and white Border Collie. He was adopted from the Stonefield Animal Refuge.

- **Benjamin 'Ben' Ashby**: A tall youth who handles maintenance jobs around town and works at his father's hardware store.

- **Bridget Evans**: Laura's mother. She's critical of Laura's move from Boston and worries about her safety.

- **Caroline**: A General Store customer.

- **Charles Wu**: Evelyn's late husband. He had a medical practice on the first floor of the Morrison

Building.

- **Christopher O'Reilly**: Runs *The Whittled Word*, and is a member of the Maplewood Crafters Club.

- **Claudia Alard**: An influential Boston food writer and guest judge at the Summer Cheese Festival.

- **Clay Elderkin**: The youngest member of the Elderkin family.

- **Clyde Hastings**: A man whose son received college tuition help from the Maplewood Crafters Club.

- **Colette Moreau**: Owner of Chez Colette, a French restaurant and one of the caterers for the festival.

- **Connor Evans**: Laura's youngest brother who lives in California with his family.

- **Dakota**: A young girl who visits the café every Tuesday with her mother.

- **Danny Evans**: Laura's middle brother, a cultural institution program director in New York, and a single father.

- **Daphne**: Laura's former colleague at Hargroves.

- **Detective Sergeant Ramirez**: The

second-in-command of the Silver Springs Police Department.

- **Diana Martinez**: Festival committee member and judge. She's the owner of Mountain Valley Dairy.

- **Dr. Patel**: A General Store customer who loves birds.

- **Edward Lee:** Judith's husband.

- **Eli Carter**: Laura's colleague and the General Store café's barista.

- **Elliott Harrington**: The director of the Vermont Food & Wine Association.

- **Evelyn Chan:** Laura's landlady, the Maplewood Crafters Club's leader, Rachel Wu's mother. Has Burmese cats: Oscar & Monty.

- **Francesca 'Fran' Palermo**: Works at Twilight Pines State Park. She's the Maplewood Crafters Club's birder.

- **Helen Mercer**: A festival vendor from Mercer Dairy.

- **Herbert Emerson**: A retired cheesemaker whose blue cheese won international awards, and a guest judge for the festival.

- **Isaac 'Izzy' Lennox**: An employee at Goldenleaf

Apple Farm and a member of the Silver Springs Players.

- **Jasmine Williams**: Laura's colleague, a member of Woodland Watch and the Maplewood Crafters Club.

- **Jeremy Blackwood:** A food critic from Boston, a festival committee member, and assistant judge.

- **Jesse O'Connor**: Laura's colleague, and an arts school graduate from Rhode Island.

- **Judith Yoon**: Evelyn's friend, a former editor, *a Maplewood Memo* puzzle contributor, and a Maplewood Crafters Club member.

- **Joyce Adler**: The Adult Circulation Librarian at the Silver Springs Public Library.

- **Kathleen 'Kathy' Quinn**: Co-owner of the General Store, Maggie Brook's wife, and a former architect.

- **Katie Fowler**: An assistant at the Village Skein, the local yarn store, and a regular at the General Store café.

- **Larry Holden**: Co-owner and front-of-house manager of Beaumont Bistro, a festival caterer.

- **Laura Evans**: The General Store café manager and an amateur sleuth.

- **Lawrence Henderson**: Martha's husband.

- **Layla Ahmed**: Owner of Red Trillium Bakery, which supplies the General Store café's baked goods and pastries.

- **Lincoln Goddard**: A former festival judge who resigned.

- **Louis 'Lou' Cooper**: Diana's husband. He helps run Mountain Valley Dairy.

- **Maggie Brook**: Store co-owner and Laura's boss.

- **Marcela Torres**: The Town Clerk, and a member of the Maplewood Crafters Club.

- **Martha Henderson**: Evelyn's friend, Historical Society vice president, Good Neighbor Guild president, a Maplewood Crafters Club member.

- **Melissa**: Rosalind's ex-partner.

- **Monty**: Evelyn's light bluish-gray Burmese cat.

- **Mr. Fleming**: A General Store customer.

- **Mrs. Lawson**: A General Store customer.

- **Mrs. Merriweather**: A General Store customer.

- **Nell Mackenzie**: Owner of the Village Skein, the local yarn store.

- **Norman Buckley**: A General Store customer

known for his legendary indecisiveness.

- **Officer Littlefield**: A senior patrol officer.

- **Oscar**: Evelyn's dark-brown Burmese cat.

- **Pete Ashby**: Ben's father and owner of Ashby Hardware.

- **Professor Harvey Lín**: A guest judge for the festival who teaches Food Science at the Tremblay Institute Of Arts & Sciences.

- **Rachel Wu:** Evelyn's daughter, chef, and a cookbook author who wrote *Spice. Steam. Stir.*

- **Rebecca**: A yarn-dyer who works at the Village Skein.

- **Rosalind Prescott**: The Festival director and committee chair. She works as a bookkeeper for local businesses.

- **Ruby**: A part-time employee at the Village Skein.

- **Sara**: Diana and Lou's adult daughter.

- **Shelly**: A General Store customer.

- **Silvia Evans**: Laura's grandmother and Evelyn's friend.

- **Thomas Whitman**: The head judge for the festival and owner of Whitman Family Dairy.

- **Toby Evers**: A vegetable farmer who supplies the General Store.

- **Todd Miller**: A local dairy farmer and Thomas' neighbor.

- **Tracy Mitchell**: The General Store's herbs and microgreens supplier.

- **Valeria 'Val' Del Solar**: A historical society volunteer.

- **Vernon Reed**: an apple farmer and supplier for the General Store.

- **Victor Beaumont**: Co-owner and chef at Beaumont Bistro, a festival caterer.

- **Yanni Petros**: Runs Wanderer Pantry, is originally from Melbourne, Australia, and is a member of the Maplewood Crafters Club.

ABOUT THE AUTHOR

Jodie Morgan is an author of cozy mysteries, short stories, puzzle books, joke books, and riddle books. Her novels welcome readers to the charming town of Silver Springs, in Maplewood County, Vermont. Jodie's books are filled with intriguing puzzles, memorable characters, and the satisfying solutions cozy mystery readers love.

When she's not plotting her next book, you'll find her reading, savoring a coffee (with cream, always!) or working on her latest knitting or crochet project. She loves to travel as this sparks ideas for her writing. Her most satisfying creative moments come from quiet evenings at home with her supportive family.

Find out more about Jodie at <u>cozycozies.com</u>.

Author photo taken by Tal at the Granny Square in Sydney, Australia.

ALSO BY JODIE MORGAN

2. Riddling In The Kitchen

Official Short Stories

- Exclusives

    a. Hope Has Whiskers

    b. Lost Becomes Found

    c. Keeping It Hidden

- Widely Available

    a. Recipe For Revenge

    b. Cataloged Under Deception

    c. Puzzles She Packed

Read A Sample
Of Murder At
Goldenleaf Apple
Farm

R ead on for a sample of Murder At Goldenleaf Apple
Farm, the next novel in the Silver Springs Mysteries!

About The Book

**In the second page-turning novel in the Silver
Springs Mysteries, within Fall's beauty lurks deadly
deception...**

Laura Evans has finally found her rhythm in the
charming Vermont town of Silver Springs. Managing
the General Store café feels like a world away from her
high-pressure Boston restaurant career, and she's building
genuine friendships with locals like Evelyn, her wise
neighbor, and Izzy, the enthusiastic young man who works

at Goldenleaf Apple Farm and lights up every room he enters.

But Laura's peaceful new life shatters when Vernon Reed, an apple farmer, is found murdered in his garage with a bung hammer—a tool used in cider production. And the weapon turns up covered in Izzy's fingerprints along with one of his distinctive handmade bracelets at the crime scene. But Laura knows the gentle soul who welcomed her to town could never commit murder.

Determined to clear Izzy's name, Laura teams up with Evelyn and her café colleague Jasmine to investigate Vernon's final months.

But the killer will stop at nothing to protect their carefully constructed lies...

This engaging book serves up the perfect blend of mystery and comfort. Every clue unfolds at just the right place, and justice is as satisfying as a refreshing glass of sweet cider.

——◆——

If happiness had a scent, it'd be apple trees during harvest. Exiting her car at Goldenleaf Apple Farm, goosebumps rose on Laura Evans' fair skin as her boots crunched on the leaf-strewn gravel. The countless tree canopies overhead cast dappled shadows across the orchard.

Jasmine Williams, her friend and co-worker, got out of the passenger seat, and they smiled at each other. No one else had arrived yet. The vehicles in the lot must've belonged to the staff. The only one she recognized was a burnt orange pickup truck, at least four decades older than all the others. A smile crossed her face.

Weathered wooden buildings sprawled across the farm, each bearing the marks of a different decade. At the center stood the cider house, its cupola crowned with smoke curling from the chimney. Nearby was the visitors center, while the office occupied a converted farmhouse with green shutters and a wrap-around porch.

Near the storage shed, a tall man with cropped hair stood beside a shorter figure. Though their voices didn't carry, the taller one was rigid, jabbing his finger toward the main building while the shorter figure shook his head. Even from this distance, the tall man's shoulders hunched forward, while his companion kept glancing around. The shorter one grabbed the other's arm, his mouth moving in an urgent whisper. The tall man jerked away, and they both stalked toward the tree line, disappearing into the apple rows. Perhaps...just a disagreement about harvest schedules? Something about the furtive way they'd acted...didn't sit right. Laura shook her head, refocusing. She'd come to enjoy herself.

"Looks like we've made good time! We're here early," Laura said.

As the roar of a distant engine grew louder, Jasmine tucked a red-tipped box braid beneath her patterned bandana, her sharp cheekbones prominent under her dark-brown skin. "It sounds like someone's just around the corner."

An older forest-green SUV pulled into the parking lot, stenciled with the Silver Springs General Store logo. It stopped beside Laura's dark-blue sedan, and a woman got out. She had dark brown hair streaked with silver cropped into a pixie cut which peeked from beneath a wide-brimmed sun hat. Her cream-colored skin, dotted with freckles from years of working outdoors, contrasted with the black maxi skirt and a light sweater that'd seen its share of early mornings. Maggie Brook, one of Laura's bosses, and a co-owner, smiled at them both.

From the passenger side emerged a taller, younger woman with olive-toned skin and auburn hair threaded with silver, tied into a plait, and tossed over her shoulder. Her ever-present tool belt was slung around her hips—Kathleen 'Kathy' Quinn, Maggie's wife and business partner.

"Good morning!" Maggie said. "How are you both?"

Laura grinned. "Great, thank you. I've been looking forward to this!"

Jasmine made a muffled noise of agreement as she sipped from her water bottle.

"Morning," Kathy said. "The weather's working in our favor."

Laura couldn't help smiling. "Is this anyone's first time at the farm, or have some of you been here?"

Maggie's expression showed feigned offense. "What sort of General Store co-owner would I be if I didn't have that covered?"

"Good point," Laura said, and she smiled. "Isn't it beautiful here?"

"Real magic's inside," Kathy replied, hands stuffed into her cargo pant pockets, hair ruffling in the morning breeze.

Laura couldn't stop a shake of her head, a grin spreading across her face. "I must say, it's special. I still find it hard to believe I'm in a role where we get to enjoy team-building exercises."

After fifteen years at a prestigious restaurant job in Boston, she'd worked fourteen-hour shifts, seven days a week, only to be passed over for her promised promotion. Silver Springs had been a welcome change of pace. It made sense to everyone she'd explained the situation to...except her mother. A month in, and still, her mother's most recent phone call made her disappointment clear. Laura had tried to explain, for the hundredth time, about burnout, needing a change, and the opportunity to be part of something meaningful in a small community.

But to Bridget Evans, her eldest daughter slipped backward, while her sons moved forward. Danny thrived as the program director at one of New York's most renowned cultural institutions, and Connor built a flourishing tech career and picture-perfect family in California. Her mother's words still stung: "I just don't understand why you're wasting all your professional experience, Laura. Danny may be divorced, but at least he's building something meaningful with his career. And Connor's providing for his family. What are you doing up there in that little town?" What was she doing indeed?

Maggie smiled. "You'll enjoy this, I promise."

Laura nodded. "I know I will. Could you tell me who's leading our tour this morning?"

"Roy," Kathy said. "Vernon's off Mondays. Always has been."

Jasmine nodded. "He hikes with the Woodland Watch, but he hasn't joined us these last few weeks."

Maggie squared her shoulders. "Come along then, let's head inside. The others should be here soon."

———◆———

The visitors center was bright and inviting, its tall windows revealing the picturesque farm beyond. Rustic wooden tables and chairs dotted the space, and an illustrated display of various apple varieties decorated one wall. A small counter sat with a sampler bowl offering candies wrapped in red foil. Behind it was a reception desk, and a pair of double doors leading deeper into Goldenleaf Apple Farm's facilities.

The thundering echo was close now. An old cruiser motorcycle, hand-painted with green-and-blue swirls across the otherwise black chassis, rumbled into the parking lot, followed by a compact red hatchback, and a station wagon in a sensible white. The rider of the first arrival, clad in leathers, cut the engine and removed their helmet. Two men got out of their respective cars and followed the first to the visitors center.

"Looks like the cavalry's arrived," Maggie said with a chuckle.

Several minutes later, the front door opened to admit three more colleagues. Jesse O'Connor entered first, still pulling off a motorcycle jacket, followed by the two men. The shorter and younger one was Eli Carter. The other, Anton Reynolds, the chef at the General Store's café, outstripped Eli's pace with his broad frame and long gait. He smiled at the group, squinting at them from beneath bushy eyebrows.

"Did I miss anything important?" Jesse asked with a grin.

"No, for once," Jasmine replied, her gaze drifting to Jesse's cruiser outside. "You must be freezing, riding that thing! Aren't early fall mornings too cold for motorcycles?"

"You can keep asking, but you'll get the same answer every time," Jesse said. "Why settle for warmth when I can make an entrance? Cars are for people with no imagination."

"Keep making excuses, sure, but you're just jealous we're comfortable," Jasmine said, grinning.

"Comfortable and boring," Jesse said, letting out a huff of laughter. They looked around at Eli and Anton. "Wow, I arrived before these two again? Shocking."

Kathy scoffed, though there wasn't any malice in the sound. "Don't get smug, kid. Showing up a few seconds earlier doesn't buy you the right to tarnish their good names. Those two are punctual to a fault!"

Jesse grinned. "Get used to it. I run on time, unlike some people."

Eli rolled his eyes. "We'll never hear the end of it now."

"You guessed it," Jesse said, grinning.

"Morning, all," Anton said. The man spoke little and was the only one of the staff who wouldn't lower themselves to engage in silly squabbling. Laura had to admit, sometimes, she was grateful for that.

Jesse's gaze settled on Laura. "So. Be honest. Are you here for the educational value or the promised breakfast?"

Laura laughed. "You've discovered my weakness! I've been excited to try those apple cider donuts."

The double doors at the back swung open, and a familiar face burst through. Isaac 'Izzy' Lennox, a farm employee, theater enthusiast, and friend. Long curls

braided back into a bun, golden-brown skin, and a
patchwork jacket hanging off his wiry frame: there was
no other way to describe the man than a whirlwind.
He bounded toward them, reaching Laura first. "Laura!
Always a delight to see you!" As if remembering there
were others present, he added, "And everyone else!
Welcome!" He rattled off their names, greeting each with
his characteristic grin and spirited handshake for all who
accepted it. Something about Izzy's animated gestures and
theatrical enthusiasm always made her smile—so much
like her brother Danny. The same inability to stand still,
the same need to fill silence with warmth. Izzy spun
around to the other man who'd followed him in. "And
this, if you're not already familiar, is the man himself, Roy
Beckett!"

Roy, a tall man just shy of sixty, with weathered ruddy
skin and a buzzcut, nodded at them. He was far less
enthusiastic than Izzy, but that was easy to do. "Welcome
to Goldenleaf Apple Farm! I'm the co-owner. Since he
didn't say so before, this is Izzy Lennox, an employee here."

Izzy swept into a bow. "He undersells himself! Folks,
you're looking at the fellow who's been nothing but
dedicated to this fine establishment. Keeps us, and the
orchards, running smoothly."

Roy shook his head with a smile. "Thank you, Izzy, but
I don't think we need that level of theatricality. It's only a
tour, after all." He turned to the group. "We might as well
get started. Please, follow us." He held the double doors
open for them, which led into a short hallway with an exit
to the farm beyond.

———————— ◆◇◆ ————————

As Roy led them toward the production facility, he explained the farm's history. It took all Izzy's strength to not jump in every few seconds to add anecdotes of his own.

From where Jesse stood next to Laura, they leaned over. "Five bucks Izzy knows every apple tree by name."

"Ten bucks he invented the naming system, and he's the only one who remembers any of it," Jasmine said.

Jesse grinned, and Laura couldn't resist smiling.

"This place has been making apple cider for decades. Vernon, the other co-owner, is the latest in a long line of people just like him," Roy said. "He was the first to work with someone outside the family." He allowed himself a smile. "Now it's the biggest operation in town." He gestured toward the press and grinder. "This is where it starts."

A series of shiny filters and buckets lined a bottling station, and a refractometer sat ready to measure the cider's quality. The sweet scents and rich colors created a different world, an escape from the ordinary outside.

"This is incredible," Laura said.

"Isn't it?" Izzy grinned, sweeping his arms wide. "We even have a new cold-pressing system now to make things faster." He pointed to a machine in the corner. "Vernon is a hard man to convince, but even he couldn't deny how well it works!"

Photos along the wall chronicled the farm's progress over the decades—images of old hand-operated presses, then newer systems, leading to the traditional-meets-modern setup they stood around now. Roy and Vernon had their feet in one era, and Izzy was pulling them into the next.

"Vernon and I have done things a certain way," Roy said, offering Izzy a smile that was more polite than inviting. "But it's worked well so far."

Laura studied the photos more closely—a progression of grainy black-and-white images of the first Reed generations to color ones of a youthful Vernon and Roy. In one, they wore Halloween costumes; in another, they stuck out their tongues, pulling goofy faces. As the years went on, their smiles grew more subdued, more serious.

Izzy caught her attention by gesturing to a wall of labeled bottles. "My role around here is to make sure we're ready for anything—new systems, new ideas! This is where we test different cider grades and styles." His voice was bright. "Roy and Vernon maintain standards, and I handle innovation."

Roy smiled a little at that. "Vernon and I have always been hands-on. We know every inch of this place." He paused as a senior employee approached him with an apologetic expression. "Excuse me for just a moment."

Jasmine came to stand beside Laura. "Pretty amazing, isn't it?"

"Yes, it truly is," Laura replied.

Izzy's voice rose above the mechanical hum as he explained further. "Besides being the steady hand at the helm, Roy's a shrewd business manager who deals with our numbers."

Roy reappeared in time to catch the last of Izzy's declaration, waving off the compliment with an abashed smile before continuing the tour.

———————◄O►——————

Want to read more? You can find this next novel on my store, <u>cozycozies.com</u>, and wherever excellent books are sold!